PRETENDING TO BE

ERICA

PRETENDING TO BE
ERICA

Michelle Painchaud

VIKING
An Imprint of Penguin Group (USA)

VIKING
An Imprint of Penguin Random House LLC
375 Hudson Street
New York, New York 10014

First published in the United States of America by Viking,
an imprint of Penguin Random House LLC, 2015

LIBRARY OF CONGRESS CATALOGING-IN-PUBLICATION DATA
Painchaud, Michelle.
Pretending to be Erica : a novel / Michelle Painchaud.
pages cm
Summary: "Violet has been preparing her entire life to step into the shoes of the missing
heiress Erica Silverman, in order to pull off the biggest inside job in Las Vegas history. She
doesn't count on having a conscience" —Provided by publisher.
ISBN 978-0-670-01497-2 (hardcover)
[1. Impersonation—Fiction. 2. Swindlers and swindling—Fiction. 3. Conduct of life—
Fiction. 4. Missing persons—Fiction. 5. Las Vegas (Nev.)—Fiction.] I. Title.
PZ7.1.P35Pre 2015 [Fic]—dc23 2014032932

Printed in U.S.A.

1 3 5 7 9 10 8 6 4 2

Set in ITC Esprit Std   Designed by Kate Renner

The author is aware that *La Surprise* by Jean-Antoine Watteau, the painting used in this
story, was discovered in 2007. The author also thinks it is the loveliest of paintings.

For PM. You don't have to be scared anymore.

*"Las Vegas is the only place I know
where money really talks—
it says, 'Good-bye.'"*

—FRANK SINATRA, *The Joker Is Wild*

PRETENDING TO BE
ERICA

1: FAKE IT

I still haven't gotten used to writing my new name.

It'll get easier with time. Most things do. But for now the word *Erica* is strange and unfamiliar as it bleeds from my pen and onto the corner of my math worksheet. It's a pretty name, a sweet name. Doesn't suit me.

"Erica?" Mr. Roth, the grandpa-sweater-wearing math teacher, smiles. "Would you like to introduce yourself to the class?"

No. I would rather puke all over your floor.

"Sure." I stand and walk to the front. The whiteboard is blank, an intimidating ghost. I don't want to turn. I don't want to face the class. I pivot.

"Hi. My name is Erica Silverman."

A murmured hush runs through the crowd of faces staring. They've heard of me. A black-haired girl in the front glares, but I avoid eye contact. I avoid eye contact with everyone—Erica is still a little tender from the betrayal. Roth clears his throat.

"That will be sufficient. Perhaps it's best you don't share personal facts with us, Erica." He turns to the class. "Please treat her with respect, as you would any other student, and keep in mind, talking to the reporters outside about Erica will be grounds for detention. The sooner we ignore them, the sooner they'll leave."

A grumbled agreement goes around the room. I settle into my seat. The window's to my right, and I can see the front lawn. The reporters pace the fence, snap pictures. More have joined them since this morning—two news vans are parked outside too. They're here for me. The cameras are easy to act in front of. It's the high school kids who are hard. I don't want to admit I'm nervous beneath it all. Performance anxiety is for greenhorns.

"Vultures."

The voice comes from my left, low and gravelly. A tall boy sits next to me, slouched in his seat. He looks like he just woke up—wavy longish blond hair sticking at odd angles, and his blue eyes heavy lidded. He's not remarkably handsome, but his face is symmetrical and pleasant and entirely forgettable.

"Vultures? Who, me?" I whisper.

He winces. "No. Them. Paparazzi assholes."

Assholes. I savor the word. I haven't heard someone swear in a month—it's all been polite speech I've imitated. I glance out the window and contrive a soft smile.

"I'm starting to get used to it. This week's been nothing but cameras and police. I'll need a Seeing Eye dog if I get another flash in my face."

It's supposed to be a lighthearted joke, but he frowns. "You can just tell them to piss off."

I wanted to. Trust me, guy, I wanted to say a hundred nasty things to them as they bum-rushed the car when I got out this morning. But I can't say that. I try to look startled, like wounded Erica might. "I don't know if I'd be that rude."

He puts his head on his arms. "Kidnapper parents taught you to be doormat nice, huh?"

I darken my expression. Any mention of my parents gets a glower. "It's not like I don't want to be rude to them; I just don't know if they're worth speaking to at all."

He smirks. "That's a better answer."

The PA system blares with morning prayers, and we bow our heads. This is a private Christian school. The shadow of the cross on the roof stretches over the lawn. The blond boy doesn't bow his head. The black-haired girl glares at the floor. Some kids in the class look straight ahead. Everyone prays in their own way. I clasp my hands and put them to my forehead, careful not to touch the tender parts of my face. My plastic surgery bruises have faded, but I can still feel the phantom ache in my muscles.

Dear God, forgive me for my sins. I'm pretending to be a girl who went missing thirteen years ago. A girl who's rich.

A girl who's dead.

―――

At the age of four, Erica Silverman was a very charming little girl—pale blonde hair, deep brown eyes with long lashes, and a smile full of baby teeth. She was the pride and joy of the Silverman family—Mr. Silverman, an aerospace engineer, and his wife, a lovely southern socialite who came from Georgia money. They settled in Seven Hills, where the savage desert of Las Vegas relented to artificially green slopes and magnificent adobe near-mansions. Erica loved to play Princess and Dragon, and she had a thing for glassy-eyed porcelain dolls.

One day, after kindergarten, Erica wasn't there when her mother came to pick her up. School security had looked away for a mere thirty seconds. That was all it took for someone to snatch her from the curb.

The hunt lasted for years, until the police force could no longer sustain an intensive search. No ransom demand came through. No trace was left. The private detectives came and went in succession, each failing where the others had—when an actual sign of the girl was needed to continue. The most they could guess was that she'd been taken out of state, possibly over the border. After the seven-year mark, Mr. Silverman broke the way parents break when their children die—frantically, messily, irreparably. One Tuesday morning, he smashed every piece of furniture in his fifteenth-floor office. Then he smashed his office window. They caught him climbing out. His psychotic break landed him in the best mental hospital Mrs. Silverman could afford. She was left in charge of everything—to suffer and wait alone.

The story branches here.

The truth: Erica is dead. She was killed forty-eight hours after being kidnapped by Gerald Brando—a thirty-six-year-old computer salesman from Boulder City who'd seen her in a newspaper article on the family and had become infatuated. He stalked her for a year, watching her schedule, learning her quirks. When he took her, his sheer amount of preparation rendered escape or recovery futile. He had a quiet IQ of 120 with no overblown pride to muck it up. My father—Sal—met him in jail, where Gerald had been arrested for a different child murder. Gerald never told the police about Erica, but he told Sal every last detail during exercise in the yard.

The lie: a couple kidnapped Erica and raised her as their

own. The couple, friends of Sal, are promised a cut from the con. They're currently fleeing the country, leaving the now-seventeen-year-old Erica—me—to the police.

Sal is a con man. I am his daughter. This is our sting.

Before today I'd never been to high school. Or middle school. Or any school, for that matter. School wasn't possible when you moved around as much as we did. Sal homeschooled me. I'd covered calculus, the classics, and Sal's personal favorite, tactical military philosophy, a year ago. The classes I'm taking now are too easy. I'd covered this stuff years ago, but I don't say anything. I don't raise my hand to offer answers, and I purposely leave some questions wrong. Just a few. Erica is going to be a smart, but not too smart, girl. Too smart makes people uncomfortable. I want everyone to be comfortable around me. Comfortable people rarely hide things.

My free period is quickly becoming my favorite part of the day. No sitting straight and pretending to pay attention. Freedom. Freedom to wander the halls and scope out the land and the people. I get furtive glances from the hallway crowd. I've been on the news all month. They know exactly who I am but are acting like it's nothing. Groups of girls watch me, glances skittering over my face and uniform before turning back like they couldn't care less. But their whispers are insistent, and their giggles, loud. They're definitely talking about me, right? I take a deep breath, trying to breathe the confusion away. Remember Sal's words. His lessons. The number-one rule of a con artist: even if you have no confidence, act like you do.

Make them believe in your make-believe.

I square my shoulders and flip my hair. Confidence. My stride is long and my steps are even. I flash smiles at the groups that stare too long, and they look away abruptly.

Confidence. Make them believe in everything and anything. Make them believe in you.

The girls' bathroom—a sanctuary against the stares. I thought being the center of attention would be easier, less stressful. The moment the door closes behind me, I feel a weight lift from my chest. The mirrors are clean; the barest graffiti scrawls down the stall doors. My new face in the mirror still stops my heart and snap-freezes my blood. I have to look at it. A normal girl doesn't avoid mirrors—they're her best friend, worst enemy, and mild obsession all at once. I stare into it and mouth my real name, like the mirror will keep the secret in its silvery depths.

Violet.

My real name is Violet.

My hair isn't as blonde as it should be, but we decided to keep it my dishwater color. Highlighting would make it unnatural-looking, too desperate to mimic a little girl's hair color. Blonde fades with age sometimes, so the color can be justified. My cheekbones are now more defined. They couldn't put in implants, since those would show up on X-rays, but they did shave the bone down to imitate the look. My eyes are bigger, rounder. They'd slit those open on the sides (like peeling grape skins, the doctor said). My nose is upturned slightly, no longer hooked (shave the cartilage down, the doctor said). Three surgeries over five years. I look beautiful, but I don't feel pride. I just feel lost, small, eaten. Erica's swallowed me whole. The more I throw myself into her life, the more convincing I'll be. I have to be on my toes, keep aware of my surroundings like Sal taught me. I can't ruin the con that'll get us enough money to retire from petty crime. From *all* crime. Enough money to buy anything we want—houses, cars, small islands. Sixty million dollars is not chump change.

Michelle Painchaud

It's not easy-won change either. In the Vegas underworld, the Silverman painting is whispered about in the darkest corners, a holy grail for every security hacker and seedy lockpick expert. It's the con no one thinks can be done—an Olympic feat. Sal's people use it in conversation—"If you can outdrink me, buddy, I'll steal the Silverman painting." "Talking to the boss is harder than filching the Silverman painting." It's Mount Everest for climbers, the Marianas Trench for divers, and the Super Bowl for football teams.

And I'm going to steal it single-handedly.

All my training and all Sal's resources have culminated here today. This moment.

I make a smile in the mirror. It looks so warm, so genuine. So practiced. I pull the corners of my lips down a little. There. Less artificial. More honest—whatever that is. I can't be honest anymore. Honesty died a month ago when I stepped out of that cop car and into this world of private schools and fancy uniforms.

Sal took me to study normal high schoolers before I went undercover. We parked across from a school and watched them flit amongst each other, laughing and glaring and kissing. They were honest. I lived and worked around people who lied with their whole bodies. I tricked those people with deceptive body language of my own. I can read people well, but there was no need to read those kids. They were open books of hundreds of mishmashed emotions—flickering to love, hate, and everything in between with the speed of an impatient child with a TV remote.

Sal looked at me and smiled. "See? It's easy to pretend to be normal. You just gotta not pretend at all."

I want to call him. I want to hear his voice and his laugh and ask him for advice. But I can't. This is the most delicate time. I have to convince everyone I'm Erica. Every phone call, every eyelash batting, every smile and wave. It's *the* acting role of my life.

The bathroom door swings open. The black-haired girl who glared at me walks in. We lock eyes, hers a deep brown with a ring of heavy eyeliner, making her gaze almost feral. She breaks the contact and leans against a sink to smoke a cigarette. I push into the stall and do my business, suddenly nervous about how loud my pee sounds. When I get out, she's still there, and she doesn't budge when I use the sink behind her. Her eyes burn into me. Her smoke clouds are in my face. I dry my hands. She might scare other people, but I've seen her type before. Acting tough to hide some vulnerability. We're both acting.

"I'm on to you." She coughs.

I put on my practiced poker face, laced with a hint of insecurity to lure her into thinking she has the upper hand. "I'm sure you are."

She stubs her cigarette out on the enamel and laughs. "You're not the first to do this whole song and dance. Two girls have tried to pull it off before you. They'll weed you out like all the others."

She's not lying—I'd read up on the two girls, three years ago and eight years ago, who tried and failed to be Erica. They wanted the comfy lifestyle—but that was their downfall. Wanting so much for so long is impossible when you're faking. You just keep your eyes on the prize, grab it, and get out before someone blows your cover. Their prize was a whole life of luxury. Mine is simpler, cleaner, and much more profitable—the Silverman painting.

The other girls got caught. But they weren't me. I have DNA—a lock of the real Erica's hair Gerald kept for himself

Michelle Painchaud

in jail and Sal swiped. I have the lab assistant who marked it as a fresh sample when Sal hung something—blackmail, I suppose—over his head. I have an identical break in my right fibula, inflicted by Sal's doctor. The break healed in the same place, at the same angle as the fracture Erica had gotten falling down some stairs.

I have Sal on my side.

Nearly a month ago, "Erica" found out her parents weren't her real ones. She found out she was kidnapped. Erica might be wounded, a little soft, but she's not a doormat. She's frustrated and angry—every police officer and reporter who visited the house has accused her of being fake in the last month. She's had it up to her pretty brown eyes with being accused.

"You're not the first to doubt me." I glower. "And you won't be the last."

She laughs, a hyena chuckle. "Like I haven't heard that before."

The heavy thunk of the door as she leaves punches a hole in my chest. It's my first day of school, and I've already got someone on my scent. Fantastic. But she's only human.

Me, I've been in training all my life.

That girl's intimidating presence was probably enough to break the previous "Ericas." I'm different. Sal chose me from the foster system because I looked like her. He raised me to be her; he knew one day I could become her, fall into her easily, like a hand slipping into a glove.

Erica was part of me before I even knew her name.

I make my way to the cafeteria and choose a sandwich from the hot bar. I hand my lunch card to the student operating the register. The buttons look worn, old. The register is on its last legs. The student taps the Open button, and the tray pans out and pulls a memory from me.

At five years old, Violet is the perfect distraction.

The smell of gasoline clogs her nose. Cigarette smoke makes her eyes water. Neon beer brands in the window blind her. She waddles up to the counter and musters the fattest tears she can, which, in a strange gas station store with scary people staring at her, is easy to do. The cashier looks around, hoping someone will claim the wailer, but no one does. He doubles around the counter and asks questions—parents, in the bathroom? In the freezer aisle? They look together; her crying gets louder. The cashier tells the girl to wait behind the counter with him until her parents arrive. Ten minutes. Fifteen. A half hour passes before a man comes tearing in, gray hair askew. He's tall and well built, aging just past his prime.

"Has anyone seen my daughter? My daughter, blonde, brown eyes. Oh God, please, someone has to have seen her!"

The cashier walks around the counter and comforts the man, calms him. The girl isn't running out to meet him, so something must be wrong. He wants to make sure the man really is her father.

The cashier's back is turned. Violet is just barely tall enough to reach the Open button of the ancient register, but short enough that the security camera does not see her. Sal's frantic yells cover the faint *ding* of the opening register. Little fingers dance over the grooves of plastic—tens, twenties. She grabs as many as she can and stuffs them down her overalls, easing the tray closed.

She shouts, "Daddy!" and runs around the counter, braids waving. The reunion is acted, faked each time they drift apart and come together again, a job well done, a meal of something other than fast food and a soft motel bed, well earned.

Michelle Painchaud

But Sal's smile is proud, and Violet's smile is happy because he's proud, because someone, anyone, is proud of her.

———

Today's the first day in a month I've been out of the house.

House isn't the right word for it. Mrs. Silverman's place is more of a chateau. Not quite a mansion, but close. The yard is three acres of prime Vegas real estate in a gated community. White stone balconies and stained-glass windows contrast like rainbows on snow. The groundskeeper dawdles among barely budding flower bushes. The landscaping is overwrought, too lush and unnatural compared to the surrounding dry desert.

Mrs. Silverman let her grip loosen for me to attend school. I almost dread getting back in the car when she pulls up to the curb in her silver BMW, but I quash the feeling and try to look happy. Her hair is blonde, cut in a perfect bob. Her dark blue suit makes her pale skin and bright red lips glow. Her nose is thin, her cheekbones high. I look like her now. Too much like her. The smile on her face as she gets out of the car is too huge too be real. Too warm.

She sweeps over and draws me into her chest. The reporters along the fence are pushing toward us, but the police officers stationed there do their best to hold them back.

Put on a good show, Violet. Lose yourself in this woman's sorrow, her dark relief that's so easy to fall into—to imitate. Become a current in the river that is her life, and the sea that has been her suffering. The emotions radiate off her in waves as her tiny sobs echo in my hair.

"I'm sorry, sweetie. I'm sorry. I missed you. It's just school, but I missed you so much—"

"It's okay." I sniff, my own tears starting to spill over. She smells like roses and expensive lotion. The brute force of her sadness, *happiness*, makes acting easy. The trick to faking anything is to believe it's real. No doubts. Just faith. The bright February sunlight spills over us, onto my face and her face, onto our entwined bodies as she cries into my hair and I do the same. I am a mirror.

In this moment I am Erica Silverman.

2: SELL IT

Erica's house doesn't *look* like a prison.

The flight of grand oak stairs shines. Paintings line the walls. High ceilings flood with sun and crystal reflections of chandeliers—dancing rainbows on a dead girl's domain. The furniture is expensive, the floors hardwood. Everything screams affluence. This is the kind of place Sal and I would rip off. Theft of a huge house is easy when they're in the dining room having dinner, doors wide open. Dress in a service jumpsuit and nod and smile as you walk in, and very few people think twice about what you're doing. Sal liked to go as a plumber; I liked the pink polo shirt of a maid service. Expensive perfume, electronics. Sometimes jewelry if you were really lucky.

But today, I'm a different girl. One who doesn't know how to pick almost every industrial lock on the market. One who can't accurately discern a personality just from the clothes someone wears. I throw my backpack on my bed and look around Erica's room. My room. Dolls line the shelves, glass eyes reflecting my new face. They've been waiting thirteen years for Erica to come back and play with them. They know. Every curled strand of fake hair and plait of silk mocks me; they know I'm not her. Unlike Mrs. Silverman, dolls don't get desperate. They don't let it blind them to the truth. The vanity is lined with nail polish and pony stickers from another time. A crayon masterpiece portraying a stick figure family is taped to the mirror.

Mrs. Silverman's been possessive.

In my heart I know it's vital to the success of the con. She looked at me when I stepped out of the car and her knees gave way. Collapsed. Started crying. I inched over to her and picked her up, and she hugged me and didn't let go for a full hour. Hands like claws into my back. She felt it—felt me. It couldn't have just been my new face—while it was eerily similar to the composite the police drew up of seventeen-year-old Erica, moms can always tell. There was something else. Desperation, maybe. Two Ericas were fakes; her hopes lifted and smashed and repaired, only to be smashed again. Mr. Silverman retreated into a shell of madness. She lost her daughter *and* her husband.

Desperation.

I am convincing. The face, the DNA. The DNA cinched it. They didn't let me see her until it was confirmed. Erica was four when she was kidnapped—old enough to be loved, but young enough that time is my ally. Time distorts the little flaws Sal worked so hard to hide, erase, and pay off. Mrs. Silverman lets time and emotion distort her hopes; she sees me as the real thing. Her heart tells her I'm real.

She canceled all her appointments, charity balls, and dinner appearances, and spent a month with me in the house. Nail painting. Talking. Mostly talking and making food, like sustenance would fill the gaping maw of lost time. She asked about every year, every birthday and Christmas. I wove a story for her, a story that had her crying and me crying. A story that'd been carefully crafted by Sal and me, rehearsed in the months before I came here. I know every detail, every supposed bike accident and pet, as if it was my own life.

If the cameras caught my performance in that month, I would've earned an Oscar. At least two. Simple acting didn't cut it. I revived Erica from the grave, pulled her soul from air. I channeled her, invited her spirit to live through me. Violet was suppressed so deeply, I started to worry I'd lost her, but being at school today brought her out. Slipping from the shadow of Mrs. Silverman's grief brought her to light a little. Just a little. I can't show Violet too much.

A knock at my door.

"Come in."

Mrs. Silverman walks in wearing a hesitant smile. "How are you doing?"

I shrug. "School was tiring."

"Were they nice to you?"

"I don't know." I finger the childish pink bedspread. "They stared. I felt like they were accusing me. Doubting me."

She winces and sits on the bed beside me, squeezing my hand.

"You have to understand: there were other Ericas. They're just confused, is all."

"Like I am," I murmur.

She squeezes again. "What are you confused about?"

"I don't know!" I stand. Anger. Confusion and anger. "How could they do that? How could they take me, not tell me for thirteen years? *Thirteen years!* I loved them. I trusted them—"

"Them." Mrs. Silverman bites her lip, eyebrows knit. She knows I mean my kidnapper parents. "I don't have any answers for you, Erica. They were just bad people—"

"They weren't!" A shout. She flinches. "They weren't bad people. They were my parents. And every time I look at you, every time I see those reporters, or see them on TV, I—" I choke. "I want to hurt something. I want to hurt something until someone gives me a reason."

"Erica—"

"A reason!" I kick the door.

"Erica, please." She sweeps over and holds me. "Breathe. Deep breaths, like we practiced."

"The reporters treat it like it's entertainment," I say with a hiccup. "It's my life! *My life!*"

"I know, I know," she chants, holding me closer. "I was hoping they'd die down. I'm sorry. They're getting worse because we haven't made an official statement yet."

"Can we just make one and get it over with?" I wipe my eyes.

"Is that something you really want to do?" Mrs. Silverman's gaze crinkles with worry. "You might not be up for it."

"I'm up for it," I insist. "I'm tired of this. I just want to go back."

Mrs. Silverman twitches, a jump in her shoulders. I went too far, too fast.

"Not back to my old parents!" I scrabble. "I mean, go back to the way things were. Quiet. Peaceful."

She relaxes but still looks on the verge of breaking. "It's going to take time."

"Sorry. I didn't mean to scare you."

She smiles and traces my shoulder. The touch is feather light, laced with a hesitance I can't place. Disbelief that I'm here. Gratitude. The intensity of the emotions in her every look and touch hasn't diminished at all from the first day I got here. Thirteen years of love is pouring out of her every day, and I soak it up. I'd never been hugged so fiercely, with so much burning protectiveness. Her hug lasts years—thin

Michelle Painchaud

arms quivering, as if she thinks the moment she lets go, I'll vanish into smoke and broken lies.

Sal was my mother and father wrapped into one. He's hugged me once or twice. More when I was younger. I had foster home mothers before Sal adopted me, but I don't remember any of them.

Mrs. Silverman is my first *real* mother. But I haven't called her "Mom." Not yet. If the real Erica were in my shoes, she'd be hesitant to call Mrs. Silverman Mom—at least for the first month or so. But that month's running dry. I've played the mentality of a kidnapped girl straight and true, and now it's time for the next step.

"I'll see what I can do." She finally lets go and makes her way to the door. "A few daytime shows want to interview us. One visit will silence them all, hopefully. In the meantime come downstairs. Marie made croissants."

"Okay." I inhale hugely. "Deep breaths."

"That's right." She breathes with me, smiling now. "Deep breaths. We *will* get through this. Together."

The hall echoes with her footsteps. When I come down, she's not in the kitchen. Marie, Mrs. Silverman's hired help, flits around the marble countertops. She asks questions without looking at me.

"How was class?"

"Boring." I settle on a barstool.

Her laugh is the sort people make to tactfully cover something up. She'd heard my fit. She's older than Mrs. Silverman by at least twenty years; her weathered skin tells the story of a long journey through hardship. Other than the occasional fast-food deliveryman, Marie was the only one allowed in on our month of recuperation.

Marie hands me a croissant, still warm. "Did you go to

high school when you were with your other parents?"

"I was homeschooled. I guess they didn't want anyone to find out I wasn't their kid. They'd have to give birth certificates and stuff. Things they didn't have."

"Did you ever—" Marie cuts off. "Never mind. It is not my place to ask."

"Did I ever suspect them of not being my real parents?" She's easy to read. "No. I didn't look anything like either of them. I thought that was weird, but they said I looked like some aunt I never met. They didn't have any newborn pictures of me when I asked for them. Small things like that. Things that didn't make much sense until now."

Marie's tactfully quiet. I clench my fists on the countertop.

"I'm never going to forgive them."

"Neither would I," she agrees, and slices through a tomato with renewed vigor.

"Are you ready to go, Erica?" Mrs. Silverman's voice comes from the hall. "The hospital closes soon."

"Yeah, coming." I wolf the croissant down, shake off the anger. "Thanks, Marie. You're a really good cook."

Mrs. Silverman hesitates in the doorway. Her eyes glaze as she stares into the distance. Reporters gather at the front gate, the security and wrought-iron fence holding them back. I grab her hand, reassure her.

"Together." I nod.

"Together." She smiles, glaze lifting and leaving a clear sapphire blue.

━━━

Erica's kidnapping broke Mr. Silverman like a toy soldier.

I put myself in his shoes; she was his angel. She was the

Michelle Painchaud

reason he worked so hard, hurried home after dusk, and bought so many dolls. She was the reason his steps were light and his mind worked like it did—quickly and cleanly. When she was gone—when she'd been *taken*—his razor-sharp intelligence turned on him, the way a shark attacks its prey, shredding his sanity. And then he was gone, too. Only his body remained, macerated by hopelessness. Mrs. Silverman put him in Whiteriver Rehabilitation Center, where he's been for four years now. We've visited him every Wednesday of the last month. He hasn't spoken a single word to me or Mrs. Silverman. It's like he doesn't even know who we are, or that he's still in the world of the living. All he wants to do is play checkers. He's held together by the shallow will to keep moving forward as a Darwinian life form. Breathe, blink, breathe, sigh. He's here, but not really here. This linoleum table in the visitor lobby is where his body is, and only his body.

"Dad." I lower my voice. "It's me."

He's balding. He was once a very handsome man, but age and emotional storms weathered him thin and malnourished-looking. Stubble tints his face a sickly gray. Dark eyes dull with a milk of apathy. He glances up, looks me over, and looks down at the checkers again. Moves a black piece. I capture it with a red piece of my own.

Mrs. Silverman watches us from afar, wrapped in a vintage fox-fur coat as she taps on a vending machine for a coffee. She looks out of place, nervous. She wants to see Mr. Silverman frown, grin, *something*. Anything. I'm supposed to be the charm that brings him back. Even I can tell he's too far gone. The nurse pity-smiled when I said he'd remember me. Anything he says is inadmissible. The police will never believe a man who's been in a crazy house for years. Maybe I can give him some comfort. Some truth. If he says something about me, no one will believe him.

I lean across the table and put my hand over his, my whisper low.

"Your daughter wasn't in pain long, Mr. Silverman."

Gerald used a knife to cut her wrists. Clinical, quick, silent. She died of blood loss, probably just felt herself getting colder and sleepier. The violation happened long after she was dead. Her soul wasn't around to feel it.

A nurse passes, dropping a cup of water and pills for Mr. Silverman.

"Just to help keep him level," she assures me. Mr. Silverman downs the pills mechanically, a reflex. His eyes rivet to the checkers game. It's the only thing he seems to care about. I envy him. This game of strategy is so much simpler than the one I'm in the midst of—the one I'm living. The one in which I'm the star piece. Everything rests with me.

For once, it would nice to be a pawn instead of a queen.

Mr. Silverman smiles sweetly and moves a checker to my king line. Eyes surrounded by fine lines look up at me, his voice singsongs.

"I win."

"Did he say anything?" Mrs. Silverman presses. I shake my head and dredge a nice lie from my mental bank.

"He said something about a ballet class?"

Hope gleams in her eyes. "Yes, you took ballet when you were younger. Maybe he's coming to. We should keep visiting him. Work him out of his shell."

I don't have the heart to tell her the truth or disagree.

Michelle Painchaud

She's still in love with him. A mother and father who love each other. I wonder if Erica knew just how lucky she was.

When we get home, I realize Marie picked out new bed-covers for me—blue with white flowers, smelling of fancy department stores. I hug her and she laughs something in Spanish. I flop onto the bed and spread my arms, feeling the high-quality softness, so different from the thin motel blankets I'd slept in most of my life. Dinner is short ribs practically falling off the bone. Dessert is sorbet. I'm in heaven. These meals are a million times better than Sal's burnt monstrosities or convenience store takeout. Mrs. Silverman pushes a glass of wine toward me, her eyes twinkling.

"Try it. Sip slowly. It's a very good wine from a very good vineyard."

Sal's let me have sips of his favorite whiskey. This is milder, more fruity. It doesn't burn as much as whiskey. I still cough. Mrs. Silverman laughs and takes a sip.

"Now that you're officially in high school, let's lay some ground rules."

"Rules," I echo.

"Alcohol, for instance." She spins the wine glass by its stem. "A few sips here and there won't do you any harm. But you're young, and groups of young people like to drink. You'll make friends soon, I'm sure. The Erica I know is loved everywhere she goes."

I want to grimace, but Erica forces a flattered face instead.

"Believe me when I say there is plenty of time for drinking in your life. You don't have to do it all at once. That's not healthy. I don't mind the occasional drink—as long as you're at home with your friends, and I have the keys to everyone's cars. Is that clear?"

I'd seen glimpses of her stern side before, when she'd

demanded to know the details of my life with my kidnappers. If it concerns my safety or my past, she becomes an iron-spined demon of willpower. I nod meekly.

"Crystal clear."

"If you ever find yourself in a position where everyone is drunk, where you are uncomfortable or feel scared about getting in the car, call me. I'll pick you up no matter what, and I won't ask questions."

"No questions asked?" I tilt my head.

"None at all. I might need answers after incident two, though."

I nod. It sounds fair enough. Sal never gave me any restrictions, really, except that I had to be home in time to pull a con or catch the bus/train/plane with him to our next port of shelter. Partying was redundant when you pulled cons in nightclubs on a daily basis. Loose pockets on the dance floor, easily blackmailed Johns with overeager libidos and the stupidity to hit on an underage girl like me. Sorority girls looking for coke and scoring baking soda instead. The possibilities were endless. But going just for fun? Just to drink and not to make money? That sounds like a waste of time.

"Did those people tell you everything?" Mrs. Silverman presses. "About growing older, and, ah, interactions with the opposite sex?"

"I got that talk. Pretty sure I know how it works."

"You should know there's always a condom involved. Always. I'll have no STDs or pregnancies from you. I want you to have the best life you can now that you're home."

Violet rolls her eyes. Erica blushes. "I'll be safe. Common sense, right?"

"If you want to get birth control, we'll schedule a doctor's appointment. Just tell me. Be open with me."

This is what parents do. It feels weird. Moving around with Sal left me little time for solid friends, let alone boys or love. It was never an option when every day was spent plotting a con for tomorrow or running from yesterday's. I'd pretended to be in love before, when it was part of a con. The emptiness bleeds through in my words.

"I doubt anybody will like me enough to do that sort of thing with me."

Mrs. Silverman's brow wrinkles. "Of course someone will like you, and you'll like them. It's just a matter of time. I want you to be properly prepared when it does arrive."

It won't arrive. I smile like it might. People like it when you're stupidly optimistic. Makes them want to protect you.

"Thanks for dinner. And everything."

"What have we said about thanking me?" She looks at me sternly.

I sigh. "Don't do it, because families help each other without expecting gratitude."

Her smile comes back. "It's just what mothers do."

That final sentence echoes in my head as I brush my teeth and then scrub my hair with the fancy shampoo and my body with the loofah that probably cost more than all the secondhand clothes I used to own. I don't know what mothers do. My real mother, the one who'd birthed me, left me on the steps of a church. She was probably too young to have a kid. The priesthood turned me over to foster care, and Sal picked me up when I was five. I don't know what *mother* really means. Sal loves me, I guess, but not so deeply, so desperately. I've seen movies and stuff, but that sense of longing hasn't hit me until now. I've gotten a taste.

My bed is cold. The dolls leer down at me from the shelves.

The plan is simple. It's not anything as complicated as a will, or having Mrs. Silverman allot me half of the estate. That would be too messy. I'd have to stick around for years to pull off that con, and possibly wait until she died.

I mince downstairs in my pajamas to get a glass of water. I stop on the last step and stare into the dark library. Mrs. Silverman inherited a very old painting. Sal knew, like all Vegas con men, that Mrs. Silverman created a safe somewhere in the house to hide it. A Japanese collector has offered a huge sum to whoever "acquires" the painting. A buyer meant we wouldn't have to navigate the black market for a willing fence, and with art, that's important. A near-priceless original is a viable theft only if you can sell it quickly. We have a buyer. All that's left is for me to steal the thing.

It's called *La Surprise*, an oil-on-wood painting done by Jean-Antoine Watteau in 1718. Sal said it'd been stolen during the French Revolution and then made its way down Mrs. Silverman's family for years. Maybe her family was too scared to turn it in, or maybe they were waiting to get the maximum money for it. Whatever the case, when Mrs. Silverman inherited the painting, right before Erica was taken, she never documented it on tax papers or house revaluation forms. She wanted to keep its existence a secret.

She failed.

Every crook in Vegas knows Mrs. Silverman has the painting, but few know where she keeps it. Most speculate in a bank in Switzerland, or inside one of the heavily guarded vacation houses the Silvermans own. No one thought Mrs. Silverman would keep such a painting in her main house—but that was exactly why no one had found it. Sal, by a stroke of sheer luck, met the man who constructed a vault off the Silverman's library. Sal bribed him for info. The library is fixed with four closed circuit cameras monitored by Mrs. Silverman's security all the time. The vault's encrypted with an eight-digit code comprised of letters and numbers. Only Mrs. Silverman knows the code. Mr. Silverman knows it, but his brain is too scrambled for any chance at reliable extraction. I only have one shot to try the library vault. If I hang around the vault, it'll raise suspicions. Once is enough to blow my cover. I have to get the correct code beforehand and use it when I make the getaway. I haven't actively started searching for the code. This code is something I'll find by listening, not asking. Questions make people suspicious. I need to keep my mouth shut and ears open while I establish myself as the real Erica Silverman. Time is my ally. Just a little more time, and the people in Erica's life will come to trust me, and with trust, the code will start to take shape.

The microwave clock spills over into midnight, and the marionette girl walks up the stairs to sleep in her puppet bed in the puppet house, filled with not-puppet people.

They are made of flesh and blood, and she is made of lies and wood.

3: STAGE IT

The small space between my stomach and heart where I keep Violet chained is churning, blades mixing the concrete that used to be my impenetrable nerves. When did I get so soft? It's just TV. Violet isn't afraid of anything—not camera lenses, not the crowd of people in the house, not the impending performance she has to act out. Erica quivers uncertainly, corrupts Violet—a patch of rust on a suit of armor. Mrs. Silverman's publicist flits around the couch, his slicked hair reflecting the light trees a few feet away. He waves a script in his hands.

"Just be natural. Katie won't ask any unsettling questions. She's usually good about that kind of thing. If she asks something you don't like, I'll jump in and stop her. Just give me a nod or a look."

Mrs. Silverman talks with the producer and her lawyer in the kitchen over coffee. She looks just as uncomfortable as I am.

"Erica, are you listening?" Publicist snaps.

I already know what I have to do out there. Don't coach the master, apprentice. Erica shoves Violet aside and smiles apologetically.

"Yeah, sorry. I'm just really nervous. I've never been on TV before."

Publicist's tone softens. "Whatever you do, focus on the fact you're glad to be back home, and how you're coping. This isn't live, so they can edit out any stumble."

"Five minutes!" someone shouts.

Publicist gets twitchy and calls out, "Mrs. Silverman, are you ready?"

Mrs. Silverman sits on the couch beside me, grabbing my hand. "No one is ever really ready for television."

Her makeup is caked on, unnaturally so. Mine is too, the concealer and powder making my muscles work twice as hard to show emotion. At least the interview is in the house. At least we can sit together. Publicist settles in an armchair just off-camera, ready to jump in at a moment's notice. The crew assumes positions behind lenses and lights and boom mics. Marie stands with Publicist, face creased with worry.

The interviewer, Katie, comes in. Her red suit matches her nails, her nods short and curt as she holds out a hand. Mrs. Silverman and I stand.

"Mrs. Silverman, Erica. It's nice to meet you. I'm Katie Tims, and I'll be interviewing you today. Thank you so much for agreeing to this."

Her grip is smooth. Practiced. She settles in a chair across from us and asks over her shoulder,

"You've got my left side, Jerry?"

Jerry grunts from behind the camera. The producer shifts in his chair.

"Ready when you are, Mrs. Silverman."

Mrs. Silverman looks to me. I nod. She gives a small *Ready*, and laces her fingers through mine. Katie clears her throat.

"On five."

The lights blare, brightening a notch. The boom mic hovers like a foam flamingo. A crane. A *vulture*. Katie goes from a business frown to a concerned, devastated look in a millisecond.

"First of all, Erica, I just wanted to thank you for talking with us. There's been a lot of controversy over your case."

"That's why we decided to tell the story . . ." Mrs. Silverman starts. "We want to get it out in the open, tell the truth, and go on with our lives."

"You've been through so much." Katie's sympathetic tone is hard beneath it all—guiding. "How are you feeling, Erica?"

The swivel in the camera tripods yanks me into the spotlight. This isn't a crowd I'm trying to blend in to or cause a scene to distract or pick which person's pocket looks best. This is the entire nation, and all I'm supposed to do is be myself—no, Erica. Soulless black lenses are watching me, not human faces I can gauge reactions of. Just pretend. Pretend they're people.

"I'm fine." I swallow, and the nerves aren't all faked. "I'm still confused. I guess that feeling will never go away."

"How did you find out your parents weren't your biological ones?"

I shift uneasily and shoot a look to Publicist. He makes a move to say something when I change my mind. Indecision, reluctance. I'm playing this pitch-perfect. I inhale.

"My old parents fought; one of them got hurt. They didn't normally fight that hard, but . . ." I bite my lip. Mrs. Silverman puts her arm around my shoulders. "My old mom got injured, fell on some glass. We took her to the ER; there was a woman there. Social services. She thought it was domestic violence. They put me in foster care, and when they asked for my birth certificate. . . ."

I flinch. Mrs. Silverman squeezes my hand and answers for me.

Michelle Painchaud

"By then her old parents were gone. Running."

"It must've been *devastating* for you. What happened from there?"

"The police took my DNA and matched it with Mom's." I incline my head to Mrs. Silverman. She looks shocked—this is the first time I've called her that. Gratitude and relief shine in her eyes.

"And how do you feel, Mrs. Silverman? How, if you'll forgive me for asking, can you be so sure she's your real daughter? After all, there was the Kara Smith fraud, and the Bethany Richmond fraud—"

"I know." Mrs. Silverman's arm tightens around me. "I can feel it in my heart—my baby girl is here, sitting beside me. DNA or no, I knew it was her the moment I saw her."

"But didn't you have those feelings about the previous Ericas?"

"No. Not so strongly. Not so purely. I know this is Erica. The world can doubt it, but to me, she is my beautiful, sweet, kind Erica, and she's home with me. That's all that matters."

Me? Sweet? Kind? She's not talking about Violet. She's talking about my fake self. I tamp down what tastes like disappointment. Katie seems taken aback at Mrs. Silverman's show of conviction, but she presses on.

"Erica, how do you feel about your old parents? I mean, when you found out, you must've just broken down. And the police haven't been able to catch them."

Clench my fists. Make a strangled noise in my throat. Mrs. Silverman pets my head like it'll relax me.

"On one hand, I want them to get caught, to suffer, you know? But on the other, they raised me. Gave me a pretty okay life. I wish they hadn't had to lie. I wish—"

Lies. This is a world, a girl, made of lies. Tears spring up that aren't forced. They come naturally, frightfully easily.

"I'm s-sorry," I stammer, and wipe my eyes on my sleeves. Mrs. Silverman pulls my head under her chin. It's just a little movement, but it makes the tears flow harder, and my hiccups resound. Why? Why am I crying?

Publicist clears his throat and waves a hand. "That'll be enough, Katie. Let's stop here."

"The truth is always hard." Katie's voice is sympathetic, even after the cameras stop rolling.

This isn't the truth. No truth could rival the prickling pain of these nesting thorns. They dig, pull back, embed deeper with every day I spend in this woman's arms. It's just a con. I've done hundreds of cons.

Why does this one hurt?

— — —

For once, Mrs. Silverman doesn't insist on inching her way into my room. I watch the reporter vans leave through the curtains. I pull the new, stiff comforter over my head and cocoon my body in it. Break it in. Break it all. Break it into bite-size pieces, something easier to understand. I'd just been acting. The tears were a nice touch. Hadn't planned them; it was Erica bleeding through too well. This Erica-only month tipped the scales. I need balance. I need Violet.

Violet pulls herself out of the cocoon and turns a lamp on. Light peeks into the dark room. She spots the ancient crayon drawing taped to the mirror—the one the real Erica drew thirteen years ago. The one Mrs. Silverman's kept up there until now. Violet pulls it down. Rips it into tiny pieces. The fragments spread on the carpet like islands in a blue sea.

Michelle Painchaud

"Erica?" The knock on my door is hesitant. "Are you all right?"

"Yeah." I sweep the fragments under the bed with my foot. "I just need . . . some time alone."

There's a pause. A stop in the flow. An eerie silence devoid of calming waves. The building rhythm of the last month is frozen. Something rests against the door, a hand.

"I love you," I try—a tiny ripple meant to soothe her.

"I love you, Erica. Forever." A tsunami of fire, resolve.

And the ocean starts moving again.

—▬▬▬—

The second day of school is easier.

Mrs. Silverman's hug is still as fierce as ever. When she pulls away, she takes something from her pocket and presses it into my hand. It's smooth, square. A touch phone, the fancy kind Sal would swipe from a tourist's pocket.

"I'm sorry it took so long for me to give you this; it just arrived yesterday. If you feel like you need to come home, or if it gets to be too much, call me. I'll pick you up," she insists. "I know high school isn't easy. Especially if you've never been to a school before. Try your best, but think of this as an emergency way out, if you need it."

"Thank you. It's amazing." My jaw unhinges a little. I'd always wanted one of these. Getting one wasn't an option, with Sal and me using money to pay rent or bribe the next Joe in the Erica scheme.

"And if you can, get some friends' numbers." She winks.

I laugh. "I'll try. Easier said than done."

She waves as she pulls out of the parking lot and honks her horn in a final farewell. People stare. It's a little embarrassing.

The reporters shout their questions from behind the police barricade.

"Erica, now that you've gone on TV, do you feel any different?"

"Over here, Erica! Is it true you don't want to prosecute your fake parents if the police find them?"

I put my backpack under an acacia tree and take my sweater off, spreading it on the grass and lying on it. Tune out the voices. Tune out the stares from the kids on the lawn around me. I put my arm over my eyes as if trying to get some sleep. The February morning is hot, but a sweet wind blows in the gray sky.

"Erica, right?"

I lift my arm at the voice. A girl with bright red hair sits by me in the shade.

"I'm Merril. Nice to meet you."

"Why so forward?" I raise an eyebrow.

"You don't like it?" She tilts her head, and it's then I notice her eyes—huge and brown, with thick lashes. Doe eyes. Pretty-girl eyes I'd undergone plastic surgery to get and still don't really have.

"Just not used to it." I roll over onto my belly, the grass tickling me through my shirt.

"You're all over the news. You should definitely get used to it." Merril picks at grass. "I saw your bit on the morning show with Katie Tims."

"It sucked." I sigh.

"You were so sad looking," she murmurs. "Made me feel bad. About ignoring you on your first day."

"It's all right. I'm getting too much attention lately. Getting ignored is refreshing."

She fiddles with her skirt. "I guess, I mean, my mom said

we went to school together. When we were younger."

"Did we? I can't remember."

"It's okay." Merril smiles. "I don't really remember it myself, but Mom won't shut up about how we used to play together when we were kids. Me, you, and Cassie. All I remember is one really blurry Halloween. Cass was a fairy. I was, like, in a puppy costume, and you were—"

"A ballerina," I finish for her.

She looks startled, but nods. It was an educated guess; Erica took ballet at a very young age. From the picture I'd ripped up, it was clear she liked the color pink. A tutu would have been right up her alley.

"You *do* remember." Merril's face softens.

"Sort of. It's a fuzzy haze. Starting in the middle of the year sucks. Not remembering the people you're supposed to sucks even more."

She points. "Cassie's over there. She's pretty popular now. Has a boyfriend in college. You might wanna say hi to her. Over in that corner"—she points at a bench—"are the scary-smart kids. The punks go behind the building to smoke in the mornings, so you won't see them that much. Just don't go in the second-floor bathrooms. It's, like, their hideout or something. Mr. Harold is a jerk, gives way too much home-work. And don't say the word *fat* in Ms. Anderson's class. She flips."

"Right." I smother a laugh.

"Nacho day is Wednesday—it's the only lunch worth eating."

"No good tacos?" I lament.

"I know this great place around the corner that has awe-some tacos." Her eyes light up. She whips out her cell phone. "Here, give me your number."

Smile a lot; be pleasant. This friend thing doesn't seem so hard. It's like conning, but without the lure of scoring money. The bell rings. Merril offers me her hand. I take it and stand.

"Your first period is Roth, right? Let's go."

Merril leads me through the crowd, all of us in the same uniforms of plaid and blazers. Paintings line the main hall, and polished wood floors gleam. Everyone in the world says hi to Merril, and she slings some intimate inside joke back to each of them. She's obviously popular. I fight the urge to smile at people. The real me—Violet—burns to talk to someone. Being in a huge crowd of people my age lights up every nerve. But I'm Sal's protégé down to the subconscious bone. I keep my eyes from meeting anyone's gaze—the more evasive and mysterious I am, the more damaged I'll seem. Erica is damaged.

Merril pulls me into Mr. Roth's class. He nods. "Good morning, Erica. Hello, Merril."

"Mr. Roth, can't Erica sit by me?" Merril pouts. "Taylor can switch into her seat, right?"

"Maybe if you get on your knees and beg my permission, popular, I'll think about it." The voice comes from the black-haired glaring girl slumped in her seat. Her eyeliner is even thicker today. She puts her feet up on the empty chair in front of her. So her name's Taylor. Merril smiles sweetly.

"It's not like I'm asking you to jump off a cliff, Taylor. But if you'd do that, too, I'm sure everyone would appreciate it."

"There'll be no need for that kind of animosity." Mr. Roth clears his throat. "Taylor will remain where she is. Erica, please sit in the seat I assigned you."

Merril shoots me an apologetic look. Mr. Roth goes over matrices, and boredom numbs my brain. I finish the sheet he assigns for homework in five minutes, but stow it away to turn in tomorrow with everyone else. James Anders, the blond boy next to me, sleeps through the whole class, but the worksheet under his head is half-finished with right answers. He obviously got bored like I did, and gave up.

Second rule of conning: set up contacts. Merril is the first of my information pipelines. She's one of the most popular juniors in the school, with friends in all grades. If I maintain my friendship with her, I'll know about everyone and everything.

———

"Taylor is the daughter of a lawyer, so she acts superior all the time." Merril sips her soda. "The kid you sit next to— James Anders. His dad's a concert pianist or something. Totally a lazy slacker. He sleeps in every class and lies to get out of PE."

"He seemed nice." I pick at my salad. Erica is skinny. Violet, on the other hand, wants beef. I try to imagine the salad as a massive cheeseburger. Merril sniffs.

"Not worth your attention, trust me. Now, Kerwin over there." She nods to a group at a table, where a dark-haired boy sits surrounded by friends. Instantly, I can tell he's the one she's talking about—too handsome to look at without getting blinded. "British transfer student. Well, technically Wales, but whatever. Captain of the varsity soccer team, takes all AP classes, and did I mention he's hot as hell?"

"You didn't have to say it; it's obviously one of those facts of life." My eyes flicker away, looking for James. Does he eat in the cafeteria? His skinny frame makes me think he doesn't eat at all.

A girl with a very noticeable chest walks up to our table, smiling. "Erica, is it really you?"

Brown hair, round face, about 5'5". My mind flicks back to the dossier Sal gave me. This must be Cassie. My eyes light up. "Cass?"

"Oh my God! You really remember me!" She hugs me with all the contained excitement of a hamster on crack, talking at relatively the same speed. "I told Merril you'd remember us. Oh my God, it's been *so* long. When you went missing, we held tons of vigils for you and stuff. By middle school we definitely thought you were—" She stops herself. "Uh, well. Gone. For good. Is that insensitive? And then those other girls—Oh, who cares, you're here now, and that's all that freaking matters!" She hugs me again. "Let's go places, do things. We *have* to catch up."

"Definitely." I smile. "What did you have in mind?"

"Maybe a dip in that huge pool of yours? Your mom kept the pool, right?" She giggles and looks to Merril. "Text her my number."

Merril gives her a thumbs-up and gets on it.

"So . . ." I start. "A boyfriend in college?"

Cass's eyes widen at Merril. "You slut, I told you not to say anything."

"Sorry! It just came out," Merril defends, typing on her phone rapidly without looking at it. She doesn't seem to take offense at the *slut*. It must be some sort of endearment, but I can't see how calling someone a slut would be endearing, ever. To be safe, I won't use the term at all, even to blend in.

Cass gets over her momentary anger. "But seriously, who wants to talk about boyfriends when you went through all that? Were they nice to you and everything? How did you find out?"

I go quiet. Merril looks like she wants to say something.

Cass bites her lip. "Sorry, didn't mean to bring up anything you don't want to talk about."

"It's fine," I assure her. "It's just hard, you know?"

She hugs me again. It feels strange. I've never been hugged this much in my life. "I bet your mom's all over you. Did you visit your dad yet? I heard he's in a hospital or something."

"Yeah, mental health place. We've been visiting him since I got back."

"That's good." She nods. "Well, listen, I gotta get back to lunch, but Merril's giving you my number, so you two call me when you wanna do something."

"Sure." I smile, and she brushes a lock of hair behind my ear.

"You're so pretty, Erica. I knew you'd be pretty, but honestly I didn't think you'd be this gorgeous."

I laugh shyly, and she trots back to her table. Merril exhales.

"She's way too hyper."

"Hasn't she always been?" I murmur.

Merril shakes her head "In middle school she was super quiet. It's when she got that huge rack that everybody started paying attention to her and she got all chatty."

I cover for my mistake by taunting her. "Jealous, are we?"

"Of course. I'll never have her chest unless I plastic it." She motions to her rather flat blazer.

"You're cute anyway," I compliment, and she flushes and punches my shoulder.

"Oh, be quiet."

After school I swing my legs on the front lawn's bench. Mrs. Silverman will be right on time, like always. She's hyper-aware of time; she always gets here exactly three minutes after the bell. Thirty seconds of those minutes were all it took. Thirty seconds stole her kid from her. I know why she's so bent on punctuality, but it's pointless—there are too many reporters watching for me to ever get snatched again. They cling to the fence, around the fence, snap my picture and shout questions.

Two people are behind the main building, wearing plastic gloves and carrying tongs. They pick up litter, throwing it in the trash bags they carry. The girl has long dark hair, the boy wavy blond. I move to a closer bench so I can hear them.

"You never talk to anyone else, Beethoven. So why the sudden yammering with the new girl?" Taylor's voice. My eyes widen.

James sighs and rubs his brow on his arm. "None of your business, Gotherella."

"Don't you watch the news? Goths died out years ago," she snaps back.

"So did Beethoven." He grunts.

Taylor's eyes shift over to me, and her smile grows. "Fake Erica! Sup?"

James straightens.

I slink around the corner and don't bother to correct her. "Believe what you want, Taylor."

"I will, thanks. Should've said something deep, Beethoven. Impressed her." Taylor cackles. She fishes a pack of smokes from her pocket and lights one, squatting behind a bush. Her skirt rides up, panties clearly visible, and James nearly drops his tongs. He covers his eyes with them.

"Show some decency, woman!" His face is bright red.

Taylor cackles again and wiggles her fingers at him. "Don't get too close, virgin. You might actually see something you like."

"You guys obviously know each other . . ." I start.

James sighs. "She's the only person who gets as much detention as I do."

"What can I say?" Taylor blows smoke. "Teachers are jealous of my good looks and endless talent. And youth. They love that youth shit. It's why they teach in the first place." Her voice gets a Dracula accent to it. "They vant to suck my youth."

"Or immaturity, in your case." James grunts again and puts a soda can in the trash bin.

Taylor takes a heavy drag. "You're especially prissy today, Beethoven. Is it that time of month?"

I nearly laugh, but the flash of a camera stops me. The school fence is close to my right, and the reporters have flanked it, their eager faces behind the chain links.

"Erica! Erica, just a few questions—"

"Any comments on what you remember from the kidnapping?"

"Why aren't you and your mother pressing your lawyers and the police harder to find your kidnappers?"

There are just a few of them, but they come with cameramen and sound people. Violet, the real me, is very comfortable with these sorts of people. These sorts of shouts and lights. Erica isn't. I flinch at another bright camera flash and fake a stutter.

"I really d-don't—"

Before I get a full sentence out, a pair of tongs violently collides with the fence, narrowly missing the fingers of a reporter. They jump away. Taylor's on her feet, arm extended in the end of a throw.

"Buzz off, fuckers."

"Who are you? Are you a friend?" A reporter starts forward again.

"Erica, are you adjusting well to your school?"

"Your kidnappers have all but gotten away. How do you feel about that?"

Taylor lunges at the fence, bringing her leg up and kicking with trained expertise—karate, maybe.

"I said leave us the fuck alone!" A reporter whistles at her lifted skirt. She flips him off and glances at James. "Back me up here, sissy boy, will ya?"

James lets out a sigh bordering on a growl. He stretches to his full height—an intimidating six feet, at least, and runs the tongs along the fence in a languid pattern.

"Don't you guys have anything better to do than bug high schoolers? This is a private school. You know what that means, right? The parents of the kids are usually well off. Let's not forget that Erica here"—he puts a hand on my shoulder; it's warm—"has a mother who's *very* high up there. Her lawyers are pretty fancy too. What would they do to your penny presses if she, oh, I don't know, suffered *mental distress* because of your pestering?"

Some of the reporters back off. Others look unsure. They still hang at the fence, but their questions are quieter. At the gate I see Mrs. Silverman's BMW pull up to the curb. I breathe a sigh of relief. Taylor spits one last time at the reporters and stubs out her cig, waving me away.

"See you later, Fake Girl."

James nods. "Later."

I start to walk away when something compels me to stop. I look back.

"Thanks. Both of you." I'm not sure why Taylor defended me. My con artist's instincts hone in on a reason—she's the sort of person who believes in the right thing to do. Even if she suspects me, she feels like no one should have to go through badgering like this. She's probably gone through it herself. Same with James.

"Thank me for what? Being myself? If you like it so much, pay me." Taylor snorts.

"She's got a point. I could use some pocket change," James ponders aloud.

"I'd make you buy better motivation." I cross my arms over my chest. "I saw your paper in math. You're good."

"I bet you say that to all the boys." His voice takes on a bitter tone. Taylor gives the same hyena chuckle.

I feel like they're making fun of me, but I'm not mad. It's the opposite—I'm glad they're making fun of me. They're not being fake. They're not pretending to be someone they aren't. It's the only true thing—that they are cruel and I am equally cruel, and we sling cruelties back and forth in all honesty.

Honesty.

I slide in the BMW, and Mrs. Silverman peers out the window. "And here I'd hoped the morning show would make them go away. Did those reporters give you any trouble?"

"No." I look in the side mirror at the two figures picking up trash. "Someone told them off."

4: WIN IT

Three people know I'm going to a shrink—Mrs. Silverman, Marie, and the man who cleans the shrink's office.

Mrs. Silverman makes sure I get there on time, but like school, she's reluctant to let me go.

"You'll call me as soon as it's over?" She furrows her thin brows.

"Definitely." I get out and give her a reassuring smile through the window. She takes me in, the school-rumpled uniform, the slightly frizzy hair. The way she smiles, you'd think I was dressed up in a college graduation gown, or a CEO suit. Something speaking of accomplishment that makes her proud.

She's just proud I'm *alive.*

I pull open the glass door and head inside. Business offices line the halls. I take the stairs two at a time and stop in front of the shrink's office, the plaque glinting in the sun: MILLI-CENT HARRIS, MD—COUNSELING PSYCHOLOGIST. The door is plain, scratches marring the wood finish.

On my first visit here, I took twenty minutes to compose myself outside this door. I'm sure that meant something to Millicent. Reluctance. I'd recalled how Sal told me to deal with psychologists—don't pretend. You let your act down, push it into the dirt, let it die—otherwise it's too easy to spot. In front of any halfway decent psychologist, a con face falls apart. They spot your every sign, and the really good ones can do it in minutes. Sal's been perceived only two times, and by internationally famous criminal profilers.

I'm not as good as Sal. It'll be a miracle if I ever *become* as good as Sal. I can't think that far ahead—or maybe I've never thought of being a con artist for that long. Sal's poise comes from fifty years of conning. I've had twelve. Millicent, while stationed in a shoddy building, is one of the best shrinks in the state. She just prefers to keep that quiet.

The door's unlocked, which means she's not in with a client. The curtains are drawn back, pale light washing over the leather furniture and stocked bookshelves. The woman herself is making tea. The steam from the water boiler puffs around her suit—gray, with brass buttons. Her hair is auburn, like burnt scrapings of caramel. She's a little pudgy and pear-shaped, but it only serves to deceive—she is not jolly. She might look homey and slow, but her brain is sharper and faster than any starving crocodile.

"Erica, do come in."

She says it without turning around. She likes to do that—say things without looking at you, like the unease it creates gives her the upper hand. I sit on the leather recliner and put my backpack on the floor. She turns, two cups in hand.

"I thought we'd have some tea. Do you like peppermint?"

"I hate tea," Violet sneers.

Millicent's face remains smiley, cheeks trying to swallow her eyes. "Very well."

There's no point being Erica. She's put on the back burner, Violet given the reins. Violet's bluntness is a perfect disguise— to Millicent, it's Erica expressing her true self: the angry, tortured self that was betrayed and shipped off to a whole new world. She has no reason to suspect Violet is my true self beneath Erica. To her, they're just two aspects of one person.

She's more right than she knows.

Millicent settles in the chair across from me with her tea and a notebook. Her pen has a stupid plastic panda on the end of it.

The first question is always the same.

"How are you feeling today?"

"Fine." I shrug and lie back on the leather. "Tired. But that's nothing new."

"What's made you so tired?"

"People. Reporters. They're never going to give up, are they?"

"You said last session, the reporters didn't bother you. What's changed that?"

"I don't know," Violet snarls. "Maybe it's the fact they've hung around for a whole month screaming at me and taking pictures of my every zit."

"So you feel as though your privacy is being invaded." She scribbles something.

"I never had privacy to begin with. First Mom, wanting to be with me all the time. And it's not like I don't like it—I like it—she's way nicer than my last mom—" I stop. "God, listen to me. 'Last' mom. People aren't supposed to have two sets of parents like this."

She's much harder to read than the average person. But the quirk in her eyelids tells me she's thinking about what I said. Two sets of parents. Of course people have two sets of parents—divorce. She's a family counselor, mostly.

"I know what you're going to say." I sniff.

"We're here to talk about you, Erica. Let's stay focused."

"What if I hate focus? What if, for a half hour, I want to be totally unfocused?"

Her face goes still. She does that when I say something interesting she can delve into. She scribbles and leans back in her chair.

"All right. Feel free to ask me questions, if you wish."

"No, I don't want to ask you questions. I just want to talk about something other than being kidnapped for four seconds. Is that okay?"

"Absolutely."

"And don't do that."

"Do what?"

"Agree with me all the time."

She writes something down again. She doesn't say a third of the things she wants to.

"It must be boring, listening to people blabber for a living," I try.

"It's not as boring as you might think." She twirls the panda pen. "Eventually, it becomes more than just listening. It becomes a way for you to step into someone else's shoes— imagine what their life must be like, and to understand their feelings truly. To say you understand is one thing. To feel understanding is another thing entirely."

The words hit close to home. I know exactly what she means.

"You don't 'feel' understanding," I correct. "It's something that transforms you. When you honestly understand something, you become it."

"In that vein of logic, when you become something, you understand it?" she counters lightly, and sips her tea.

"No." I lace my fingers and unlace them. "You can become something without understanding it."

"I don't think so." Millicent smiles over the cup.

"I think so," I assert. I know so. I've become something right now without really understanding it. *Her.* Erica. "I can become this happy girl. This pretty, popular girl, if I try really hard. If I smile a lot and try to laugh, I'm someone different, and no one knows otherwise."

The panda pen scratches across the clipboard.

"Do you feel like you can't be yourself around the people in your life?" she asks.

I smile. "I can be both of my selves. But just one at a time."

I don't know what she'll make of that. It gives her something to think about, because she doesn't ask any more questions as she scribbles madly on the clipboard. In these pregnant pauses I'm supposed to keep talking, but I have nothing to say today.

Finally Millicent breaks the silence with gentle words.

"Who hit you, Erica?"

My head snaps up from the carpet. Her eyes are still sharp, but cautious.

"Who hit you when you were little? Your old mother? Old father?"

My fingers twitch. I force them to relax. "No one hit me."

She watches me, unblinkingly, for a good thirty seconds. That stare says it all. Violet's stomach gives a twinge.

"I'm sorry. Let's stop for today." Millicent smiles and stores her clipboard. "Are you sure you don't want any tea?"

I grab my stuff and push through the door, heart thrumming in my ears. Two stairs at a time, and then freedom, fresh air free of the smells of cloying tea. The bench is cold and hard. Across the street is a restaurant, bustling with the dinner crowd. Cars pull up. Families get out. The golden squares of the windows are bright and welcoming.

———

On Violet's eighth birthday, Sal takes her out to a nice restaurant.

She's wearing a Dorothy-style dress with red plaid. The waitress asks Sal if she's his daughter, and he nods, his proud smile perfectly insincere as she compliments Violet on her beauty and says their orders will be coming right up.

"I *am* pretty, right, Sal?" Violet creases her brows and stuffs bread into her mouth. She doesn't know when they'll be able to stop for another meal like this. Puts an extra roll in her pocket, just in case.

Sal chuckles. "Prettiest girl I know."

She's satisfied with that answer. He leans forward and filches packets of sugar.

"But you know, Vi, your face isn't gonna last for long."

"Right." The girl tucks her napkin in her collar. "Because I'm gonna get changed. More pretty."

"That's right. Even prettier."

"Even more like Erica," she presses.

Sal's hands freeze, putting his napkin on his lap. Blue eyes glance up, flinty. "What did we say about her name, Vi?"

Violet shrinks. "Don't say it at all."

Her soda comes then. She sips, looks dejectedly at the tablecloth. After polishing off half of his Arnold Palmer, Sal sighs.

"I'm not mad. But you can't forget these kinds of things. Remember, every—"

"Every word is a tool. Use it too many times and it gets dull."

"There you go." Sal nods. "That name is something we can't make dull. It has to be sharp. New, fresh, so that in a few years, you'll be able to use it well."

"I'm sorry."

"Hey, don't worry about it, kiddo. Rather have you slip up now than later, you know? Drink up. Are you gonna use your fingernails or hair?"

"Hair."

"Smart choice."

The waitress comes back with two plates of steak dinners. Sal digs into his. Violet waits forty-seven seconds before she starts wailing.

"Ew! Ew, get it off!"

"Violet, honey, what's wrong?" Sal feigns worry.

"It's sticking to my fork!" She squirms. On the tines dangle a few greasy hairs.

The waitress rushes over. "Is everything all right?"

"My daughter found a hair on her steak." Sal glowers. "This is unacceptable."

"I'm sorry, sir." The waitress scrambles. "I'll take it off your bill and get you a new dish right away."

To Violet, the free steak tastes infinitely more satisfying, and Sal's proud thumbs-up fills her with that same satisfaction.

— — —

Every morning at school, we pray. They pray. I bend my head and mouth the words but don't feel anything. I feel Erica's need to pray, to be seen as a good girl. If she'd grown up, she would've been a Goody Two-shoes, striving to please her parents and keep them off her back simultaneously. A sweet girl. A rich, pampered, pretty girl with an equally popular boyfriend, both of them crazy in love and destined for some Ivy League college. When I complete this con, I'll have more than enough to go to college too, if I want. I can travel around the world instead. Invest it in something. Anything is possible. That painting is my freedom.

Today, I am not going to pray.

The reporters wait for Mrs. Silverman to pull into the school parking lot, and then they rush me. Screamed questions, loud lightning flashes of cameras. Mrs. Silverman nearly gets out of the car, Coach handbag clutched as if she's ready to use it to beat them, but a police officer persuades her to get back in the car. The officers escort me through the stifling ring of lenses, microphones, and shouts. I cover my face with my hair until we leave them behind at the school fence. Merril laces her arm through mine.

"When will they learn to give up?"

"They'll do anything for a story." I shrug. "It's a hard life—scraping up rumors and stalking tragedies." *Vultures*, James had said. "They're like vultures."

Merril shudders. "Vultures are gross."

I'm in an even shadier business, Merril. I'm an even more grotesque vulture.

"Oh my God." Merril giggles and buries her face in my arm. "Kerwin's coming over."

The dark-haired boy she'd pointed out yesterday is walking toward us. The small visual cues tell me who he is before he can tell me himself—too many buttons undone from the top of his shirt, showing off the beginnings of his pecs. One button is confident. More than three is stupidly overconfident. He wears silver jewelry—a cross around his neck and silver rings. Vain, and comes from a religious family. He's from Wales. Probably Roman Catholic. He keeps his hands unclenched, arms relaxed at his sides. He's open and eager. Doesn't expect anyone to hurt him.

"Hey, Merril." He smiles. His accent is crisp and lilting, and he rolls his *r*'s. Merril practically squirms.

"Kerwin! What's up?"

"Came to say hi. Who's the friend?"

"Erica." I smile at him. "But you already knew that."

"Not really." He keeps his smile on too.

"Huh. I've only been all over the news."

"My host family doesn't watch much telly." He blinks and looks to the left. He's lying.

"Telly!" Merril squeaks the word and covers her mouth. "Sorry, it's a funny word. Good funny, not bad funny."

She laughs and I nervously laugh with her. Her crush is about as subtle as the reporters screaming my name a few yards away. Something's off about this guy. I'll play nice and try to get him to let his guard down so I can see what's behind his façade.

I extend my hand to him. "Nice to meet you, Kerwin."

He and Merril look at my hand like it's an alien's. Do teenagers shake hands? My heart lurches. I'd messed up—greeted him like one of Sal's contacts instead of a teenage boy. I put it down with a sheepish smile. Quick, come up with something. Small excuse. He's from overseas. Make something up.

"Sorry. I figured you Welsh are more proper than us Americans."

"Proper's too stuffy." He chuckles. "Just call me Ker. Everyone does."

"Ker!" Merril jumps in. "You can call me Mer if you want. Our names sort of rhyme."

"So I guess I'll call Erica, Er, then?" He shoots a smirk at me. "What's up with the reporters following you, if you don't mind me asking?"

He's not very good at acting. He already knows why—his easy posture and the tone of his voice are *too* relaxed. He's playing dumb for some reason.

"Back when Erica was little—" Merril looks to me. "I mean, it's your story to tell."

"I was kidnapped." I tilt my chin up. "I'm back now. The news is going a little batshit over it."

"Kidnapped?" He looks me over. "You look fine to me."

"I *am* fine," I insist.

"Right. Of course you are." He chuckles. Merril laughs with him.

"Is something funny?" I quirk an eyebrow.

Kerwin's smile fades. "No. Sorry. I'm being a right asshole, aren't I? Look, it was nice meeting you. Just wanted to introduce myself properly. I'll see you around, yeah?"

"Yeah!" Merril chimes. When he's gone, she clutches at my arm. "Did I have cereal in my teeth or something? He wouldn't look at me."

She bares her teeth for me to check, and I shake my head. "Your teeth are fine."

"Weird." She runs her tongue around in her mouth.

Taylor flashes me a devilish smirk as I walk into first period. A reminder that she's on to me. I ignore her and sit in my seat. James's wavy-haired head is on his desk, his breathing shallow but steady. Sleeping this early? He sits up groggily for morning prayers and then goes back to sleep. Mr.

Roth doesn't seem to notice, too deep in his integer lecture to look around the room. I extend my pencil across the gap between our desks, poking James in the arm.

"Psst."

He doesn't move. I poke him more insistently, and his eyes crack open.

"If you're going to poke me, use the soft eraser end, would you?"

"Is that your special talent or something? Falling asleep at inopportune times?"

He yawns, eyes tearing. "Girls who look like you shouldn't use big words."

"What's that supposed to mean?" I hiss.

"People get jealous of beautiful and intelligent people. You can be one, but not the other. You can be a little of one, and a lot of the other. But both extremes at once is trouble. Too much hate and envy. But hey—your life. You wanna make it hard on yourself, feel free." He puts his head back down.

Did he just call me pretty? I can't tell if that was a compliment or an insult.

"Mr. Anders, would you repeat back to me what I just said?" Mr. Roth's voice cuts between us.

James raises his head and sighs. "You were saying something about reverse engineering the problem?"

"No. I'd like you to stay after class." Mr. Roth's words are short.

James sinks, defeated, on the desk. The class murmurs amongst themselves until Mr. Roth raps the board to get attention.

The paper under James's head—our worksheet—is mostly blank. He's done a few problems. I blink. They don't have any work scribbled next to them, yet the answers are clearly there. Seventy-two. I do the problem myself, scribbling my work in the margins of my own sheet. Seventy-two exactly. The next problem, he's put thirteen. I do that problem, my work scrawling down the page. Lots of written work, but it comes out to thirteen. My eyebrows raise. Is he really that good?

I look for him at lunch, but he's nowhere to be seen. Cassie comes over, chest heaving. It's a show the boys appreciate, elbowing each other and laughing as she passes. She seems oblivious, or maybe she's gotten used to it by now.

"What are you two doing on Saturday?" She slides into our table.

Merril shrugs. "I have to go pick up Dad's car from the shop in the morning, but after that I'm free."

"What about you, Erica?" Cassie smiles.

"I'm free."

"Awesome. Bowling. Lucky Nine Lanes—third exit off the interstate. Totally trashy, totally cheesy, absolutely perfect. I'll bring Alex—boyfriend." She winks at me. "And you guys can meet him. If you wanna bring other boys, that's cool too."

Merril grabs my arm. I have a bruise in the shape of her hand by now. "You have to invite Kerwin!"

"What? Why me?"

"He's into you." Cass flashes me a smile. "Would *not* stop asking about you in first period."

Merril pouts, but I pat her shoulder. "If you want, I'll invite him for you."

Her face brightens, doe eyes unable to hide much.

— — —

Tracking Kerwin down is easy. He has a small crowd of people around him at all times. Popular? Without a doubt. He slouches against his locker, his soccer buddies shoving each other and laughing.

"Um, hi, Kerwin."

His dark-haired head turns to me, and his smile is contagious. Would be, if I were the kind of girl to fall for it. It's a very, very fake smile, but just honest enough that it fools most people.

"Hey. What's up?"

"Cass is having this thing, a sort of get-together at Lucky Nine Lanes. I just wanted to know if you wanted to come."

One of his buddies snorts, and Kerwin smacks him on the back of the head.

"Are you gonna be there?" he asks, suddenly all smiles again. I nod. "Then definitely. What time?"

"We're meeting at noon."

"All right." His accent drags out the word. "Look, I know the area, but not well. I might get lost. Give me your number just in case."

"I don't know the area either." I smile. "I'm new too."

He laughs. "Right. I'm transfer-new and you're kidnap-new."

"Something like that. Here, this is"—I take a marker out and motion for him to give me his hand. I scribble Merril's number on the back of it—"Merril's number. She'll be with me, and she knows the town like the back of her hand."

I look up. In our new position, his eyes are riveted into the top of my blouse. I pull away and clear my throat.

"So, I'll see you then?"

"Yeah. Brilliant." He struggles to form words. "Thanks for this."

His friends whistle as I leave. Violet wants to snap at them to cut it out. Erica wants to ignore them. I mumble threats under my breath—a happy middle ground.

When I tell Mrs. Silverman I'm going bowling, she beams. There are tears there, just barely hidden beneath a veneer of wine and eye-dabs with a napkin.

"I'm so happy for you, Erica. You're making friends so fast."

"I had friends before." That's a lie. Violet's never had friends—what kind of con artist has friends? "So it's not like I never had them."

"I know." She smiles. "I'm glad you're making them here. That I get to see you make them."

I pick at my broccoli.

Her voice is small. "Do you miss them? Your old friends?"

The friends I've never had, you mean? "Yeah. I miss everything. But everything back there was a lie. So I shouldn't miss it."

Mrs. Silverman doesn't say anything. Marie comes in with tea and a plate of fruit for dessert. I pick at a peach slice when she starts talking again.

"There will always be two parts of you, Erica. There will be the one who had the life with your kidnappers—however good or bad a life it was. And there will be your life with me, and I intend to make it the best life I can for you. Those two sides don't have to be at war. Both of them are important. Both of them make up the whole that is you."

Violet sneers. Erica chews peach silently. The precipice between the two grows larger with Mrs. Silverman's words.

A flower dangles, roots clinging to both sides as the fissure widens.

— — —

Sal covertly writes a Dear Abby–ish love advice column in a queer magazine under the pseudonym of Ms. Maple, and it's how we communicate. The magazine is nothing graphic— mostly articles on the gay community, notices about events and art showings. Sal's third column response is usually encoded with a message for me. Before I left, he gave me a phrase I use as a substitution cipher—SEEING RED AND BLUE—that strips away the unneeded letters and leaves his words for me. I submit seemingly innocent romantic questions to Ms. Maple via the Internet, and they contain my coded message using the same cipher. It's a Cold War system that, while convoluted, keeps anyone off our trail.

I buy the magazine from a bookstore. Mrs. Silverman handed me two hundred dollars and dropped me off at the mall to buy something nice to wear to Cassie's bowling party on Saturday. I barely kept my eyes from bugging out at the sight of two hundreds just for me. Not for food or rent or to pay someone off to keep them quiet. For frilly, frivolous clothes.

The mall. To Violet, it's a place of infinite opportunity. I have to stop her from leaning over and picking the pockets of unsus- pecting families or taking advantage of the security guard's turned back to sneak items into my oversize purse. To Erica, this is a place of endless temptation—pretzels, cinnamon buns, greasy fast food that looks as good as it smells. Her thin waist growls. Her eyes roam over the clothes—she wants to feel them all on her skin. She wants to wear and eat it all, because she's dead and hasn't eaten or worn anything for thirteen years. I buy Sal's magazine and settle in the food court with a soda.

I spread the pages and jot on my notepad. First, I reverse the entire advice column, spelling the words backward. Then I apply the cipher. Sal's words grow. I can hear his hoarse cigar voice reading them.

Michelle Painchaud

Violet,

Hope you're doing well. I've been
watching you on TV. Can't even
put into words how proud I am. You
walk like her, talk like her. Even your
heart's a little like hers, I reckon.

Not gonna talk specifics, in case
someone cracks this. Ricebowl's full,
as always.

Count on Sal to talk in half code even after I've decoded
his words. "Ricebowl" is the Japanese businessman art buyer
who's waiting eagerly—still "full."

Silverman based code off important
memory shared with Erica just before
she got kidnapped. When you've got
dirt, lemme know.

P.S. Mama Silverman's hired a
private investigator. Been snooping.
Convincing evidence trail placed in
your "hometown." Will keep PI busy.
Silverman won't turn him on you until
you mess up. Did that to other girls.
He busted them. PI goes by Mr. White.
Bald, ex-military, you know the type.

Lady Luck's with you, sweets.

"Didn't peg you for the creative writer type."

The deep voice startles me, and I whirl in my seat. James stands, hands shoved in his pockets and blond hair flyaway as ever. He's wearing baggy jeans and a dark button-up shirt, cuffs rolled. I want to scream at him: *Don't you dare stand behind me again. Don't you dare read over my shoulder.* I bite my tongue and quash Violet, bringing Erica up to coat my surface with a pretty polish.

"I'm taking notes." I hold up the magazine. "Social studies class."

"You're doing a project on homosexuality?" He quirks an eyebrow. "Didn't expect that sort of thing from you."

"Care to elaborate before I take that the wrong way?" I smile broader.

"It's just open-minded of you. Not something you usually see at a private Christian school. Might not get you the grade you want."

"It'll get the grade it deserves"—I close the magazine—"which, if I can brag, will be an A."

"That good, are you?" He chuckles.

"English is easy. School is easy. People are hard."

He tenses up. Blue eyes get a flinty edge. I hit something in him with that last sentence. But what?

"You can sit if you want." I motion to the chair across from me.

"No, thanks." He clears his throat, the jump start of a machine that temporarily broke down. "I've gotta go."

The bag at his feet is full of guitar strings, lots of batteries, a strange synthesizer-looking thing, and an extension cord.

"Building a terminator?" I nod at the bag.

"I've got a recital coming up."

"That's right. Your dad's a famous musician or something, right?"

His eyes go dark. "Piano. It's his life."

"And yours, too, apparently."

I hit that thing in him again. A heavy silence smothers us. James's hand tightens into a fist. He gives a dismissive little laugh and picks up his bag. "Good luck on your project."

"Your recital. It's not tomorrow, is it?"

"It's next month."

"So you're not doing anything tomorrow?"

He tenses again. Picking up on people's quirks is my career. James tenses when he wants to say something but holds himself back.

"No," he says carefully. "Why?"

"Some of my friends arranged a bowling thing. None of them are interesting to talk to. You should come entertain me."

"Then why are you friends with them?" he interjects, almost accusatorily.

"We were together when we were kids, or so I've heard."

"But they bore you. Why hang out with them?"

"Look, I don't know why I do. I'll probably never know. This isn't about philosophy. I just wanted to invite you."

"Why me?"

"Why not you?" I smile and tilt my head. He shifts his weight on his feet.

"You'll regret asking me."

"No. I don't think I will."

He stares at me, into me, and finally says, "Lucky Nine Lanes, right?"

"How'd you figure that out?"

"Simple deductive reasoning—the cheapest alley that's also nearest."

"Don't start getting smarter than me. It hurts my pride."

He shakes his head and walks away with a small smile. I get up and browse a rack of shirts in the department store. No Salvation Army this time, just fresh new clothes I *didn't* have to shoplift. I pick out a ruffled tank top and black skirt—short, but I'll wear tights with it. James might like it.

My hand freezes picking up the clothes hanger. I scrub that last thought out of my head with the strongest mental bleach I have. He can't like it. I can't want him to like anything about me. Why did I even invite him? I only need to *pretend* to make friends to convince Mrs. Silverman I'm her daughter and get the code. I'm not Erica. I'm going to mysteriously disappear into the night with *La Surprise* and never come back. I'm not real.

I'm the shadow of a dead girl. A shadow does not have friends.

A dead girl does not feel guilt.

5: BET IT

The slowly rotating bowling pin that serves as the alley's sign drips with rust and neon. Mrs. Silverman stops the car and I get out, smoothing my hair.

"Have fun."

"I will." I pick at my outfit. "Thank you for the clothes."

"I wish you would stop thanking me." She smiles sadly.

"I'm sorry. It's just a habit, and—"

"I know." Her makeup looks perfect in the hot, dry air. Her hair is so blonde, her skin so pale. She's a statue of porcelain, glass, and platinum, like one of the angelic dolls on Erica's shelf. The cracks don't show so much when she smiles.

"I'll get a ride home with Merril, so—" I cut off awkwardly.

She thinks something over, eyebrows wrinkling, and then leans in. She hesitates, and my breathing goes shallow. Soft lips press to my forehead. When she pulls away, she has tears in her eyes, her fingers rubbing off the lipstick on my forehead.

"God, I'm like a leaky sink. I must be embarrassing you. I'll go."

"I'm not easily embarrassed." I smile.

"Got that from your father." She laughs. "I'll see you at dinner, then."

I wave until she pulls out of the parking lot. She nearly runs over the curb, trying to wave back. I laugh as she straightens the wheel and gives me a thumbs-up out the window.

The alley engulfs me in loud music, the crash-bang of abused pins, and smoky air smelling of wax and sweat. It's dark inside, lights from vending machines and arcade games flashing. I scan the crowd. James isn't here. I deflate. Why would he be here, anyway?

"Erica!" Cass runs over in a colorful dress and hugs me. Her monstrous chest tries to suck me into its oblivion-crevice. A redheaded older guy slinks up behind her. Cass pulls away.

"Erica, this is Alex. Alex, Erica."

He nods, I nod. Not as handsome as Kerwin, who I can see talking with Merril at the cashier, but pretty cute. Cass grabs my hand.

"Let's go get the lanes and shoes. What size are you?"

"Seven and a half."

"Day-umn, Bigfoot." Alex smirks. The average American woman's shoe size is eight. But I laugh and put my money into the pool on the counter. Kerwin flashes me a smile.

"Erica! You made it."

"Who would pass up the chance to throw balls at things?" I close my purse. Everyone laughs.

The cashier snorts. "Wow. How lame are you?" I get a good look at her. Long dark hair, thick eyeliner.

Next to me, Merril lets out a hiss. "Oh my God, you! *You* work here?"

Taylor takes our money and pats it into the register. "Yeah. So?"

"Be a little more polite to customers. We *can* complain, you know," Cass says with a sniff.

Michelle Painchaud

"It's fine, Cass." I smile. "Everyone has their bad days."

"Except you, Miss Perfect," Taylor sneers, and ducks into the rows of shelves where the shoes are kept. Kerwin and Alex don't seem nearly as fazed by Taylor's snarky attitude as the girls are. She was nice to me a few days ago. She's messing with my head.

"It's totally suspicious she's working here." Merril sighs.

"Why's that?" Alex raises an eyebrow.

Merril lowers her voice, and we all lean in to hear her. "Her dad's a lawyer for the mob. He probably pulled strings, and this place is probably owned by them."

Cass grimaces.

Kerwin whistles. "Like, the American mob? The machine-gun-and-bootleg-rum kind?"

"No," Alex says patiently. "Like the owns-every-casino-on-the-Strip-and-cuts-off-fingers kind."

Kerwin doesn't lose his excited look.

Merril punches his shoulder. "Don't even joke around, Ker. It's serious."

"I know, I know." He laughs. My eyes narrow, but I force them wide and friendly again. Taylor comes back with our shoes, and we lace them up. The others finish before I do, but Kerwin keeps messing up purposely, waiting until I've finished to finish. Amateur move. Too obvious.

"You don't have to wait for me," I offer.

He looks up from his shoes and grins. "I want to."

Above our heads and from behind the counter comes a Taylor gag.

"My shoes are too small." I wince.

Kerwin stands and looks at Taylor. "Get her a bigger size, will you?"

"I'm fine. Go join the others," I insist as sweetly as I can muster. Violet wants to growl at him to leave. The undue attention makes me uncomfortable. He's obviously crushing on me. It could be innocent, but it could just as easily have an ulterior motive to it. He has poor control over his zygomatic major muscle—the crease around his mouth as he tries to hold back smiles gives away something. I'm not sure what, but it's still there. A sign. A hint that not all's right.

He ignores me. "Let's try a size eight."

"Go join the others." My voice is stony. "Please."

"You heard her," Taylor sneers. "She can put her glass slippers on herself."

Kerwin shoots her a nasty look and starts off. I hand my shoes to Taylor.

"You know . . ." She smiles. "There's a rumor kicking about a baldy hanging around school. Outside of it. Watching the reporters who watch you. Any idea who it might be?"

"Is he buff?"

"Yeah. Is he your partner? Do I get to call the police and tell 'em about you yet?"

Taylor smirks and ducks into the shoe rows. My heart skitters across my ribs. Sal said the PI is the bald military type. Is Mrs. Silverman on to me already? What had I done to make her suspicious?

Taylor hands me size eights. I slip them on, and she glances out the doors.

"Holy shit!" she swears. "What the hell is he doing here?"

In the doorway is James, looking nervous in a plaid shirt and jeans. He takes a deep breath and pushes into the alley, and Taylor shouts, "Oy! Over here!"

I finish tying my shoes and stand. He sees me, and his eyebrows become just a little undrawn.

"Hi." I smile.

"I'm really not good with places like this . . ." he starts.

"Any music that isn't perfect hurts his delicate little ears," Taylor simpers, and points to the speakers blaring rock above.

He throws her an exasperated look. "I'm just bad at bowling."

"So am I," I insist. "We can be bad together."

Taylor's wolf-whistle transforms my words into something dirty. James rolls his eyes, a flush sprinkled across his cheeks.

"Cut it out, Taylor."

"Did you hear her?" She laughs as she fishes out his shoe size. "You can be *baaaad* together."

We walk to the lanes. Cass rolls a ball and knocks a single pin down. Merril and Alex boo.

"So who's who in this tragic play?" James asks me. "I'm not up on the more popular actors."

"Alex is the technical pedophile, Cass is the balloon-chest, Merril is the other girl, and Kerwin—"

"I know Kerwin. Hard not to when everything with XX chromosomes in the school can't stop talking about him."

I shrug. "He's got very stylish dark hair, the right height and build, and is very charming and easy to talk to."

"Top it off with that accent, and I'm surprised you aren't all over him too," James murmurs.

"Not my type." I smile. "I don't even know if I really have a type."

"Every girl has a type. It usually starts with 'tall' and ends with 'handsome.' Why don't you have one?"

I need to lead the conversation away from my lack of romantic ideals. I can't let him see I have no type—that I've never had romantic interactions. I'd never thought about dating. Living with Sal wasn't the sort of life that permitted stable relationships. I never asked, but it was an unsaid rule that I could do what I wanted as long as I was ready to move, pull cons, and jump to complete what Sal asked. Normal teenage girls usually have relationships, and . . . *types*. I need to seem as normal as possible. "How'd you get here?" I ask.

"I put gasoline in the tank of my car, got in, closed the door, turned the key, and drove, like everyone else." He smirks.

Merril waves. I wave back. James and I browse the bowling balls. Kerwin is still watching us. James palms a green bowling ball and tests its weight.

"Thank you." I pick a purple ball.

"For what?"

"Coming." I put my fingers in the ball's holes and mimic a throw. "I thought you wouldn't."

His shoulders square, and his arm muscles tense. He wants to say something that's hard for him but opts for the easier words instead.

"Thanks for inviting me."

"Erica! You and your friend, get over here! It's your turn," Cass calls, all smiles.

"James." Merril nods. He nods back.

Kerwin gets up and slaps James on the back. "Your turn, John."

No one bothers correcting him. Merril grabs my arm and whispers as we watch James walk up to the lane.

"*He's* the guy you invited? Why?"

"Is there something wrong with him?" I raise an eyebrow.

"No. He just never talks to anyone in class. I mean, he's okay and all, but you can't be friends with someone who doesn't talk."

"He talks to me."

"I'm telling you, he's a weirdo. Your choice, I guess." She sighs. I want to tell her Kerwin's weirder, but instead I cheer with Alex when James gets a spare. I run up and high-five him coming off the lane, and he smiles, his hand warm and soft.

If I were going to stay, I would tell James to say what he means more. I would ask Kerwin what his deal is. I would tell Taylor to stop doubting me. But I'm not going to be here for long. Erica is a pleasant face-value sort of girl. She doesn't tell people off or get involved deeply. She can't risk people disliking her or growing too attached, because she's not real.

Erica has to stop smiling at James.

Violet has to stop burning to touch him, touch Merril, touch someone, anyone, and make sure they're really here.

Because she's not.

"I beat you," I inform James, collapsing on the chair beside him when the last round finishes.

"Did you?" He quirks a brow, smile barely there. I point to the score screen—148. His is 122. He sighs. "Bowling's hard."

"Don't whine." I slap his knee and rub my hand. "Ow. You're all bony."

"Self-defense mechanism. Darwin is a cruel master," he says jokingly, and leans his head back on the chair.

"Wow, John." Kerwin claps him on the shoulders. "This must not be your game."

"It's obviously yours." James shrugs him off.

Kerwin got seven strikes. He sighs. "What can I say?

Sometimes people just have a *gift* for things. But, hey, you'd know all about *that*."

James goes quiet. Merril sees an opening and dives for Kerwin's arm.

"Let's get drinks! What does everyone want?"

"Lemonade," Cass calls, fanning herself. The alley is stuffy.

"I think I'm going to go." James stands.

I stand with him. "Home?"

"Yeah." He nods, staring at Kerwin. "I'm pretty tired. Thanks for having me, guys."

Alex gives him a thumbs-up—the only one to even acknowledge he said anything. Cass and Kerwin don't look at him.

"I'm going too." I grab my purse. Cass straightens.

"What? Erica! Why?"

"I've gotta get back. Mom wants to do stuff together. It's been like this since I got home."

Merril sighs. "Okay, but call us tonight, yeah?"

"For sure." I glance back—James is already at the entrance. I jog to catch up with him. Taylor leans over the counter and grabs at James's sleeve.

"What did the populars say? You look fucking angry."

"Nothing. I'm fine," he murmurs to her, and pushes out the doors.

Taylor sees me and sneers. "You shoulda known better. Bringing him to your popular people get-together? That's like sticking a fish on the ground and expecting it to run."

"I just—"

"Yeah, you *just*. Didn't for a second think about his feelings, did you? Selfish bitch."

I flinch and rush outside to gulp cold air. "James! Wait up!"

He slows. "What?"

"I'm sorry. Whatever Kerwin said to make you want to leave, I'm sorry for it."

I follow him to a beat-up Cadillac. It has to be a decade old, at least. The brown paint is worn dull, the inside scattered with music things—a guitar, empty packages of picks, and music books. He unlocks the car and reaches in for a half-finished bottle of soda. He takes a gulp and makes a face.

"Warm. Disgusting."

"I'm sorry," I try again.

He shakes his head. "Don't be. It's me. You're the only one who doesn't know. Even transfer boy found out. I guess I should've expected it."

"Found out what?"

"If I tell you"—he pours the soda on the cement, the splash loud—"I'll look pathetic. That's the last thing I want right now. I'm sort of cool in your eyes, right? At least one percent?" His voice is pleading. I nod. "One percent is good. Let's keep it at that."

"No matter what you tell me—"

He cuts me off. "You have secrets, right?"

I freeze, my heart contracting painfully. Yes. A really, really big secret. I have secrets on top of my secrets in order to make my secret look less like a secret. I'm made of secrets.

"I have a secret too." He opens the car door. "Everybody in this town knows it, so it's not much of a secret, but for four days, five days, a week, maybe, I want you to still see me as a pretty cool guy. You'll find out eventually, and I'll look like a moron. But for now just stay oblivious, okay?"

You'll find out my secret eventually too, James. But by then it'll be too late.

"Do you need a ride?" His offer breaks my silence.

"If it's okay with you. My house is in Jefferson's Creek."

"Not too far, then. Enter the chariot of fire and grandeur." He smirks and motions to the passenger seat. I slide in. The car rumbles to life, a massive beast waking from winter hibernation.

"Sorry about the smell." He reverses out of the parking spot. "Brought takeout Chinese home last night."

I sniff. "I don't smell anything."

"I swear, I'm practically re-eating the beef broccoli every time I breathe in."

I laugh. He waits until we hit the freeway to turn music on. It doesn't so much cover our silence as enhances it. It's electronic—alternative and sparse with lyrics.

"I thought you played piano?" I ask. "What's with the guitar in the back?"

He tenses.

I let out a breath. "It's so obvious when you want to say something that's hard for you." He says nothing. "Your shoulders get high, your arms get straighter, and your mouth curls down. Like this." I make an ugly face. He glances at me and chuckles. There's a silence the music helps fill.

"Piano is the ultimate instrument. To my dad. Everything else is inferior," James finally says.

"But you like guitar."

"I'm in a band. Sort of." He shakes his head. "Dad doesn't know that."

Michelle Painchaud

"Do you play gigs?"

"A guy I met on the Internet and I do collaborations. I play the guitar and piano; he does the electronic stuff."

"Let me guess—your band name is James and the Giant Peach."

"Close." He smirks.

"Giant Fig?"

"I lied. No name yet. But Giant Fig is pretty interesting."

"Have you told your dad?"

James sighs. "And give him a coronary? I don't want to kill the guy. Telling him what I really want will just hurt him. I've learned that now."

He sounds so despondent, so resigned to his fate. He doesn't want to do what his dad wants him to. Violet always wanted to do what Sal said. Conning. She likes it. But she likes this life of normalcy also. Telling Sal that would just hurt him, too.

"I know this is a dangerous subject," he starts. "But what kinds of music do you like?"

I have to think up something quick. Sal played lots of Elvis and old music in the car.

"You're going to laugh," I murmur.

"I won't. Honest to God."

"And you won't hate me?"

"I'm not a music Nazi."

"The Ink Spots. Billie Holiday." I sigh. "Elvis. Janis Joplin. Bob Dylan. My dad—the guy who used to be my dad—loved all those older bands."

"Whoa, you covered at least three separate decades there."

"They're all old to me," I say with a huff.

He laughs and switches lanes. "All right. So, favorite song?"

"Ever?"

He nods. I bite my lip and watch the just-budding trees flash by outside.

"I don't think I've found it yet."

His mouth twists with a smile I've never seen before. And I've seen every smile.

"That's the right answer."

6: CHEAT IT

The desert stretches on forever, the lights of the Strip faded against the twilight sky. Bare fingertips of light hovering on the horizon are all that are left of the world's luckiest place. The desert is pale sand, khaki and dry and spiny with the bones of dead things and cactuses—saviors of the thirsty and the masochistic.

Ten-year-old Violet waits by the side of the road, her thumb out. Her braids are long and pale. It's been two weeks since she slept in a real bed. Five days since she had a bath. Seven hours since she last ate. Sal paces the shoulder lane. Their stolen car is a smoking husk, having been driven until the gas ran out, over the sands and potholes of off-road Nevada until the police lost them. The bumps had been fun, but Violet's tired now. She can't show that though. Sal might get mad. She blinks back sleep and holds her thumb higher.

"Let's play the face game, Vi"—Sal looks to her—"on whoever picks us up."

She nods. The headlights of a truck cut the ribbon of cooling asphalt. At a distance they are two white fireflies, flickering in and out of the night. Embarrassed. Shy. They get more confident the closer they rumble, and Violet's pupils shrink to pinpricks. The lights slow. Sal gathers Violet up and opens the truck's door.

"You headed to Dallas by any chance?"

The driver smiles. "Yeah, hop on in. Car trouble?"

"Damn thing just blew up. It's been on its last legs for years now." Sal sighs. "I'm George, by the way, and this here's my daughter, Abigail."

The driver kicks the truck into gear. Sal is a natural at conversation—not distracting, and mildly stimulating. He asks what the trucker's shipping (furniture), where he's from (Salt Lake City), and what's the longest he's gone without sleep in this job (twenty-seven hours, though, legally, it's supposed to be just fifteen).

"We just got back from a funeral," Sal says. Violet watches his face carefully, keeping an eye out for which muscles he uses to make his lies or truths convincing.

"You twitched your corrugator supercilii," she murmurs. Sal squeezes her hand—a *good job*.

"We weren't expecting the car to break like it did, really," he keeps on.

"Depressor anguli oris," the girl mutters again. Another hand squeeze.

The truck driver looks at her. "Is she all right?"

"A little Tourette's. She's on meds for it, but she still says strange things sometimes," Sal lies, and smiles.

Violet watches as he says it. "You gave it away with your zygomatic major. Too pinched."

"Those are some awfully big words for a girl your age." The trucker laughs nervously.

"How many kids do you have?" Violet asks. The trucker scratches his head, smiles, and shifts gears. The eighteen-wheeler gives a little stutter.

"None."

His smile doesn't crinkle his eyes. Violet picks up on it. "A flat orbicular oculi. You have a kid. Maybe one you don't want to have. Or maybe you lost it. Did it die?"

"That's enough, Abigail," Sal whispers. "Don't push it."

The trucker goes quiet. Sal makes apologies, squeezes Violet's hand hard to let her know she needs to be quiet.

But she's curious. "Did you love your kid?" she asks.

The trucker pulls the brim of his hat down, uncomfortable.

"Did you hug it? Did you ever get to kiss it? Was it a boy or a girl?"

"Abigail, I'm warning you—" Sal begins.

"How did it die?"

The truck screeches to a stop. The trucker, so genial before, puts his face in his hands.

"Get out."

"We're sorry," Sal says, scrambling for words. "She's just so uncontrollable sometimes—"

"I said get out."

"We don't have any way to get back—"

"We're close to Dallas. Someone will pick you up. Get out."

Violet watches the trucker's face—drawn, his muscles taut. He's honest. Broken and honest. He cared about his child enough to break down at her prying. Would Sal ever break down if she died? Sal exhales and yanks Violet from the seat with him, watching the truck sputter exhaust as it drives away. Reality seeps in with the cold night air. Streetlamps are faint, the darkness heavy. Sal rolls his sleeves up calmly.

"Sal, I didn't mean to—"

Terror. Cold terror grips her intestines and twists them around each other. Sal keeps rolling his sleeves, slowly, and finishes at the elbow. Takes his first step toward her.

"No! I'm sorry! I won't do it again! I just wanted to see—"

The sting of a palm on her face. Everything condenses to those five points of white-hot acid on her skin. Stars shatter themselves in her eyes.

Just once. It's always just one hit. One hard, unforgiving warning.

"When I say stop, you stop."

He pulls her by the arm into town. Miles and miles of cold air nipping at the red slap. It fades. Nothing too permanent. Sal is never that messy, that uncontrolled. At the first gas station he walks into, he rips off a disposable phone.

The little girl watches him work, the sickly light of the gas station showing his bones—white on black on muscle on sunspots on death. Sal's face is never angry. Even in the darkness, even when he hits her, he never shows his real emotion. The face game is useless on him. He hides everything too well. Or he just has nothing to show.

After the discipline comes the apology. The worst part isn't the pain—it's the fact that he always tries to make up for it. To pretend he's sorry.

He comes out, beaming, a candy bar offered to her in his hand.

Violet plays poker with Sal and only wins when he lets her.

Red and blue chips in the pot.

In a different world, Violet is a girl like Erica. Maybe not as rich as Erica, but just as well loved, by a mom and dad who are around and have jobs and a small but tidy house. Maybe that Violet's had a few boyfriends—blushing, stolen glances, smoldering hearts, smoldering afternoons on a sunlit bed, exploring, hands, mouth, crooks of necks, crooked smiles.

This one has only read cheap romance paperbacks out of boredom, desperation—there is very little to do in an RV park. She reads on a bench littered with beer cans and gets weird looks. A neighbor woman smoking, hanging lingerie to dry, sings some Dylan: "Get born, keep warm."

7: GIVE IT

Michael Anders, age forty. Labeled a child prodigy at the age of seven. Toured the world playing concert piano for various orchestras at ten. Got into Julliard at seventeen (same age as James is now) and won a string of major awards for composition. Married a dance major and had James.

That's what Google says. I twirl in my computer chair. Having a huge fancy desktop PC like the one Mrs. Silverman gave me is a new experience—Sal had a laptop on its last legs. I hold my breath and type James's name. James, at the age of six, had also been labeled a prodigy. His first major recital was at age eight. He sat at the piano and didn't move, just stared at the keys. Started shaking, trembling so bad that when he touched the keys they wobbled in a sour note. His father withdrew him from the concert piano scene. The media had a field day—famous young composer's son, someone everyone pegged for a success, flubbed his recital.

No wonder James hates reporters. There are dozens of articles on his "failure." Some writers used it as a platform to point out how parents shouldn't pressure their kids; others used it as an example showing that familial ties aren't everything in the music biz. But all agreed that James had been pushed into something he wasn't prepared for.

His family must've been disappointed. Everyone must've been disappointed. He'd learned to cope with it by keeping to himself. But James wouldn't have stuck with music through so much shit if he didn't love it. There's no doubt he loves it. He's just probably not the kind of musician his dad wants him to be.

I have to stop. Stop reading these things, stop looking on the Internet at Merril and Taylor and everyone else who's talked to me. I'm doing what a con artist would do to potential contacts—scope out their backgrounds and figure out how they can help you. These are not resources. They are people. Potential friends. Friends I can't keep.

There's a soft knock on my door.

"Come in."

Marie pokes her head around. She's bearing a sandwich and a glass of milk. "How's a snack sound?"

I nod.

She puts both on my desk and looks at the scattered textbooks. "What are you studying?"

I don't need to study, but scribbling on paper and leaving said papers on my desk gives the illusion of a girl who tries hard.

"Algebra." I hold up the textbook, my arm drooping. "It's so heavy, though."

"Your mother never stopped telling me how good you were with math. So small, but you loved to do lines and lines of addition and subtraction. You are so naturally gifted at it, just like your father."

Sal knew that too. Talked to Erica's old tutors—yes, of course she had them almost from birth. It's why he put the emphasis on math when teaching me, I suppose. Marie puts the plate down.

"The sandwich is turkey."

"Thank you." She looks like she wants to say something.

I clear my throat. "Is there anything else?"

Marie starts. "Oh, no, it's just"—swallows hard—"my cousin lost a child."

"I'm sorry to hear that."

"An accident on the subway. I thought to myself, 'Marie, there is nothing worse than losing a child.' I have two, grown up. I came here to work for your mother three years ago. I saw everything clearly. Losing a child may be hard. Losing a child and burying no body is harder. The unknown . . . it does things to the mind."

"Everybody needs closure," I agree softly.

Marie nods. "Closure. That's it. Your mother had none. It is good the body still lives." She pats my hand. "But if it hadn't, I would pray for the police to find it and put your mother's suffering to an end. A mother should hold her child in life, and in death, too."

I stare at the sandwich, my lungs burning.

"Closure," Marie whispers. She smiles and gets up. "Do you have any laundry?"

"Just some shirts. I put them in the basket."

"I'll do a load. Study hard and well."

"I will. Thank you for the snack."

She closes the door behind her. I wait until she walks down the hall to wrench my bathroom door open and dry heave into the toilet. Marie's words made me want to scream it all—that I was a fake. That the body is still rotting out there. The body is still out there. Erica is out there somewhere. Her mother has false closure.

Michelle Painchaud

That night, I mince through the night-fallen hall, the paintings glowing in the soft guide lights. Mrs. Silverman's door is left open a crack. I make my way to her queen-size bed. Pillows are scattered on the floor. A forest of makeup bottles crowds her dresser. She's a lump beneath the covers, pajamas silk and face smooth. Her wrists peek out—thin and weightless-looking, like a malnourished bird's leg.

Wake up. I need to tell you something.

Nobody really likes the truth, sweets. Sal's voice. *They just like their version of it.*

"Erica?" She yawns and looks up at me. "Is something wrong?"

Erica's still out there.

"I couldn't sleep. My room feels too big."

"You can sleep with me if you want."

I hesitate. Sal and I never slept in the same bed, not even when I was little. But Mrs. Silverman seems to expect it. Do families sleep in the same bed without incident? A normal girl, a girl raised by a normal family like I'm pretending, wouldn't be afraid of people in her bed. I slide under the warm covers and watch her back as she turns over. Breathe naturally. In, out. She won't hurt you.

She shifts, turns over to look at me. A spindly leg brushes against mine. My neck hairs stand on end, and I fight the instinct to leap out of the bed.

Mrs. Silverman's sleepy eyes look alarmed. "Are you all right? I'm sorry, I didn't mean to—"

Be normal. Make up something normal. "It's fine. Your feet are cold, is all."

"You used to sleep between your father and me all the time when you were little."

"I had nightmares?"

"Bad ones about clowns."

I shudder.

She feels it through the bed and laughs into her pillow. "Try to get some rest, honey."

The blankets are so soft. The sound of Mrs. Silverman's steady breathing becomes comforting after a while. I'm so warm.

Erica is out there, cold, alone.

———

Cassie has to explain Sadie Hawkins Day, and even then I don't get it. A whole event just so girls can ask boys to dance? Why can't they do that every day?

"It's not like males choose females in the wild." I poke at my cafeteria meatloaf, which, not surprisingly, looks like a burnt rat. "The females of almost every animal species have the first say in who they want their mates to be. And if you think about it, it works the same with human females. We choose who we let kiss us—"

"Erica, I love you, but I'm not in the mood for Brainiac 101 right now. That's how Sadie Hawkins works, and how it'll work until the end of time. No one cares about it anyway, not when prom is right around the corner." Cass exhales and pulls out a bottle of painkillers. She swallows two and chugs chocolate milk.

"Cramps?" Merril asks.

"If by 'cramps' you mean 'end-of-the-world tornados in my ovaries,' then yeah." Cass groans, putting her head on the table. She immediately recoils and sits up. "Gross."

The bell rings. We get up, and Cassie holds on to my arm for support. "Come with me to my car, guys."

Michelle Painchaud

"We can't be late for Gray's class," Merril whines. "There's a test today."

"It'll just take four seconds. God, Merril, think about someone other than yourself for once," Cass snaps.

"It'll be real quick," I assure Merril. She rolls her eyes and follows us to the parking lot. People are returning from off-campus lunch. We use the crowd to our advantage, and slide into Cassie's black Buick. Cassie fishes around in the glove box and pulls out a silver flask. She uncaps it and takes a sip, holding it out to Merril.

"Well? Go on," she urges.

Merril sips it, making a disgusted face. "What the hell is that? Cow pee?"

"Brandy." Cass takes another sip and then offers it to me, wiping her lips. "My dad's got the really old stuff. He never misses it when I fill this thing up."

I take a tiny sip. My nose burns and my throat is on fire.

"Not as good as whiskey," I mutter. It just falls out of my mouth. Merril stares, and Cass laughs.

"And you'd know all about whiskey, huh?"

"In health class they said not to, like, mix and match," Merril chimes in. "Pills and booze aren't good—"

"Whatever," Cass says with a huff, and pushes herself out of the car. We get out too, and she locks it behind her.

"Cass is just under the weather," I assure a sulking Merril. "Cheer up."

"She's such a diva."

"And you're not?" I tease. Merril's sour face lightens.

"She's a one-hundred-percent diva. I am less than, like, fifty."

"Seventy-five," I say, and smirk.

"Sixty-one, and I am not going a single percent higher."

We walk in silence, Cass calling to upperclassmen she knows. The bounce is back in her step, and her chest bounces with it. I smother my laugh every time a freshman boy goes wide-eyed and stops to watch her in the middle of corridor traffic. People I don't know say hi to me, and I say hi nervously back. They all know me—I'm the reason their school is surrounded by vultures. In the distance I spot a sheet of black hair: Taylor. She came to school late today wearing an uncharacteristic amount of foundation. Merril commented on it, asking who she was trying to fool, but I'm not sure Taylor put the foundation on just for show.

"So, how was the ride home from the bowling alley?" Merril's sharp elbow nudges me. Her doe eyes are voraciously curious.

"Fine. James is a really careful driver."

"That's not what I meant!" She sighs. "Sometimes I think you need to get your subtlety radar fixed."

I pause. She was being subtle? About what? Cars, a boy, and me in a car—oh.

"We didn't do anything if that's what you're implying."

"I am not implying, I'm *asking*."

"The answer's no."

"I think he really likes you."

I fight hard to keep the red tinge in my cheeks from blossoming to a skin-tingling wildfire. "No way."

"He always sleeps in class. I used to think he was trying to ignore us or something. Like, he talks if you talk to him, but he doesn't start stuff, you know? Not my type of guy. But with you, he got all chatty the very first day you came."

"He just didn't like the reporters outside school."

"Well, whatever the reason—" She interrupts herself. "His talking to someone first is totally a big deal. He must really like you. He might be a loser or whatever, but if you wanna date him, I'm totally for it."

Her eyes flit over to Kerwin, who flashes us a smile before he goes into his classroom. "Hi, Erica!"

"Kerwin." I nod.

Merril waves. "Hi, Ker! It's Mer!"

He holds up a hand and ducks inside. She likes him. I can't keep up with these people and their love triangles. It's driving me insane trying to keep the threads straight—who likes whom, who hates whom. Conning is so much easier—it's who pays whom. That's it. No likes or dislikes, just who gets the money, when, and why. It's so simple compared to this minefield of emotions I'm wading through, every step laced with the possibility I'll blow myself up.

"Merril, if you like Kerwin, I'm okay with that."

She blushes to the roots of her hair. "What are you talking about? I do not like him—"

"I don't like him. He's all yours."

Her eyes get even wider. "Oh. You don't have to do it for me—"

"He seriously gives me the creeps." Her face darkens. I rush to cover my mistake. "I'm just not used to so much attention from one guy, you know? It weirds me out. He'd probably be a really sweet and attentive boyfriend."

She sighs. "Yeah. But he doesn't even know who I am."

"We went bowling together, remember?"

"He was looking at you, Rica, the whole time. It's like I was a wall."

"I'll tell him." I pat her shoulder. "I'll tell him I don't like him. Maybe that'll help him see you better."

She bites her lip, a squeak behind it as she hugs me around the waist. "Oh my God, you are the best friend ever."

Is honesty what makes people best friends? Or do girls come to like you the more you help them pursue their romantic interests? Maybe that realization will come in handy later. I can use it to my advantage. I'm just glad she likes me, period. She pulls away from me and opens the door to the classroom.

"After you, madam."

I laugh and make a fake curtsy, slipping past the door.

<hr>

The bald head is easy to spot from the windows of the classroom.

The PI, Mr. White, is sitting in a café across from the school. He reads a paper and puts it down when he hears the bell ring. The large glass windows of the café let him see the campus clearly. They let *me* see *him* clearly.

The reporters are dwindling by the day. If he decides to stand on the fence, he won't be mistaken for a reporter. He'll be seen as suspicious. Maybe that's why he's in the café now. Sal was right—the guy is certainly ex-military, his walk trained and limber. There's a slight lope to his gait, though, the kind you see in people who spend a lot of time on the water. Navy, maybe special branch. Why would someone Navy turn to being a PI? An injury of some kind, most likely, that forced him to retire into civilian work.

A con artist is the world's most desperate actor.

A PI is the world's most desperate truth seeker.

He watches me as I wait for Mrs. Silverman to pick me up. I stand on the curb and shift my weight from one foot to another. Fiddle with my bag. Turn my head and glance at him out of the corner of my eyes without moving them,

Michelle Painchaud

the first trick Sal ever taught me. Baldy is watching me very intently—an intent with more than money behind it. Doesn't take his eyes off me. When people are being paid to watch you, they usually look away, take a drink of something, blink. He doesn't. He's doing this because he wants to, because he has some personal motivation. I doubt he was even asked by Mrs. Silverman to follow me. I can be wrong, like any human can, but I'm usually very right.

"Hey there, Fakey!" Taylor walks up. "Who are you looking at?"

"The bald man you told me about."

"He looks real serious. Could be trouble."

"I've got him under control."

"So he's not your partner, then," she muses. "Must be your informant."

"I don't know him, okay? He's just stalking me."

"Couldn't have anything to do with the fact you're a fake and he busted the other two fakes before you."

I whirl to face her. "Why do you care so much?"

"I don't care." Taylor shrugs. "I just want to see how far you get before someone busts you. I've got money on a month."

"Sorry to disappoint," I snarl. "But I'll be sticking around for years. Get a refund while you can."

The acid in my voice ricochets and hits me. Not years. *Years* is a lie. Saying *years* makes me feel worse. Heavier.

Taylor looks taken aback, her expression going soft, amused. "And here I thought you were just a spineless, whiny, rich-girl crybaby."

"We rich-girl crybabies have our moments too."

She laughs. No hyena cackle or half sneer tints it. It's a normal laugh. One that isn't condescending or cruel. Mr.

White is staring at us now. His eyes flicker between Taylor and me, trying to work out our relationship.

"You're not so bad when you aren't being . . ." I trail off.

"Go on, say it," Taylor challenges.

"Bitchy."

She throws up her hands. "Bitchy, lesbo, emo—it's always something. It's like a girl can't be sure of herself and not be called names."

"Anger is a fire. Passion. It's not a bad thing at all." *Violet is like you, Taylor. Very much like you.*

Taylor quirks an eyebrow. "Erica Silverman—Queen of the Masses and prodigal returned child, telling me it's okay to be me. Good thing you said it, otherwise I never would've known."

The sun peeks out from behind a cloud. In the bright light Taylor's hair looks even glossier. She's proud of it. Takes good care of it. For all her sass, she still cares about what she looks like, what people see when they look at her. The heavy makeup she wore today covers her pale skin, hides it. It's a shame. She doesn't need surgeries like I did to be beautiful. She just *is*, naturally.

"Hey, do me a favor. Go ask that bald guy if he's doing this for my mom," I say.

"What's in it for me?" she sneers.

"Fame. Love. Gobstoppers. Whatever you want."

"I want the truth."

I give a neutral shrug.

"Then no dice, Fakey."

There's a moment of quiet. She steps off the curb and spans the crosswalk.

"Where are you going?" I ask.

"Doing your shitty little favor." She doesn't turn around.

Michelle Painchaud

I watch her slip into the café. She stands over Baldy's table and sneers my question. I watch his face. The corners of his mouth twitch. He looks outside, at me, and we stare through each other. I finally break into a smile and wave. It intimidates him more than the staring, because he severs eye contact. Taylor trots back across the street to me.

"What did he say?" I ask. I don't need to know—that look told me enough. He's definitely doing this for Mrs. Silverman.

"Told me to get lost. But, hey. Now you owe me, Fake Girl."

"I'm thrilled," I deadpan.

"You know, you're not the happy little popular star when no one's around. It's like you're another person entirely."

My heart skips a beat painfully.

She laughs. "But that's no different from anyone else in this school. In this *world*." She holds her hands over her face and opens one like a door. "One face." Opens the other hand. "Two faces."

I take out a pen and grab her arm.

She recoils. "Oy! What are you doing?"

"Hold still." I write my number on the back of her hand. "My number. I hate being in debt to someone. Call me when you think of how I can pay you back."

Mrs. Silverman's car pulls up then, and I jump in.

"Who's that girl?" she asks.

"Taylor. I just gave her my number."

"She looks awfully mad. Did you say something?"

"No, that's her default expression." I chuckle and strap myself in. "And, not to freak you out or make you worry, but do you know that guy?"

I point to the café. She glances at Baldy. They lock eyes. Or I think they do. Baldy gets up abruptly and leaves the window. Her face instantly pales, and she grips the wheel hard. Checkmate.

"He's been following me. He's just a little creepy. Probably a reporter." I keep my voice light. "Mom? Are you okay?"

"Yes." She smiles but doesn't say anything more until we get onto the highway. "I don't want any secrets between us, Erica. I want us to be honest with each other. That man back there was a private investigator."

I look up from playing with my phone. She turns her blinker on.

"I hired him to look into the previous Erica. And the one before that."

"Mom—"

"I didn't hire him this time, honey. At least I did, but I hired him to look into your old parents, not you. I wanted him to find them. You have to believe me. I don't know why he's doing this; maybe he feels obligated? He's the type of person who'd feel it was his duty."

"You should talk to him."

"Oh, I will," she assures me. "I most certainly will be talking to him."

We pull into the parking lot of the mental hospital. Mrs. Silverman tightens her coat around herself.

"He's a little touchy today, but when I told him you were coming, he looked very happy."

"He'll want to play checkers again probably."

"Probably." She smiles, and her milky fingers search for my hand. I clasp it around hers.

— — —

Michelle Painchaud

The nurse sets up the board, and I settle in the seat opposite Mr. Silverman. He's shaved recently—a step up. Today he's the red side, and I'm the black. He bites his nails and drums his fingers on the table, but otherwise he makes no noise. Mrs. Silverman stays at a distance. It's like she thinks I'm some miracle cure—a cure that can only be worked when Mr. Silverman and I are alone.

"I think I like someone, Dad," I try. He moves his piece wordlessly. "A boy."

Dads are supposed to hate the idea of their little girls going out with a boy. But Mr. Silverman's protective instinct seems about as present as his mind. He sighs and motions for me to hurry up and make my move. I jump over a piece and capture it.

"He's not very social. But then again, neither am I. I just pretend to be. Erica is social. Violet isn't."

My voice is too low for anyone but Mr. Silverman to hear.

"The boy doesn't know who I am. He thinks he does. He's good to talk to—challenges my brain. Seems like he's always trying to look inside of me. It's nice. To have someone try to figure you out. He never will, but the effort is nice."

We play until I capture his last piece.

"You win," he murmurs, disappointed.

"Not yet." I pat his hand.

8: BURY IT

Sal,

No reports on the surprise yet. Going to ask about those special times and see if I can't get her to remember the right one. It's in the library—behind the right bookshelf. Can see the indent marks where it opens up. You'd think they'd put a rug.

They feed me too much—getting fat. Not body fat. Happy fat. Forgetting what it's like to go hungry. Dull. Not sharp. Need sharp.

Don't work good alone. I'll do my best. This is the final exam. Won't let you down. So many rules here. Don't smile, smile, pretend you like this kid, help this girl go out with this guy. A sting is easier than one day in high school.

Will get code.

Violet

I track down Kerwin between chem and study hall. He's leaning against a locker, chatting up some girl.

"Sorry to interrupt." I smile. Kerwin straightens; the girl throws me a glower.

"Erica? What's up?" he asks. "Sorry, Ruby, let's talk later, yeah?"

The girl turns on her heel and sniffs. I smile wider.

"A friend of yours?"

"Something like that." He grins nervously. "What's up?"

"You like me."

For ten seconds I think he's gone comatose, but he blinks, his eyes growing dark. His depressor anguli oris goes slack and tightens again—a dead giveaway that what I said startled him. He wasn't expecting it. It looks true, but some part of his face is holding back. There is something false here. He puts his hand over my shoulder and leans into me.

"So what if I do? Is that a problem?"

"I don't like you." I look up at him.

"And I can't do anything to change your mind?"

"No. I already like someone else. But I do know someone who likes you."

"Your friend Merril by any chance?"

"She's pretty transparent," I say, and laugh.

"But I don't want her." He leans in farther, nose brushing my cheek, his cologne flooding my sinuses. It doesn't ring true.

It's not the motion of a simple high school playboy—rather of a worldly and experienced young man. "I want you."

You want a lie, liar.

"Where are you from, Kerwin?"

"I thought it was obvious. Wales."

"Where exactly in Wales?"

The corners of his mouth crimp. "Swansea."

"Do they know the meaning of *no* in Swansea?" I smile and duck to the side, breaking free of his shadow. "Merril really likes you. You might want to try her."

His eyes get a hard edge. I walk away, four steps, and turn. "Oh, and Kerwin?"

He glances up, the hardness sharpening into a knife of something I can't quite pinpoint. I'm not afraid. This isn't sweet mutable Erica talking anymore. Violet is a raging fire burning out of my eyes, snapping the flaming reins.

"I know your game. I know you're hiding something. If you hurt her, I'll destroy you from the inside out."

Kerwin Howell. I bring up the Google map of Wales, and find Swansea. He was lying, I'm sure. When people lie on the fly like that, they tend to stray just a bit off the truth. Instinct. It's not Swansea, but there's a good chance he's from a town around there. Swansea is the biggest city in the county, and it's a port city. A nearly as large port city is just south. Port Talbot. I scour the online newspaper, and get three years back before my eyes start to hurt. Nothing on Kerwin. Not even an obituary for anyone with his family name.

My phone dances on the table in vibrating circles. A strange number is on it. I pick up.

Michelle Painchaud

"You called, mistress?"

Taylor groans. "Don't call me that. How'd you figure it was me?"

"I'm smart. You should try it sometime."

"Whatever."

"How can I help you?" I shut down the PC.

"That thing you owe me—meet me in two hours, in front of the Green Foods."

"Just letting you know now—I'm not the best shoplifter." Another lie. It's the one thing I'm better than Sal at.

"Just meet me there, Fake. Wear something halfway nice."

The line goes dead.

— — —

"A friend? That's good, don't get me wrong. I'm happy for you, but what are you two going to do at Green Foods?" Mrs. Silverman raises an eyebrow.

"Taylor's dad is picking us up. We're going to the movies. If that's okay."

"Of course it's okay, I just—" She cuts off. "I'm worried. Just you and Taylor? That angry-looking girl? She didn't look like your friend when I saw her, sweetie."

"I'm getting to know her better." I nod. "I promise, I'll be home in a couple of hours."

"Before eleven. I'll pick you up," she asserts.

"And I'll text you her address." I smile.

She sweeps over and kisses the top of my head. "I'm so glad you're making friends. Just be careful, all right? I trust you."

"I know."

—‑—

If anything, Taylor is starting to become my frenemy. I'm still unsure about her and what she wants from me. Mrs. Silverman offers to drop me off. In front of Green Foods, standing out among the pulsing families darting in and out with their dinner groceries, is a girl in all black, dark hair almost touching the bench she sits on. Taylor smiles and waves as we approach. *Smiles. Waves.* She's better at faking happy than I thought.

"Hi, Mrs. Silverman."

"Hello, Taylor, was it?"

"Yeah. It's good to meet you finally. Erica's told me lots about you. Good things, mostly."

"Has she?" Mrs. Silverman shoots a look at me, and I nod. "It's a pleasure to meet you. Your father will be here shortly?"

It's Taylor's turn to glance at me. "Yeah. In ten minutes. He's getting off work, so—"

"Of course." Mrs. Silverman smiles. "And what movie are you going to see?"

"The new vampire one." Taylor shrugs. "Erica said she really wanted to see it."

"Well, I'll leave you to it, then." Mrs. Silverman turns and hugs me. "Stay in touch."

"I'll text," I assure her, and pat her back. She leaves hesitantly, walking backward a few times to wave at us. We wave back, Taylor's mutter disgruntled.

"Nice lady. Little clingy."

"You get used to it." I sigh, and settle onto the bench. "Wanna tell me why you called me out here?"

She plunks a paper bag onto my lap. I peer into the

dimness—bright rainbow hair extensions, lines of beads, and sticks of makeup.

"You called me out here to give me unicorn vomit?" I quirk an eyebrow.

She ignores my jab and stands. "You ever been to a rave?"

"No."

Her smirk is wide. "First time for everything."

We wait an extra twenty minutes, just in case Mrs. Silverman's still around. Taylor leads me to the bus stop. Soon we're mashed together in one plastic seat, watching the world sway by in rose-blush twilight. Lights sprout. Radio towers, closing shops, rows of houses. The lady in front of us snorts and sleepily adjusts her knit beanie. When Taylor gets out on the south side of the city and leads me to the line of people around the block, Violet feels a wave of nostalgia hit her. Sal didn't fit in too well at younger clubs like this, so I used to go alone and try to score something for the night. People don't bring much to clubs, but you can always count on a wallet or a tip that lingers too long on a bar counter-top. The line of waiting people are Lite-Brite meets My Little Pony, every color wrapped around them in neon hues. Stripes on pants, necklaces, hair dye. Taylor's extensions peek out as highlighter orange feathers in a raven's wing.

"Candy," she says, and grunts, passing an armful of beads to me. "Put them on."

I try to mimic what everyone else does—wrapping them on your arms and around your neck in a choker style.

"So I'm here because you needed someone to party with?" I ask.

Taylor snorts over the music thrumming from the open doors. "You're here because I want you to be here, and you owe me. Isn't that enough?"

I push back Violet's trembling excitement and bring out Erica. "I've never really done anything like this. I mean, raves mean drugs, right?"

"You don't have to do them if you don't want to. Just stick with me, Fakey. You'll be fine."

As we get closer to the bouncers—huge guys in black with bald heads—the stuttering synth and heavy bass crescendo. I act flustered and nervous.

"Do you have, like, IDs to get us in?"

Taylor just laughs and pushes me forward into the bouncer's view. She puts her hands on my shoulders and smiles.

"Evening, Jeff."

"Taylor." He nods. "Your dad doing all right?"

"Fat and insufferable as ever. I'll tell him you said hi."

He motions for us to go in. The darkness inside the doors swallows us whole, the music screaming across my eardrums. Needles of rainbow light flicker over the heads of the crowd, waves of purple and red flashing with the epileptic strobes. The club is doused in black light, every white shirt and shoe glowing bright sky blue.

"My dad's client owns the place!" Taylor shouts in my ear as she leads me to a table tucked along the side. Merril's words come back to me; Taylor's dad is a mob lawyer. Taylor's father is the spokesman for some very dangerous, very wealthy people. Sal and I never messed with the mob. We took careful steps to keep out of their territory and never rip off businesses that were mob fronts.

I watch Taylor go to the bar and order drinks. All around her people are dancing, neon pants swirling and lurid glow-in-the-dark bikini tops flashing. Cat ears, glow-straw haloes, and rainbow Mohawks bob in the sea of heads. Ravers hold glow sticks and flash them around their bodies in pseudo martial arts waves and twists. I spot the drug dealers immediately—hanging around the bathrooms with big hoodies. Big pockets. Enough space to hold bags of drugs. I'm willing to bet it's the pure stuff too. If this place is mob owned, they'll have the best dealers with the best stash drumming up business.

Third rule of conning: always know where your exits are. The front door is one. There's an exit tucked behind the bar, and another behind the DJ table. Everything was obviously just thrown together in this warehouse, but thrown together by pros—fantastic lighting and sound systems.

Taylor comes back with three shot glasses between her fingers.

"I don't drink . . ." I start. Besides occasional sips of things, I've never gotten hammered. A con artist needs her senses. A con artist can pretend to drink, but unless she's alone, in the safety of her apartment with no one looking to take advantage of her, she doesn't drink. I'm in a strange rave club and I don't know what Taylor has planned for me. Drinking now would be begging for trouble.

"Who said any of these are for you?" Taylor downs all three shots, one after another. *Chug, clink. Chug, smack lips, clink.*

When the last one's gone, she points in my face. "If you see me go for a ninth one, stop me. In two hours ask the bouncer outside for a cab. I'll be in the front of the dance floor. Come get me and we'll go. Don't drink. Don't take any pills anyone slips you. The only time you should get worried is if I start twitching. Everything else is fine. Absolutely *everything*. You got that?"

It all starts to fall into place as I watch her walk away into the crowd, throwing her arms up as the bass rocks the walls.

She wants me here to watch her. The designated driver, so to speak. I watch her twist and turn in the arms of some guy in bright green pants. Her dark hair melds into the shadows, the extensions peeking out like tiny sunsets. She moves on and dances with a girl in a tiny bikini, laughing. It's like she's an entirely different person. This is her element. She's obviously been here before—I see some people smile and wave at her.

Taylor has two faces. Just like I do.

She goes for shot number four. Five. Six. Goes back to dancing. The music changes, vocal stutters churning my brain. One of the dealers pushes a bright pink pill at me. I crunch it under my foot when he turns. The dealers always give free samples to try to make repeat customers out of you. I consider getting up and dancing myself, but Erica is timid. Violet wants to join, to writhe with the masses, but tonight is Erica's night. Erica's chance to make Taylor believe she's real. Good girl Erica would do exactly as she said.

With a twist.

Rebellion. Erica's never tried it. Violet hums with the possibility, whispers in her ear like a temptress. Like a coach. A friend.

You can do it. It's just dancing. Just move your body a bit. Ignore the people watching. Ignore everybody; listen to the music. Nobody cares what you look like. Nobody cares about you; you're just one girl in a crowd of scantily clad ones. No one will look your way twice.

Erica gets up, a little wooden. She flinches as a group of boys rush past her and into the crowd. The music is hard, fast, people jumping up and down. I stand on the edges and watch the DJ spin—his headphones cupping one ear and his laptop open and glowing. Erica sways, one foot to another, the dance of an unsure girl. She doesn't move furiously—it's

Michelle Painchaud

not her style. She puts her arms up and lets them dip with the music. If she closes her eyes, the lights flash against the darkness of her eyelids in rhythmic imprints. If she opens them, her sight explodes in stars and colors, a galaxy being created—smoke, heat, noise, light, expanding into the dark space of the warehouse.

A hard jolt brings Erica out of her reverie and Violet to the foreground. I crash to the floor, polished stone unforgiving on my butt.

"Hey! Watch where you're—" I choke off the shout as the person I collided with pulls me up.

"Sorry, didn't see you—" His eyes widen. He's not wearing any candy or glow paint, but his white shirt glows eerily, and in the flashes I see his long blond hair.

"James?"

"Erica!" he shouts. "Are you okay?"

"Yeah, I'm fine." I motion toward the table. We sit. The music is still loud, but here you can use a seven-decibel voice to be heard, instead of a ten.

"I didn't know you went to things like this." I smirk. "I guess it makes sense. You like music."

"I'm here for my friend." He nods to the front, where the DJ is clicking away on his keyboard. "It's his first gig. He asked me to come down and support him."

"Nice of you."

"And what's your excuse?" His eyes narrow, but just barely.

"Taylor brought me."

"She's here?" His eyebrows rise.

Taylor staggers out of the crowd. I stand on instinct, and James does too, as she stumbles into the table and clutches the edges. She rolls her head slowly, smile huge, and spots James.

"Virgin! What's a good boy like you doing in a place like this?"

"Was that a pickup line?" He sneers.

"I wouldn't pick you up even if you were the weight of a puppy." She laughs, messes her hair up—disheveled angles. "*Puppies?* I'm a mess."

"Maybe we should go, Taylor," I offer.

Her dark eyes flash, and she slams her hand on the table. "I say when we go. You still owe me, Fakey. So just shut up and roll with it."

We watch Taylor edge her way into the crowd again.

"We're leaving in two hours. She said so, anyway. Before she got all . . . crazy." It's the only word I can think of to describe her.

"This is *not* her crazy mode," James interjects.

"And you would know?"

"She's overdosed twice in school. Pills. First time she collapsed in English. Second time in a bathroom stall. Hit her head on the back of the toilet pretty bad. Ambulance. Stitches. She picks fights with anybody who looks at her the wrong way. The only reason she hasn't been thrown out is because of her father's . . . *influence.* She knows he'll bail her out of anything, so she does everything."

Is that why everyone treats her like she's got the plague? I'd wondered why she was such a loner when she was so pretty and obviously well-off.

James glances at me. "I'm glad she's got someone with her this time at least."

We're quiet. Taylor stumbles in and out for another shot. That makes seven. She waves sardonically and pushes back into the crowd. James stands.

"I should get back."

"No!" My hand shoots out and pushes his onto the table. Too fast. What am I doing? Play it cool. Let his hand go. He looks at our hands, his gaze traveling up my arm and to my neck, rippling like liquid fire. My chin, my eyes. The gaze lingers there.

And before I can catch fire in the best way, the crowd parts. Shrill screams come from two figures entwined. Punching, kicking, hair pulling. One of the girls is Taylor, her opponent a brunette in a rainbow-striped skirt. The crowd swallows them again, the fight moving inward as people cheer or try to get between them. James looks at me as I look at him, a wordless agreement.

We need to break up some bitches.

James's tall, bony figure cuts a path through the crowd. I press my face into his back and fist his shirt to make sure I don't lose him. He smells like pepper and aftershave and sweat—a heady combination. A sudden jerk of his body jolts me out of my mildly creepy sniffing moment. He reaches over and pulls Taylor off Rainbow Skirt Girl. James isn't the buffest guy, so wrestling a thrashing Taylor takes all his concentration.

"Come on! Let me go! I swear to God, I'll fucking pull her tongue out—"

Skirt Girl goes in to jab Taylor's nose while she's restrained. Before I can stop her, Violet socks Skirt Girl's cheek. The hit is hard enough to make her stagger.

James holds Taylor tight the whole way through the crowd and to the exit. At points I grab Taylor's hair to keep her from biting James's face, neck—anywhere she can get at.

"Put me down, asshole! Did I ask you"—she kicks at him—"to do any of this hero shit?"

When we get free of the crowd, I dash outside and look for Jeff the bouncer. Tap his meaty shoulder.

"Uh, hi, we need a—"

"Jeff! Tell these cunts to put me down!"

Jeff's eyes roll. He takes over for a relieved-looking James, having a much easier time pinning Taylor's arms behind her back.

"Mark, get a cab, will you?" He jerks his head to another bouncer. Taylor alternates between screaming obscenities and muttering under her breath. I must look worried, because Jeff sighs.

"Just drunk tonight. I've seen her on everything else— this isn't her doped-up look. Don't worry. Just get her home, give her a glass of water."

"She comes here a lot, then?" James asks.

Jeff sniggers.

The cab pulls up, and Jeff pushes the squirming Taylor inside and tells the cabbie to child-lock the doors so she can't get out. He sticks his bald head in the dark taxi and mutters something to Taylor. She stops trying to claw at the door handle and huffs, crossing her arms over her chest.

Jeff nods. "She's all yours. Cab's already paid for."

"Thanks." I smile. "Good customer service around here."

"Just for her." He motions for us to get in.

I turn to James. "You coming with?"

"I think I did my part." James shoves his hands into his pockets. "It would be a little weird, a guy going home with two girls. I don't want to freak her dad out. Call me later, okay? She has my number. Lemme know you're all right."

"Definitely. See you later, then?" My voice sounds more timid than I'd like.

"Later." He bends and looks through the cab window. "Be good, Gotherella."

"Fuck off," she spits.

I slide in beside her, and James closes the door. Through the back window, I can see him watching the cab until it turns the corner, face twisted with something I can't pinpoint.

Taylor's house is a chic split-level on a hillside overlooking the lights of the Strip, the kind with windows that take up the entire wall. Glass walls. Walls that let in the city and night sky and endless desert. Japanese landscaping—miniature banyans in pots, gardens of raked sand and bamboo. By the time we pull in the driveway, Taylor's swearing has quieted.

"Thanks for the lift." I try to be as cheerful as I can. The driver nods and unlocks the doors. I get out and hold the door open. "C'mon. Out."

Taylor watches something in the distance, forehead pressed against the glass. She's a mess—hair tangled and makeup smeared in raccoon rings around her eyes. I clear my throat, and she winces.

"Fine, fine. Jesus."

She shuffles behind me as I take the stairs eagerly. The door is black and shiny. And unlocked. I open it—wood floors and sparse but stylish furniture. Expensive sculptures line the tables.

"Anyone home?"

"Oh God," Taylor says with a groan. "Shut up. Don't encourage him."

"Tay? That you?" a man's voice calls. Female giggles start, stop, and start again. Taylor winces again and hides behind me as a man comes out—short, rotund, and in a leopard-print bathrobe and little else. His black mustache twitches.

"Oh, sorry! Didn't know we had company. Warn me next time, Tay."

"I'm Erica." I smile. "Taylor's friend."

"Right!" He squints. Knows I'm the kidnapped girl, obviously.

I walk in, and Taylor kicks the door closed behind her, then lies on the couch with her back to everyone.

Taylor's dad shakes my hand. "I'm Barry Mansfield. Good to meet you, *Erica*." He puts the tiniest emphasis on my name. It isn't much, but it's a con artist's job to be paranoid. Did that mean something? Does he know something?

"Your mom call?" Barry directs the question to Taylor.

"Wouldn't know," she says with a grunt.

"If she calls the home phone, tell her to stop. She's been bullshitting me all day with legal agreement crap."

"Whatever."

"I've got some, uh, guests. I better get back to them. Nice meeting you, Erica." He nods and scuttles down the hall. He opens a door, the sound of girlish giggles wafting out. The door closes on laughter and faint simpering *stop*'s.

"Disgusting." Taylor growls, and straightens. She goes to the kitchen and opens the fridge—chock-full of beautiful fruit platters, pastries, and carefully arranged meats and cheeses. I think I see caviar. But none of it is touched—not so much as a bite. It's perfect, beautiful, but ignored. Taylor takes out a bottle.

"You shouldn't drink anymore, Taylor—"

"Relax, Goody Two-shoes. It's water." She pops open the

Michelle Painchaud

cap and chugs it, wipes her lips. I lift a stack of magazines from the coffee table and run my fingers over the table's surface. When I pull away, traces of white powder stick to me. I touch my tongue to my index finger. Sharp. Coke. I'm willing to bet dozens of other surfaces in the house are dusted similarly. Taylor's dad tried to hide it with magazines.

The female voices from the other room giggle louder. Taylor strides to the patio and opens it, slamming it behind her. Sort of lost, I follow. A patch of grass with a small pool has a perfect view of the diadem of jeweled lights that is the Strip. Taylor sits on the grass, knees up to her chest. I sit by her. We're quiet. A lighter clicks and shines in the corner of my eye.

"You shouldn't smoke. It'll kill you," I say.

"Life will kill you," she counters, and blows smoke.

I pull out my phone. "James said you'd have his number."

She bites down on her cig to steady it as she takes out her phone. Grumbles the number. It rings twice before James picks up. The boom of music is a muffled pulse in the background.

"Hey, Erica?"

"Hi." I sound breathless. "We got home okay."

"Great." A pause. A huge crevasselike pause. "Do you need a ride home or anything?"

"Mom's picking me up." I texted her the address earlier.

"Right. I . . . guess I'll see you on Monday."

"James, I—"

Taylor shoots me a look at the desperate tone in my voice. Violet cringes at Erica's inability to control herself. Erica wants to thank him for helping, thank him for things he doesn't know he does, the shaky influx of heat and inflating heart. But if she says that, it'll move something forward.

Everything should stay where it is. The less I move, the less my absence will be missed.

"Thanks . . . for helping tonight."

He sounds a little disappointed behind the assurance. "It was all you, Kidnap Girl."

The nickname, coming from him, doesn't make me cringe. It makes me smile. We hang up. Taylor rolls her eyes and blows smoke rings into the night air.

"Just get married already."

"You go to that club and get wasted a lot?" I ask.

She shrugs. "Better than being in this fucking house. A new set of whores every day, going through my fridge and using my shower. Calling him *Daddy*."

I'm quiet. I pick at the sparse grass under my legs.

"Thanks, Fakey. For sticking with me. It's nice having someone haul your ass out. I'd considered hiring someone to do it, but they wouldn't have the same dedication, you know? I won't blame you if you don't talk to me on Monday. Your prep friends wouldn't like it."

"I don't care about what they like."

"Of course you do." Taylor exhales, smoke cloud spiraling. "You care about what everybody likes. That's why you're popular. That's why you're Erica."

"So you finally believe I'm the real thing?" My chest swells.

She laughs hoarsely. "I don't believe anyone."

That quiet settles in again. There's no more grass to pick.

"Look, I know you aren't Erica," Taylor finally says, stubbing her cig out on the ground. "Dad knows. You don't think his bosses haven't tried to get in on that woman's money too? One of the two fakes was their plant. Just like you're someone else's plant."

I stifle the urge to suck in a sharp breath. Just as I open my mouth to argue, she sighs.

"I don't know how you did it, but you've done it. I'm not gonna bust you. Dad's not gonna bust you. He and his buddies had their chance at that painting like every other scumbag in this town. They failed. They're gonna stand back and watch to see if you fail too. They don't care. There's no evidence. At this point nobody freakin' cares, you know?"

She knows about the painting? I guess she would, if her dad was involved with the kinds of people who tried to steal it. The safest thing to do here is neither confirm nor deny. Just breathe. Breathe now, figure it out later. Listen now, worry later.

"I feel sorry for you, Fakey. You and me, we could've gotten along if you weren't such a criminal. You seem like a decent person under that rich-bitch front."

I shrug. Neutral. Shell-shocked, on-the-edge-of-freaking-out-but-somehow-managing-to-hold-it-in neutral.

"So." She lights another cigarette. "You gonna go out with Beethoven?"

"I have no time for boys." I sigh. "He's a distraction I don't need right now."

"But this is the most important time. You know, when we're supposed to figure our romantic shit out—what we like in a guy, what we don't like. We're supposed to have our firsts and get them over with. That's what high school is for. Figuring stuff out and getting rid of embarrassing first times."

I'm silent. She coughs. In the low light from the house I can see the bruises from the girl fight on her face—red patches. An older bruise, purple, sits on her cheek, blurred with rubbed-off makeup. Is that what she was hiding beneath the caked-on foundation earlier? A mark from another fight?

Taylor just coughs again. I hear Mrs. Silverman's car pull up in the driveway.

"Later, Erica."

It's the first time Taylor uses my name.

On the way out, I can hear the giggles of the women as far as the stairs. There are no family pictures on the wall—just pretentious art. Empty booze bottles stuff the recycle bin. When Mrs. Silverman asks about what Taylor's parents are like, I just squeeze her hand.

Michelle Painchaud

9: FOLLOW IT

My ears ring all weekend from the club. When I calm down, I realize Taylor was right. She doesn't have any evidence, or a truly personal motive to see me busted. If she accuses me, she'll be just another doubter among thousands. It doesn't make me feel secure, but it eases the gnawing a little. Nothing of my life as Erica makes me feel secure anyway. It's all pins and needles hidden in silk cushions.

Sunday dinner is pizza on the couch—Mrs. Silverman chooses a DVD and pops it in. She looks out of place, delicately munching on string cheese while dressed in a kimono-style robe.

"Your hair's a little too perfect to be eating pizza." I toy with one of her flawless curls.

She pushes my hand away. "*Au contraire.* I may be over-dressed for pizza, but I am certainly underdressed for a night on the *Titanic.*"

The title of the ship movie blares. I laugh and settle next to her.

"I'm also far overdressed for Leonardo DiCaprio," she croons. I gag on my pizza, and she pats my back. "No choking! Choking is not an option."

"Can I vomit?"

"Your mother likes celebrities as much as the next woman. Is that so weird to imagine?"

"Would you cheat on Dad with Leonardo?" I tease.

"Oh, it would take more than Leo. Your father and I used to joke that I'd only leave him for Clooney. A time-travel Clooney from the eighties. He wouldn't be jailbait then, right?"

I snort Pepsi up my nose.

She laughs and hands me a napkin. "Oh, dear, I'm sorry. Here."

"I'b fibe." My accent is thick. "Eberything sbells like soba."

Her laugh is loud. I've seen *Titanic*. But the DVD was scratched, so I never quite saw the ending.

"Now see, if this was a romance novel"—Mrs. Silverman leans over after the love scene—"she would be pregnant, and when he dies, she would have his baby."

"Isn't that what happens?"

"Goodness no. She goes on to have a family with another man."

"That doesn't seem very romantic," I say, and sniff. "If they wanted to make it really romantic, she'd be a spinster until the day she died."

"It's hard to be alone" is all Mrs. Silverman manages.

As far as I know, she's been alone since Mr. Silverman went into the mental hospital. I'm sure she's had tons of suitors—she's beautiful and still fairly young, and rich on top of it all. Hundreds of guys would love to date her. But she's stayed married to Mr. Silverman. She hasn't divorced him. It's a testament to their love for each other.

She cries and cries when the ship goes down, and I tear up. She wipes my tears, then sighs.

"The ending always gets me." She turns the TV off and a lamp on. "Wait here while I get something." Comes back with a thick book—a photo album. Photo albums were part of the daily ritual when we'd spent that month together alone, but this is a new album. One I haven't seen yet. It's so big, it takes up both of our laps when open.

"Here's you when we got that Slip'N Slide thing. Nearly gashed your shin on one of the stakes. Your father spent the whole afternoon redesigning safer ones. You can't take the engineer out of a concerned father." She smiles.

Hundreds of pictures of Erica. Mrs. Silverman looks so young. Mr. Silverman looks like an entirely different man— healthy and clean. Erica in a bib, Erica opening Christmas presents, Erica riding a horse with little cowgirl boots. Erica playing in the sprinkler, Erica's face smeared with rainbow cupcake frosting. I can see her—the real her. Not the semi-stiff picture in the MISSING poster. In these pictures she's always alive. She's a real girl.

I stop Mrs. Silverman's hand from changing the page— there's a picture of Erica and two other girls. They're like the Three Musketeers, all dressed in varying shades of pink as they look up for the picture. They were playing dolls, the parts and clothes scattered in the space between them.

"Who are they?" I ask.

"Cassandra Sandford and Merril Breton." She traces the picture. "They used to come over after preschool, and you three would watch cartoons. There's another of you guys in our pool. And there's you three at Merril's family barbeque. She had a bouncy castle and you were quite jealous, so for your fourth birthday we got you a bigger one."

I roll my eyes. She laughs and hugs me closer. I turn the pages on my own, and Erica's life unfolds. She was spoiled rotten. Erica probably peed her bed and threw fits. Not everything was sunshine and rainbows, but her family loved her anyway. Despite her flaws. Despite her tantrums.

They didn't hit her for messing up. For speaking out.

There, on the left side of the page, is a picture of a young Erica and a dark-haired little girl. Erica laughs and pulls the girl along by the hand. The dark-haired girl looks unsure and scared.

"Who is that?" I whisper.

"Oh, I remember you helped that girl more than once." She ties her robe tighter. "Tiffany? Talia? Something like that. She was such a timid thing. The teachers said you made every effort to stop the others from picking on her."

Taylor. Does she remember? No, they were young. But it's ironic that Taylor and the real Erica were friends, as friendly as you could get at age four, anyway. It's a string I never knew about, a thread that makes so much sense in a way.

The little Taylor looks so different from the wounded raccoon-eyed girl I know now.

I murmur, "I left you both alone. To suffer."

Mrs. Silverman draws me into her chest. "Don't say things like that, Erica."

"I'm sorry. I won't leave you again."

I will leave you again.

"I won't leave you, either, sweetie. It wasn't your fault. You know that, right?"

"Everything's my fault."

Everything will be my fault. You'll see.

"No, honey. No." She chants it over and over into my hair. I clutch at her robe and put my head on her lap. This time the tears are real. But they aren't mine. They are clearly Erica's. Violet knows this. In the back of my head,

Violet rolls her eyes and folds her arms over her chest. Waits for the deluge to stop. Sleep comes before it stops, my pillow soft, painted with cranes, and murmuring comforting nothings into my ear.

———

This is the light part, the white sugar and sparkles part, the part where I—grand pooh-bah of serious business—have to pretend to be not-serious. Not-dedicated. Not-driven.

I shouldn't complain. Hanging out with Cass and Merril is simple compared to hanging with Taylor, Mrs. Silverman, or the shrink. Being with Cass and Merril is easy, being with everyone else is hard, and being with James is natural—somewhere between the two. I am Goldilocks in a suburban forest, eating the most complicated porridge ever.

Merril and Cass drag me to the mall.

"This one's nice." Merril holds up a purple thong. My face heats.

"There's more cloth on a Kleenex, Merril."

"Pink would look a lot better on you." She hands me another thong, this one with frills. I watch her sift through piles of underwear. Her smile is bright, unconscious. She's been like this since she announced she and Kerwin started going out. Part of me is happy for her; the other is watchful and alert, waiting for Kerwin to do something underhanded. I still haven't figured him out, and he annoys me. Scares me.

"Are you guys ready?" Cass chimes.

"I don't think I'm getting anything." I smile.

Merril rolls her eyes. "You have to get some nice underwear for prom, Rica. It's like buying a prom dress—a must."

"Regular old underwear is fine?" I don't sound so sure.

Cass nods. "Oh, it's perfectly fine. If you plan on going to prom alone." She snickers. "Aren't you bringing James? He's never gone to a dance before, but I bet he'd go if you asked."

My face lights red. Both faces. Erica and Violet are burning at the same time, in the same way. We walk out of the store, the mall humming with the late-afternoon weekend crowd.

"You have to go with someone to the prom, Rica. If not James, someone else," Cass insists, hefting her bag higher on her arm. "Let me introduce you to some guys, okay? Alex has a ton of friends."

"I'll be okay alone."

"No, you won't!" She stomps her foot. "You're coming with us in our limo and we're going to the Hilton for the night and you'll be with someone like the rest of us. We'll crash the pool and order a ton of room service. You don't have to make out with him or anything; just go with him to prom. Come with *us* to the prom."

"Cass—"

"You were gone for everything else. You have to be here for this one. You have to experience it like the rest of us, okay?"

I don't say anything. Cass and Merril lead me to the food court. They get salads. I glance longingly at a burger before settling for a salad too.

"Thank you," I murmur.

"What's up?" Cass glances up from a crouton.

"We were too young. You don't remember me, but you're so nice to me."

"We might not remember you, Erica, but we know you. This whole town knows you." Merril stabs a tomato. "The police searches, the sort-of sightings. The memorials. Just when we would start to forget, a fake you would show up and stir up everything. You were always here."

"That must've been annoying."

Cass shrugs. "You can't say a missing girl is annoying. People get mad and call you insensitive."

"It was like nobody could move on." Merril sighs. "But hey. It's over now. You're alive, you're the real deal, and you're here. We can all keep going."

I'm not here.

I move my lettuce leaves around. I'm not here. I'm going to go away, and the Erica-shaped gap in their lives will come back. Stronger than ever. The last nail in the coffin that never existed.

Merril looks behind me, her smile growing. "Hi, Kerwin!"

My throat contracts. Sure enough—Kerwin in a polo shirt and a smirk walks over. She gets up and kisses him on the cheek. He sits across from me.

"Just thought I'd come by and say hi. Hope I'm not ruining a girls' day out."

"Not especially." Cass keeps the fork on her lips thought-fully. Coolly. She, unlike most girls, tends to play it cool around Kerwin. Unnaturally so. Could she, like me, suspect him of something? Or maybe that's just how she treats guys who're prettier than she is.

"So, Erica"—Kerwin smirks—"how'd you like Club Riddler?"

I freeze.

Cass quirks a brow. "Riddler? Isn't that the super-grungy one on the south side?"

"I spotted Erica there. With that girl you guys don't

like—Taylor is her name?" His brown eyes are guarded.

Merril frowns. "Why were you hanging out with her, Rica?"

"I— I just met her." I shrug. "She said she knew a good place to party, so I went with her. I didn't stick around."

"You got in a cab and went home with her," Kerwin interjects.

Merril's mouth falls open. "Where? Back to her house?"

"She was drunk," I defend. "She needed help getting home. And besides"—I shoot a nasty glare at Kerwin—"why were you there anyway?"

"I was trying to find a good place for Merril and me to go out, of course."

Fat chance. He was following me. Coincidence is null and void with this guy. But why the stalker routine? What'd I do? What does he want from me? Merril sighs lovingly and kisses Kerwin again. Lip on lip, a bit of tongue.

Cass makes a grossed-out face at me. "Who you want to hang out with is your business, Rica," she assures me. "But Taylor's bad news. She's been into some weird stuff over the years. And she's not exactly the easiest person to get along with."

"She's just lonely," I murmur. Cass shrugs.

Kerwin excuses himself early. He stopped by just to tell me he'd seen me, hiding under the guise of coming to see his girlfriend. One of my friends. It's too much of a coincidence. It's too confusing. I can't even put a finger on his motive. He doesn't like me romantically enough to stalk me and use Merril to keep an eye on me. There's no longing in his gaze. I need to find out his deal, and fast. I feel like he is circling me, like a rope is going around my feet, and the only time I'll see it is when it cinches and drags me to the ground.

After lunch we walk to the parking lot. I'm getting a ride home in Merril's Volvo, but halfway across the pavement I spot a man standing at his car. His bald head shines in the weak sunlight—Mr. White.

Merril glances where my eyes are riveted. "Who's that guy? Is he staring at us? What a creeper."

"He's a police officer," I lie. "He came to the house and asked questions. He thinks I'm not Erica. I'm going to go talk to him."

"I'll wait for you." Merril nods.

Mr. White balks when he sees me walking toward him. He ducks into his car and starts the engine. I dash up and wrench the passenger door open, slamming it and facing him. Up close, his square jaw and the scars over his right eye are obvious. His arm muscles are the kind that have been accumulated over decades. He clutches the wheel—missing three fingers on his left hand. Like I thought—injured ex-military.

"Hello, Mr. White. I'm Erica."

"Get out of my car." His voice is gravelly.

"I told Mom about you." I look at my nails and flick my hair like I'd seen Cass do when acting flippant. "She told me your name. Said she was going to talk to you."

"Your mother hasn't said anything."

"She didn't hire you to shadow me. That means you've been doing it on your own. Why? What did I ever do to you?"

His brown eyes narrow. I can read him so easy, even if he is ex-military. He was trained to be stoic under fire, but that stoniness gives him away. None of the other Ericas ever approached him. They probably noticed him at some point, but they were afraid of him and of what he could uncover. I'm pretending like I have nothing to hide—it's either the worst bluff ever, or the best. Depends on how deeply he thinks on it.

"You think I'm not the real Erica."

"I never said that." He grunts.

"You're obviously good at what you do." I pat the inside of the car, a Saab. "Pretty fancy wheels."

He doesn't say anything.

"And you're obviously in love with Mom." It's a risky thing to say, but the rapid succession of questions lets me gauge his reactions—the previous two statements had been false. His lack of emotion proved that. But the final statement made his mouth twist and his leg jump. My gut was right—he has a deeply personal motive. He's known Mrs. Silverman for years, seen her at her worst. He protected her from betrayal that would've grown if left to fester in falsity. He's in love with her.

"You need to get out of my car." His voice strains to stay level. He's a man of few words, but not few emotions.

"I understand that you want to protect her again." I soften my voice, making it soft. "But I want to protect her too. She's in love with Dad. You know that, right? He's coming back slowly but surely."

Mr. White adjusts the collar of his trench coat.

"You don't have to believe I'm the real Erica. You can keep following me if you want. But give up on Mom. Please. I'm going to put my family together again. I can't do that if you get in the middle."

"What were you doing at Club Riddler?"

"Not you, too." I exhale. "What the hell are you doing stalking an underage girl?"

"It's my job," he deadpans. "I'm sure you didn't tell your

mother you were going to the club. Shall I break the news to her, or will you?"

"She doesn't care," I spit. "It's what teens do—rebel."

"I have pictures. Of you and that Taylor girl."

"I was helping a friend."

"You were getting drunk with a friend in a club well known for the paramount quality of its drugs."

"I wasn't drinking, and I didn't take drugs! And you're stalking without someone paying you to. Isn't that technically a crime?"

"Not as much as fraud. As pretending to be someone you're not."

I don't dignify him with a confirmation or denial. That club was a mistake, a huge oversight. Erica would've never gone. I never should've gone. I have to clean up my mess—now. I make my voice low, hoarse, wounded.

"You're right. I'm not the Erica I should be. I should be more proper. More refined. I should be less selfish, more open. People don't say it, but it feels like they want to. They want to say I'm not what I should be. But you can't forget the life you've lived. I can't just forget everything that made me who I am today. So you're right. I'm not Erica. Not yet. But I'm learning."

Even though he's a hardened ex-military man, suspicious of me and clearly having been through a lot in his life, the insecurity in my words seems to reach him. His eyes soften.

"Give her those pictures if you want. I don't care. I wanted to get out, get away from her, from everything crushing me. Smothering me. I can't tell her that. She'd hate me for saying it."

I swallow hard. There's nothing left to say. I get out and close the door, and he pulls out of the lot.

— — —

Merril drives me home, and I hug her before I get out.

"Thank you. I mean it. For being my friend." For being the first friend Violet's ever made.

"Hey, you're welcome." She pats my back and pulls away. "Is something wrong? You're not usually super-touchy."

"I'm fine. See you on Monday."

"Don't hang out with Taylor anymore, okay? You're all bummed-looking. She gets to people like that."

I wait until her car leaves the curb. I don't press the button on the gate's admittance panel. I don't wait for it to swing open. I don't walk up the path lined with freshly budding apple trees and the barest of spring grasses. I leave the huge white house and the manicured lawn behind.

I pull the black hoodie I bought at the mall over my head. The sleeves hang over my fingertips, warming them. The zipper clinks, and the ties around the neck flicker across my face in the wind. Old friends. Violet welcomes them. The hoodie is too clean-smelling, too new, but it has a soothing effect on her heart, like a child's blanket.

I run.

Down the street, the sidewalk, past houses just as big and prestigious as Erica's. Past expensive cars and hired help unloading groceries and trimming hedges. Always hired help. The really important people stay inside their castles and sit on their thrones. Violet laughs. Laughs and runs until her legs burn. Until she reaches the highway and the overpass that connects the gated community to the rest of the world.

Michelle Painchaud

She laces her fingers through the chain-link fence that keeps people from jumping into traffic, and she looks at her nails— pink with faint glitter. She makes a face. Erica wants to come out, bleeds out from between her eyes, but Violet craves air before she goes dormant for another month.

Violet shakes the fence. The freeway pulses with cars and speed and wind. The Strip can be seen from here—a faint line of neon signs that grows brighter as the daylight dies. Sucking light. Hotels and casinos, too, but mostly signs. The Strip is a world of signs: low-price, half-price, sale, two-for-one, Violet and Erica for one. Violet shakes the fence and lets out a scream, but the rush of traffic drowns it out. Erica winces and covers her ears. Violet breathes in exhaust and exhales carbon monoxide, and she lives for another second, another day. She lives to pretend to be someone else for another day.

10: LIGHT IT

Today Millicent is even wider. Today her pen has a teddy bear on the end.

Today she asks me what I dream about.

"Lights," I murmur. The leather divan is cool against the bits of my skin that stick out of my uniform. "Red and blue lights. Police, I guess."

"And what do you think those lights represent?"

Fear. Worst-case scenarios. What will happen if I mess this con up. Mess my life up. One wrong slip of the hand, one wrong pair of eyes, one wrong thing said to Mrs. Silverman by Taylor, Mr. White, Kerwin, and I'm gone, taken by the flickering ruby-and-sapphire lights.

"The tightrope is too small and my feet are too big," I mutter, "but the show must go on. Be happy, smile, wave. Pretend to get better. Pretend you know how to be the person who'll make them happy."

Millicent scribbles, sips her tea. It smells like charcoal and weeds.

"The lights in my dream," I lie, "represent the day I found out they weren't my parents. The day I became Erica."

It's not the first time the police chase them.

Sal holds his hands out obediently, a soft smile in place. Makes small talk with the officers—knows them all by name. Asks after their families. Introduces himself to the young cop who's new.

Violet goes back to foster care.

Sal's lawyer—mob lawyer—pulls strings. There is no cloth of justice green bills cannot dye. Violet waits like a good girl in a strange house with strange food, strange people.

Sal hires a woman. She comes to the door one day, pretending to sell makeup. Pushes her way in. Sal slips into the kitchen's back door and takes the stairs like a panther. Rushes into Violet's room (she was coloring a picture of a ballerina), and she wordlessly grabs the Mickey Mouse backpack they gave her (stuffed with electronics the couple wouldn't miss). The woman yells at the husband for spilling concealer, covering their exit with noise.

The two of them don't get caught by the police often. But when they do, it usually hurts Violet.

Red-and-blue rotating lights in the rearview mirror mean being alone.

11: SHAKE IT

Mr. Silverman doesn't ask anything of me.

He doesn't need a false face. He doesn't ask me to pretend so hard. I still pretend (force of habit), but it's at a minimum with him. Erica only barely needs to be here. With just her smile and tone of voice, I can coast through a blissful hour or two, or however long the checkers match lasts. He just wants me to play. I play very well and with all my heart, because games are second nature to me. Games are my blood. I am a player for a living.

Mrs. Silverman dropped me off and left, saying she had to get something from the cleaners. I can relax even more. He moves a checker forward and throws his hands up.

"Two!"

"Two." I smile, and his fingers snatch my board pieces. He's on the verge of winning.

"My real dad, Sal . . ." I start. "He used to let me win at poker. Sometimes. But I never managed to beat him in an actual game. He liked challenging me, but he always some- how won. Still does. I'll play him until he dies, and I bet you, he'll win every game. Until I figure out his strategy. Then he's toast."

He moves his next piece, victory forefront on his mind. He practically dances in his seat. Crusted soup stains the front of his shirt. When he wins, he explodes, running to my seat and clutching me around the neck in his version of a hug. The nurse looks nervous, but I motion to her that it's fine. I hug him back. He smells like anesthetic and the muted musk of sleep. As abruptly as the hug starts, he ends it and sits back down. He sweeps the board clean and rearranges the pieces for another game. I settle in and sip my bottled coffee as he works. He pours all his concentration into it.

"You were having problems controlling it before Erica vanished, weren't you?"

He doesn't acknowledge my question, but his hands twitch a little as he moves his first red piece.

"You must've been incredibly smart for it to corrupt you. You must've loved her a lot for her disappearance to change you so drastically. You went crazy imagining what was happening to her, and being unable to do anything about it. You thought of a hundred smarter ways the police could be doing things. But you were just a civilian. What could you do? What would they *let* you do?"

I play the game with him for a few minutes. He's not so happy anymore. I'm winning. He finally glances up and spins a piece of mine in his fingers.

"Zoo. In *Robinson Crusoe*, there was a zoo. Pandas and a zoo."

More than three words. He spoke more than three.

I keep my breathing even. "Zoo?" I lead.

He spins the piece faster and fumbles with it. He puts it back down, as if fearing it'll slip from his grasp.

"What are you talking about, Dad?"

"I'll get better when you come back." He shakes his head, like a fly is buzzing around it. "When you really come home, I'll get better."

He means Erica. He's been listening—he knows I'm not her.

"Dad—"

He cuts me off. "It's your move."

I move. I try to get him to talk more, but he presses his lips shut and only smiles when he wins for the second time. He carefully puts the game away. "I am the rat in the maze; you are the chameleon in the trees."

I'm afraid. For that one second, I see the twinkle of consciousness in his eyes. I underestimated him—dismissed him as near comatose like everyone else. Mr. Silverman's heard everything anyone's ever said to him. He pats my shoulder like a regular person would and follows the nurse back to his room.

Finally, after sixteen years, I've met someone better than I am at pretending.

"Dad, wait!" I start after him. The nurse closes his door, but I see a slice of the room for a second. Unlike the white walls outside, Mr. Silverman's room is covered in ink, pencil, Magic Marker. Numbers crowd his walls like swarming ants. The nurse shoots me a look.

"Can I help you?"

"Let me in Dad's room. What's all that writing on the walls?"

"He likes to scribble random numbers, I'm afraid. But if you want to go in, that's up to him."

"Dad!" I pound on the door. "Can I come in for a minute?"

"I'm busy." He grunts.

My brain races. How can I play this and get in there? Those numbers looked too interesting to pass up.

"Dad, you didn't even hug me good-bye," I whimper.

There's a silence. The door creaks open, and I push in. Mr. Silverman throws his arms around my neck and squeezes. I stand on my tiptoes to see over his shoulder. The room looks like a mathy Picasso gone wrong. Numbers stretch over the walls and nearly onto the ceiling. Every white space is used up. I take the numbers in as fast as I can—these aren't random numbers. There's *structure* in this mess. Eight or nine equations are repeated, interrupting each other, clashing, their answers melding. It's advanced stuff far beyond my capability, but I can deduce, from his scribbled margin work, that he's trying to find a common integer. No, more than one common integer. Exactly *eight* integers. But the long division is wrong.

It hits me as he pulls away and pats my head.

He already knows the integers. He's working backward— making equations that equal separate numbers. There's binary to hexadecimal conversion, and vice versa. The integers aren't just numbers, but letters, too.

Somewhere in these equations is an eight-digit letter/ number code.

The safe code.

It's a long stretch. It could just be the ramblings of a former engineer's addled mind. But it's too coincidental. The nurse ushers me out of the hospital as Mrs. Silverman pulls up to the curb. I have to come back. I need to write these equations down without drawing suspicion to myself . . . somehow.

When I get to the car, I see a dress bag in the backseat. I quirk an eyebrow.

"Is that yours?"

She smiles. "No. Yours."

"What?" I watch her unzip it—blue silk glows up at me.

"Try it on when we get home, okay? I had it tailored, but your measurements might've changed."

"Oh my God. Is that what I think it is? A prom dress?"

She ushers me into the passenger side and laughs. "Home first."

I can barely contain myself. That was the most beautiful dress I'd ever seen, and I'd only seen four inches of it. I dart up the stairs with the dress bag over my arm, my Converses pounding on the stairs.

"Ah, Erica! There's a friend of yours waiting in the living room."

I only faintly hear Marie's words. I peel my shirt off and wiggle out of my jeans. The dress's skirt is short in the front and long in the back. There are no ruffles, but it's strapless and tight around my chest. Perfect fit. It feels heavenly against my skin. The zipper's in the back.

"Marie!" I call, and start down the stairs. It's easy to move in with bare feet, but high heels will be another matter. I dash into the kitchen, and Marie sweeps over.

"Oh, what is that gorgeous thing?"

"Prom dress." I smile, breathless. "Zipper's in the back. Ah!" My hand slips holding up the right side, cold air hitting my exposed skin, and I blush and grasp for it. Marie clucks her tongue.

"Patience, patience! I'll zip it in a moment."

The front door opens, and Mrs. Silverman trails in bearing more tailored suits of hers. She sees us and laughs.

"You look lovely, dear." From across the kitchen, her head tilts to look into the living room. "Oh, hello there. Marie, who's the visitor?"

I look into the living room for the first time. Wild, longish blond hair grows tall as the person stands and shoves his hands into his pockets.

"Uh, hi, Mrs. Silverman. I'm James."

I freeze and look over my shoulder at Marie, panic running claws down my throat. "You didn't tell me he was here!"

"I did. You weren't listening." She sighs.

"Erica, greet your guest," Mrs. Silverman leads. "It's rude to leave someone waiting."

I nod and regret stripping so quickly—my hair is wild. I walk slowly into the living room, leaving Mrs. Silverman and Marie in the kitchen.

"Hi."

"Hey." His face is carefully kept blank. I pray to whatever God watches over liars and thieves like me that he didn't see anything.

"Sorry. I was really excited." I motion to the dress. "It's the first time I've ever worn something like this. It's incredible. Like Cinderella."

"Belle," he corrects. "You look more like her."

"Except I'm not French."

"To be fair, everyone in the Disney version spoke Midwestern American English. Except the candlestick."

He smirks. I smile. He shuffles. I shuffle, but in the dress I can disguise it easier.

"So . . ." I start.

"I—" he blurts.

I wave my hand. "You first."

"No, you go ahead. Nothing I have to say is very important."

"Don't be so hard on yourself. About roughly ten percent of the things you say are interesting."

"Just ten? I'm wounded." He clutches his chest.

"I'll settle for twelve if you tell me why you decided to pay a house visit."

"Right. House visit. You can say no if you want; it's up to you. I won't get offended or anything. I'll probably crawl in a corner and question everything I've done in my life up until now, but it'll be fine."

I laugh, and he seems to get braver at the sound.

"Friday night they have these deals at this pizza place downtown. I'm a cheap-ass, so I usually go alone and get some, but I was . . . wonderingifyou'dcomewithme?" He winces and says the last part so fast, I have to concentrate to understand it.

"This Friday?"

He nods.

I smile. "I think I can do that."

"You will?" His mouth opens a little, but he shuts it. "You will. All right, I'll come pick you up—"

"I'll meet you there. Give me the address."

I'm busy typing the address into my phone when I hear the faint sound of a piano. I glance up—James is standing at the grand piano by the fireplace, hesitantly playing with one of the keys. His fingers are long and graceful.

"You can play it if you like," I offer.

He starts. "I was just looking—"

"All this talk of you being Beethoven from Taylor, but I have yet to hear a single song from you."

"Your mom's okay with me playing it?"

"Are you kidding? No one touches this dusty thing. She'd love for it to get some exercise."

James slides into the seat, and I lean on the piano's back, watching him over the music stand. He falls into the music so quickly and easily—hands dancing over the keys. I don't know what he's playing, but it's beautiful. The notes whisper at first, then begin to sing louder. Sometimes he makes them shout; sometimes it sounds like they're mewling in pain. The piano is talking. Telling a story. I'm no critic, but I can tell James does something special with the music. To him, it's not just music. I see that in his face—set and serious, but at the same time, completely free of self-deprecation and doubt.

Mrs. Silverman leans in the doorway, watching us. James finishes, the last chord reverberating mournfully. She and I clap, and he stands suddenly.

"Mrs. Silverman, I'm sorry—"

"Don't be." She flashes her best people-smile, a golden thing. "You play beautifully."

"Thank you."

"Your father is that composer fellow, right? I remember hearing the Anders name thrown around at an opera I went to this winter."

His nod this time is curt. Mrs. Silverman picks up on it too, because she changes the subject.

"Regardless, your talent stands on its own. You have a pleasant style. Very emotional and crisp."

"Thank you."

"And Erica looked like a lounge singer, standing at the end of the piano in that dress." Mrs. Silverman smiles.

I flip my hair and make a sultry face. "Marilyn Monroe?"

"Or that woman from *Chicago*." She laughs. "I'll leave you to it then. It was nice meeting you, James."

"You too." He smiles.

I wait until she's upstairs to pat his shoulder. "Seriously. You're not half bad."

His smile turns wry. "You're so stingy with the compliments."

"You're a pretty big deal. I read about you. On the Internet."

I don't say I know he failed his debut. I don't say I know he's more or less a disgraced prodigy. The clock in the hall ticks through our silence. He finally blinks and puts his hand over his face.

"That's it, I guess. My secret's out. All my cool points out the window."

"You're still cool in my eyes. Even cooler than before," I assure him. "Cool doesn't even matter. You're just you. And you're a good person. Going through that sort of thing, with the media and your parents, who I'm sure are hard-asses—"

"That's putting it lightly," he scoffs.

"It's nice to know I'm not the only one going through hell," I finish. "I shouldn't be so dramatic. It's not hell, not really. But sometimes it feels like it."

"I know" is all he says. Two words. He doesn't have to say anything more. It hangs there, a comforting string tying us together. He inhales. "I always thought the real Erica would be different."

"Oh really?" I fold my arms over my chest.

He backpedals. "Not in a bad way. You're fine. You're great. Better than great—fantastic." A beat. "Forget I said that."

"Already filed away under 'endearing mistakes.'" I smirk.

"The fake ones were always too happy. Everyone could sort of tell they were fakes, but no one wanted to believe that, you know? They wanted you to be back, the big mystery of the town solved and wrapped up in a neat package."

My phone buzzes with a text message at the worst time.

I roll my eyes. "Taylor."

"She likes you."

"Taylor doesn't like anyone," I say with a snort.

"She's mean, but she's not a bad person." He traces the

piano's keys. "She's the most purehearted person I know. Burns with only one thing—her desires. No lies, no scheming. She tells it like it is, even if you hate her for it."

"That's the perfect way to describe her." I laugh. "You're a lot better at this 'people' thing than I am."

"Don't be modest. Every girl in the school wants to be your friend, and every boy wants your number."

"That number I gave you is worth a lot on eBay, I bet."

"The reporters might want it too."

"Don't go getting any ideas about selling it." I wag my finger at him.

He laughs and puts his hand over it to stop me. "Wouldn't dream of it."

His hands are soft—silk smooth with light calluses. I guess they come from playing the guitar. Or maybe it's hereditary. Either way, it makes touching his hands a nice experience. A new experience. His fingers widen, and in one movement—one suspended, hesitant, shaking breath—his hand encases mine.

This is Erica's *and* Violet's first time holding a boy's hand. Both of our hearts beat thunderously under the same blue-silk-clad chest. He's looking down at me. He's so close. He smells clean and natural. No cloying cologne like Kerwin. Just soap and skin.

"Erica? Does your friend want—"

Marie rounds the corner, and at her voice our hands fly apart. We put space between us, and I laugh to cover the awkward break.

"No, thanks, Marie. I think he was just leaving."

"Yeah." He nods. "I appreciate the thought, though."

Marie herself looks a little flustered, and she shuffles back into the kitchen. I lead James to the door, and he grins.

"I'll see you on Monday," he says.

I watch him drive down the gravel road, the Cadillac grunting the whole way. It gives a sputter at the end of the driveway, and I laugh. I can practically see him cursing in the car, hoping I don't hear it.

I sit at the island in the kitchen. Marie has a bowl of fresh strawberries out, and she's slicing pineapple into even cubes. A bowl of chocolate chips sits by the oven.

"Chocolate fondue," she explains without looking up. I pop a berry into my mouth. Her knife flashes expertly. "Who was that boy?"

"James. From school."

"You like him?" She's straightforward.

My face heats. "I don't know."

"You like him." This time it isn't a question.

"But this isn't the time to like guys! I've got to help Dad. I've got to get used to living with Mom and going to a normal school. It's a distraction I don't need."

She eyes me. "Those are excuses."

I groan and swallow the strawberry. Marie's serious face lightens a little. She turns the stove on and puts the chocolate in a double boiler to melt it.

"You should not string a nice boy like that along."

Her words cut deeper than the knife in her hand ever could.

———

That night, after the fondue and dinner and a shower but before sleep, I dial Taylor. She picks up with a sleepy voice.

"Yo."

"You were sleeping? Sorry."

"I just passed out in front of the TV." I hear a shuffling as she rights herself. "Why're you bugging me?"

"On Friday—" I swallow. "James invited me to a pizza place."

"I'm *so* surprised." She yawns. "I couldn't see this coming—"

"I've never been on a date before," I blurt. Violet and Erica say it at the same time, with the same urgency.

There's a silence, and Taylor starts laughing. "Oh God, this is golden."

"I was wondering if you could, you know, give me tips, or something. I don't know what to wear. You've known him longer than I have. Does he like heavy makeup? Curled hair? Skanky clothes or not skanky?"

"Why don't you ask your bimbo friends to help you? They're better at this stuff."

"Because I don't want to go looking like I'm trying out for Miss America?"

She laughs. "Touché. All right, but you owe me again after this."

"I can't go clubbing again, Taylor. Kerwin saw me there, and he's just the type to tell my mom and ruin everything—"

"Kerwin? As in crumpet boy with the girly face?"

"The same."

"Huh. That's weird."

"Why?"

"He transferred here two months before you, right? Club Riddler moves from warehouse to warehouse and district to district. Sometimes it's on the other side of town. It's a local thing—locals usually know where it is and when. I didn't even know about it until Jeff texted me where it was."

"What's your point?"

"My point, Fakey"—she sucks in a breath—"is the jocks

he hangs out with aren't the raving type. They don't know about it. A handful of students know when Riddler happens, and they graduated last year or don't talk to him."

"Maybe he overheard them?"

"No. He had to do some digging. Or he had to follow you real close. Like, from-when-we-met-at-Green-Foods close."

"He wasn't on the bus with us."

"No. Look, I'll help you with the James thing, okay? But you can pay off that debt right now."

"How?"

"Stay away from Kerwin and watch your back. A guy that determined to follow someone has something up his sleeve. It's creepy."

He might know about me being fake. That'd explain a lot. But if he knows, what does he want from me? Why does he care? What is stalking me going to get for him? Is he police? Undercover, maybe? No, he looks too young. But there are some undercover cops who have baby faces. Maybe he isn't on the good guy's side. Maybe he's trying to get in on my con.

"Promise me, Fakey, that you'll be careful." Taylor's voice is low.

"Why do you care?"

"You're the only halfway decent asshole in this place, even if you are a fake. I'm not going to lose you."

We hang up. Her gruffness means she's getting more comfortable with the idea of me being a friend. She won't admit it. It'll take her a long time to trust me. But by then I'll be gone. And she'll be bleeding that trust all over the floor.

I creep downstairs to get a glass of water. The kitchen hums. There's a light on, coming from the library. I grab my glass and head for it. Mrs. Silverman reads a book in an armchair, glasses on her nose. She's wearing some green face mask made of clay. I clear my throat.

"So that's the ultimate method to look young." I pass a shelf of books. "Secretly be a Martian."

Mrs. Silverman looks up and sips her tonic. "Ha ha. I laugh hysterically about every joke centered around my age."

"You're as beautiful and young as a new rose."

"That's more like it." She grins, the clay cracking around her mouth, and buries her nose in the book again.

My fingers slide over the spines of the books, reading each one. Do I dare go to the shelf where the safe is? If I don't, it might look suspicious. If I do, she might get jumpy. I decide to risk it. My fingers pass over the books. I can't see Mrs. Silverman's reaction, if she has one.

Robinson Crusoe.

I see it briefly, gold letters flashing under my fingers. It takes all my willpower to keep moving, to not stop and do a double take. I pour over the other shelves and finally pick out a murder mystery.

"Agatha Christie." Mrs. Silverman nods appreciatively. "Good taste."

"Genetic good taste," I chime. "I can't read in stuffy chairs like you, though."

"Is your bed comfortable?"

"It's heaven compared to the twin bed I slept in at my old house."

"Good." She smiles.

"I love you," I try.

She puts the book and tonic down and gets up to hug me. Her face mask smells like cucumbers.

"I love you more than you will ever know," she murmurs.

We part, and she gets a mischievous gleam in her eye. "That boy James was awfully nice to meet today."

"I'm glad you thought so."

"Condoms and the pill, remember?" She jumps right into it airily, but threateningly.

"Mom!" I groan.

"Ah-ah, promise me."

My face is bright red even in the cool night air of the house. "I promise."

She chuckles and pushes me gently toward the stairs. "Sleep. School is tomorrow."

The calendar on my wall has to be lying. It hasn't really been a month, has it? We're almost into April. Prom is just around the corner. I still haven't gotten the code. *Robinson Crusoe.* Mr. Silverman said something about it—in *Robinson Crusoe* there was a zoo. What did that mean? The *Crusoe* book is on the shelf that hides the safe. It can't be a coincidence. I've been in this business long enough to know there are no such things as coincidences. And those numbers? Do they connect to the safe somehow?

Mr. Silverman is twitchy, focused in his own insane way. A rat in a maze. My pajamas are in the same style as Mrs. Silverman's—fluffy and pretty. My nails are like hers, perfectly painted. My hair is the same blonde.

A chameleon in the trees.

12: KILL IT

Sal,

Have lead on the code. Need to confirm. Barry Mansfield, the mob lawyer, suspects. His daughter said one of two fakes mob planted. You know about that?

Transfer student following too closely. PI still on tail. Won't talk to you for a while. You're always real with me. I'll be real with you: I like it here. Too much. Violet and Erica argue. Not good at being two people. Can only be me, and that person's getting lost. Have to get out of here. Can't rush, won't rush.

But gotta get out of here.

Vi

The week leading up to Friday is a blur of excitement and guilt. I shouldn't be happy I'm going on a date. James should go out with someone else. I'm going to be gone as soon as I work out the code to the painting. I've gotten the first couple of clues. It's only a matter of time before I crack it.

Even if I like James, he needs to not like me. He needs to smile more at another girl. Any other girl.

Because they are real and I'm not.

I won't complain. I won't complain. I am Erica and I'm popular and pretty and sweet and I have perfect grades and a loving mom and a fancy house. I shouldn't complain. I am Erica and I have everything. I am Erica and I have everything. *I am Erica. I have everything.*

I am Violet and I have nothing.

The inside hem of my plaid uniform skirt is shredded— threads torn by my nails. Sitting in class with an already perfected homework sheet leaves me little else to do except mangle my clothes. I already know the formulas Mr. Roth introduces. It's not hard to pretend to pay attention, but it is mind-numbing. I sneak glances at James's face when he isn't looking—he still sleeps through classes, but not as much anymore. I catch him looking at me one time, and I rivet my eyes to the floor. Everything in my body goes on point, every pore tingling. He's still staring. I can feel it. The hairs on my arms only flatten when he looks away.

I can't have this reaction.

Your face, Violet. Where the *hell* is your game face? Thrown out the window, along with your common sense. You went to the club and that messed things up. Going on this date is going to mess things up even more. You can't go. Make up an excuse. Your dad's gotten worse. Your mom needs you at home. You have chicken pox, something, anything!

You're stringing him along for your own selfish ends. You want a date—something Violet and Erica have never had. Just because you want to experience it, because you like him, you're wrapping barbed wire around his feelings, which will tighten when you're gone.

Because of you, there will be blood.

"Close your eyes," Taylor orders. She dabs something on my eyelids.

"I know how to do makeup, you know."

"You're the one who asked for my help, Fakey."

I sigh. When she's done, I glance at my long mirror—jeans, a comfortable blue sweater, and matching eye shadow.

"Not too shabby." I turn and eye my back. "I thought I was going to end up looking like a Hot Topic mannequin."

"Whatever." She chuckles and puts the makeup back in my drawer. A soft knock resounds.

"Come in," I say. Marie pops her head through the crack in the door.

"Is your guest allergic to strawberries at all?"

I look at Taylor. She shakes her head. Marie smiles timidly. I've never seen Marie so hesitant, but tall, dark, scowling Taylor has that sort of effect on people.

"Good. Well, come down when you're done. I've been baking."

When she leaves, Taylor snorts. "I hate strawberries."

"Why didn't you tell her?"

"I'm an asshole, not an idiot. Being rude at someone else's house is for morons."

"You have a heart after all." I smirk.

"Shut your mouth and put your shoes on."

I slip into the ballet flats. "For someone who wears all black, you have good fashion sense."

"I've just seen lots of bimbos out on dates."

Date. The word rings in my head, makes itself real and known. Taylor thumps me on the back.

"Your face is all white. Relax. You'll be fine."

We walk down to the kitchen, where Mrs. Silverman and Marie are conversing over a plate of strawberry tarts. Mrs. Silverman smiles at us.

"Don't you look all dressed up?"

"Taylor helped," I murmur.

"Thank you, Taylor. She looks wonderful."

Taylor's glance skitters around, everywhere but on Mrs. Silverman's face. "No prob."

When I asked Mrs. Silverman if Taylor could come over, she looked hesitant. *Taylor, the girl in all black? Taylor, the girl with just a father?* She doesn't seem to know anything about me and Taylor going to the club. Did Mr. White keep the pictures to himself? Or is he planning to show them to Mrs. Silverman later? Whatever the case, she treats Taylor as nicely as she can, but there are lines of wariness beneath her eyes. Taylor seems just as wary of her, but she tries to be nice. And Taylor trying at all means heaps.

Marie breaks the tension between Mrs. Silverman and Taylor by sliding the plate of tarts into their view. "Eat up before they get cold."

Taylor grabs one and nibbles. Mrs. Silverman doesn't touch them.

"So you're taking the bus there? Is James going to meet you?"

"At the pizza place, yeah." I nod and bite—the pastry is

warm and sweet. Taylor's face is frozen. I'm worried she'll say they're gross, when she reaches for another.

"Holy shi—" Taylor glances up and corrects her swear. "I mean, wow. These are amazing. I don't even like strawberries, but these are great."

Marie smiles. "Thank you."

"Are you going with her, Taylor?" Mrs. Silverman asks coolly.

"No, going home. Gonna let the lovebirds work it out on their own," Taylor says back, the same coolness in her voice. Mrs. Silverman looks to me.

"I want you home before eight."

"Right."

"If you start to feel uncomfortable, call me and I'll pick you up."

"He's not that kind of guy," Taylor murmurs.

Mrs. Silverman stiffens. "I know. I met him. But it's better to be safe than sorry. Promise me you'll call, Erica."

"I will." I shoot Taylor a look.

When we're on the bus, riding into downtown and laughing at the businessman snoring across from us, Taylor's chuckle fades. She leans her head on the back of the seat and looks at the tin roof.

"She's going to smother you."

I look at her. In the fluorescent bus lights, her jet black hair shines with jagged white lightning.

"She's going to suffocate you. You can't hide your true self forever just to please her."

"People do it all the time," I grumble.

"You really like her." She laughs softly. "She's the best mom you've ever had. Maybe the only mom you've ever had."

I stare out the window. Taylor rubs her eyes with her fists.

"They leave. They all leave eventually. They pretend to like you, love you. They tuck you in and braid your hair and kiss your father, but they all leave, and the new one is different from the last. Sometimes better. Sometimes worse."

Her words echo from the dark precipice of experience.

"Mom will never leave me," I assert.

"No," Taylor agrees. "You'll leave her."

A sword, punching a slit clean through my torso and out my spine. Just pull the blade up a little more, and my insides will spill out. Taylor stands to let me by as the bus halts at my stop. She keeps reminding me of who I really am. Of what I'm really here to do.

This date is just a distraction. A fake. I shouldn't get so wound up about it. It's just a con—like everything I've done so far.

He likes a fake girl.

———

I walk into the pizza place, a warm little shop, quiet in the golden afternoon glow. An old woman behind the register is doing a crossword. James sits at one of the tables, texting. When I come in, he looks up, his smile nervous.

"Hey."

"Hi." I slide into the seat opposite him. "Cute little place. Did you find it all by yourself?"

My words are rushed and saccharine, the tone too sweet. Too Erica. James shrugs.

Michelle Painchaud

"I came here one day after band practice. The rest is history."

"How boring was Roth's class today?" I laugh. "I couldn't wait for him to shut up. Taylor looked even more bored than you, and that's saying something. I couldn't decide if I should try to sleep like you or doodle."

"Erica—"

"I mean, who even listens to him? Arnold, but he's in the front and a nerd. I guess it's good there are people like that in the world, otherwise you wouldn't be able to sleep behind him and I'd actually have to take notes—"

"Erica!" He puts his hand on mine. "Slow down."

"There's no time to go slowly." I smile and pull my hand away. "It has to be today. Let's order. I'm starving. Should we get half and half or can we agree on toppings for the whole thing? I don't like peppers or anchovies, but that's about it."

His blues eyes go soft. "You don't have to be so nervous."

"Nervous? Me?" I laugh. "No way. I've never been nervous in my life. I'm stone-cold."

He sighs. That little motion tugs my heart around, but I quash the feeling. That's good. More. I need more of that. He won't like me after this date is done. Frustrate him. We manage to agree on olives and pepperoni. He gets up to order, the old woman muttering something in Italian and toddling to the kitchen. I talk about nothing and everything until my throat is sore. Interrupt him when he tries to say something. The pizza arrives and we eat in dead silence. While he finishes, I look out the window to the dimming streets and brightening lampposts. Vegas comes alive at night, breaks out of its daily cocoon. The splendor of its lights is hidden by the sun, and when darkness falls, Vegas can show its true beauty. Grime. Indifference. Dazzle.

Even in the middle of my first date, Violet is somewhere else in my head—turning over the idea of a zoo, *Robinson Crusoe*, and numbers on walls. She holds those three clues up to Erica, like she's trying to say they're more important than James. I force both of them to focus—what we need now is to focus on this moment. One goal. One face. Just get through this stupid date, and we can get back to what we really came for. The painting.

"You don't have to be like this," James murmurs.

I know exactly what he means, but I tilt my head and smile at him instead. "Be like what?"

"You can be yourself with me. You know that."

The smile on my face falters. I steel it. "I don't know what that is anymore."

He flinches. I rip a napkin to shreds.

"I know you're going through a tough time—"

"Not really," I singsong.

"But I'm here for you. I'm your friend. If you need to talk about it, or hit something, I'll be here with open ears and a punch-ready cheek."

I want to laugh. I want to laugh so badly. I want to take his offer, but I can't. It would blow my cover. He's looking at me with those soft blue eyes, his unguarded face. He cares about me. If I opened my mouth, I would spill everything.

I stand and grab my purse. "I— I have to go. Thanks for the food."

"Not yet. I've got one last thing planned." He grabs my hand. It pulls me back. "Please."

I'm the one who's been shutting him down the whole time. Carry it through, Violet. Be the bitch. Shut him down once and for all. Push the kill switch. Make this easy on yourself, painless for him.

My inhale shudders as I nod. He smiles and pays the old woman before tossing our trash and leading me outside by the hand.

"Your fingers are cold." He frowns as we wait at the crosswalk for the light to change. He puts my hands in his and rubs them together, working friction into them. All my thoughts on the painting and the code and being mean to get him to dump me fly out the window. "There. Better."

"Th-Thanks," I stutter, the sudden contact jarring. I'm used to faring for myself—mittens or pockets.

"C'mon. It's just a little farther."

He leads me through the dusk, past the couture shops and to the park. It takes me three blocks to realize we're acting like a couple—hand in hand. People walk the paths and sit on benches amidst sparse trees. The fountain burbles. James walks over to a man sitting on the grass, a keyboard on his lap. He's older than us by a few years—college student. His beanie flops as he turns to look at us—dark eyes and dark hair.

"Sup, James? Is this her?"

"Yeah." James grins. "Erica, this is Marley. He's the other member of our band I told you about."

"Hi." I put on my best smile. Marley shakes my hand. He doesn't say anything about my being kidnapped, which I'm grateful for.

"So this is where you guys practice?" I ask.

Marley laughs. "Nah. We practice over the Internet, mostly. It's a powerful thing."

"So I've heard." I smirk.

"We get together once a month and collaborate in the park.

And beg for change." James bends, pulling the guitar case closer and opening it. He cradles the instrument and pushes the empty case toward the sidewalk, just in front of them.

"I'm your first fan," I declare. Marley chuckles and runs his hands up the keyboard.

"You can dance. Probably get us a bigger audience."

"No shedding clothes." James tunes the guitar carefully. "We're a legitimate business here."

I snicker and pull my sweater around me tighter. A chill is setting in, but it gives the park atmosphere. James and Marley count in and start playing, the tune stutter-y but melodic. James's voice is warm, but not confident or loud. It's a tempting, hoarse speaking voice. Mellow and sweet, but with hidden energy, like a subtle mix of icing and espresso.

"And I never wanna see the sun," he sings, "if it means our time is done."

A few people stop to watch. A family with a little boy. A couple. A lone man taking a rest from his jogging, earbuds hanging around his shoulders to hear James's song. A rushing businessman taking a shortcut through the park hears a single bar, walks past, and comes back to throw a dollar in the case.

I know the chorus after listening to it a few times, and when it comes next, I join in hesitantly, my voice mixing with James's.

"Something's gonna change. I heard it said by the man who sings. You and I will change, and in the end it's just dew in rain."

The world gets darker, the family leaves. People start going home. Marley takes out a trumpet and plays it, the sable wailing a bridge. When it ends, James strums the guitar one last time. Our eyes meet.

Michelle Painchaud

"And I never wanna see the sun if it means our time is done."

Marley thumps him on the back and says it's the best rendition ever. We say good-bye to Marley, and James drives me home in almost complete silence, my every mistake replaying through my head.

This is a mistake.

"Thanks." He smiles, stopping at my driveway. "For giving me a chance today."

"I'm sorry . . ." I start. "I'm sorry I ruined everything. You have to understand—No, you can't understand, I just—"

"I know you need more time. Everybody needs time," he interrupts softly. "But not everybody gets it."

I sense I should kiss him, but I don't. Because I'm a coward. Because I'm a fake. I want to kiss him—to thank him for being everything I'm not: polite and enduring and honest with me when I'm not with him.

Honesty.

I silently watch him go, his taillights two bloodspots in the night.

On Monday it's like nothing happened.

Taylor asks me how it went. I shrug, and she pulls a frown but doesn't press me. Merril and Cass are none the wiser—I never told them, for fear they'd berate me. James smiles politely when I talk to him, but it feels too forced. We both know we can get along spectacularly, but it's a matter of me wanting to. James made his feelings clear. It's just a matter of *me* allowing *us* to happen. Telling him how I feel too. Evening out the scales that were imbalanced from the start.

To make matters worse, Mr. White's watching me. He sits in his car parked opposite the school. Wears a hat today, like it'll make him harder to recognize. He's just begging for me to talk to him.

I tap on the driver's window. He rolls it down and eyes me over his sunglasses.

"Mr. White"—I clear my throat—"what brings you to this neck of the woods?"

He opens the glove box and pulls out a magazine with a familiar title. The cover is of two women standing on either side of an apple tree and smiling.

"*Brackish.*" Mr. White flips through a few pages. "A magazine for the gay, lesbian, bisexual, and transgender community."

The one Sal's column is in. The one I've been buying to read his words.

"Now." He coughs. "Why would a girl like you buy something like this regularly? Unless you're a lesbian. Bisexual. You're not transgender—the medical records say that much."

"There's nothing wrong with a little curiosity," I fire back. First the club pictures, now this? The guy is good, I'll give him that much.

"Of course not," he agrees. "But if you were really curious about lesbianism or bisexuality, you'd probably buy something more brazen—something with pictures in it, if you get my drift. This is strictly esoteric: articles by professors and civilian contributors. Art pieces with gay themes, theater productions. Reviews about gay movies."

Good call on my bluff, Baldy.

He'll never find the column. There are hundreds of articles, and no reason for him to suspect any of them are coded messages. The chance he knows I write Sal is slim—lots of

Michelle Painchaud

people submit, but only one is chosen, and never my sub-mission. Sal reads and decodes my message independently. I send the submission via computer at the library during study hall. I always log out and clear the computer's browser history and cache. I'm thorough and nothing less than perfect. I am Violet. There's no way he knows.

Which means he's guessing—going on a hunch. Poking the body to see if it'll twitch. And my reactions to what he says now will either prove my guilt or my innocence. High school relationships are dizzying, convoluted, bloodthirsty. Lying to save my skin is so much easier. I've done this countless times before. Adrenaline keeps my face perfectly calm and makes my tongue limber. It's time to shine.

"I haven't told Mom you like her," I start. "Not yet, any-way. Let's make a deal. You don't tell people I'm gay, and I don't tell her you've been stalking me out of some misguided sense of protection."

"I'm not a high schooler. You can't threaten me or use me by manipulating my love. And you're not gay."

"Says you."

"I've been watching you for more than a month now. I've seen you look at that boy. James Anders."

"What do you want from me?" My voice tips up, shrill. Violet cringes. I broke my composure at the simple mention of his name. I'm losing my touch.

"You can't hide forever. It might be a nice change now—the money, the big house, the friends. But it won't last forever."

I know that. Goddamn it, I know that! You don't have to remind me, you bald fart. He's desperate. He's got nothing on me, and it's driving him insane. His gut tells him I'm not her, and he's right, but he can't prove a lick of it. I win this delicate game. For now. I smile like a nice girl. To the experienced con artist, that smile would give it all away—that he was right. Maybe he can see that. It doesn't matter. I'm winning.

———

I make small talk with Mrs. Silverman when she picks me up, but my mind is on that painting. The code. The zoo. *Robinson Crusoe.* I'm putting it together in my head as I trace patterns on the windows of the BMW. Mr. Silverman gave me a hint, a hint about the zoo. Sal said the code pertained to a fond memory only Mrs. Silverman and Erica shared. The memory—I'm willing to bet it took place at the zoo.

I have to get inside Mr. Silverman's room and write those equations down.

I watch Mrs. Silverman's face as she talks over dinner— pork sirloin with onion relish that melts in my mouth. She makes jokes, touches my hair. It felt so natural before, but now there's something between us, a tiny flame of resentment. Violet. Violet is there, eclipsed before by my professionalism. Violet is getting tired of pretending. No con has ever been this long. Violet can bow her head and take a few hits, but not so many. Not so many, so fast. Not so many hits directly to her heart.

She hates Erica. Everything Erica has, she covets. Violet wants to stop pretending and still have the things Erica does. But that's impossible.

Not impossible—she can have it if she gets *La Surprise.* With enough money, she can have it all. That's why she's stealing it in the first place, why she agreed to the con. She agreed because Sal is her father, and the gypsy life of crime is her milk, her blood, her song. Before this con, she didn't know what high school was or what friends were or how it felt for a boy to hold her hand. Normal was a fantastic desert illusion—spices and water and figs and honey she tasted on the tip of her tongue.

And, because Erica is sweet and kind and perfect, she does not hate Violet in return. She envies her. Violet is alive in ways she will never be, in ways that'll cease after the curtain on this con lifts and the crowd applauds themselves deaf— after Violet takes her bow and exits stage right to a bouquet of roses and a good chunk of sixty million dollars and a life emptied of the people Erica never really got to love.

13: TURN IT

I let Mr. Silverman win today. But he knows it. Instead of cheering in his fidgety timid way, he frowns. I smile and clear the board.

"You did great, Dad."

"My name is Brandon," he corrects softly. I arrange the pieces for another game.

"I really want to call you Dad. Is that okay?"

He doesn't say anything. Heavy silence makes our hands work harder to move pieces. Every black checker feels like lifting a ship anchor.

"I saw those numbers on your wall," I try. "They're very pretty, all jumbled together like that. What do they mean?"

He fiddles with his shirt cuff. "Nothing."

"They looked really important."

"Nobody should know." Mr. Silverman shakes his head. "Nobody will ever know; it's not good to know."

"Okay." I nod. "I don't have to know. I just thought they looked pretty, is all."

I let him capture a few of my pieces. His face grows angry, dark.

"Play seriously," he demands. I look around for any nurses. None. Mrs. Silverman's listlessly looking out the window.

I lean in and lower my voice. "I'll play seriously with you if you'll be serious with me, Dad. What are those numbers on your wall?"

Mr. Silverman hisses something under his breath.

"I can't hear you."

"Don't trust myself," he finally murmurs.

Doesn't trust himself with what? Numbers, obviously. Did he make those equations to hide something—to keep himself from giving them away? When the nurse walks him back to his room, I stop at the front desk.

"Hi, I'm Erica, Brandon Silverman's daughter."

"Oh yes." The receptionist smiles. "I've seen you in the— That's insensitive of me. I'm sorry. Did you need something?"

"I'm just curious: how long has Dad been writing those numbers on his wall?"

"I'd say since about"—she taps her chin with her pen—"a year after he came here? We're under orders to let him scribble randomly—the doctors say it's therapeutic for him."

I bite my tongue to keep from saying his scribbles aren't random. At least, not all of them are. There are eight or nine equations in that jumble that are suspiciously well focused.

"Is it okay if I go in his room and take a few pictures?" I put on my prettiest smile. "I've got a school report, and I decided to focus on mental illnesses. My shrink said it'd be good if I used Dad as the focus."

Her face collapses in a sympathetic grin. "I'm sorry. Family can only enter a patient's room with permission from either the patient himself or the patient's supervising nurse."

"And who would that be?"

She points to the nurse leading Dad away. "Nurse Rodriguez."

I thank her and start after them. Nurse Rodriguez rounds the corner without Dad by the time I catch up to her.

"Hi." I smile. "I'm Erica, Mr. Silverman's daughter—"

"I know," the nurse deadpans. "What did you need?"

I already know the answer before I ask—this lady is hardcore. Late forties, no-nonsense tight bun, and the nurse who I've noticed spends the most time checking lists, papers, and all other legalities. Plays by the rules. I've caught snippets of other nurses talking about her snitching on them for taking shortcuts on duty. It's better not to ask, period. I know her type—suspicious to the core. If I ask, she'll be watching me, cued to my interest in those numbers. Her personality could be lethal to my con.

"I just wanted to thank you." I smile wider. "For taking such good care of Dad for so many years."

Her eyes remain dull, compliment taken in stride. "Thank you. If you'll excuse me, I have other patients I need to check on."

Sal's voice sounds like he's right next to me: *If flattery doesn't move them, work around them.*

———

Sal watches his daughter carefully from the playground bench. She's young and bone-thin, even after being with him for four years, but she's perfect.

Sal knows she's something special. Not many kids have the guts to pick his pockets within ten minutes of meeting him. Even fewer kids admit to it once confronted. But she did. Sal's been in the business of scoping people out for decades, and he knows a talented kid when he sees one. He

Michelle Painchaud

convinced a friend—another con artist—to pose as his wife and help him adopt Violet right away.

Maybe it's the face—the placid face free of most emotions. She doesn't smile as much as she should. A blank slate. A catatonic slate. Her emotional reactions are left wanting, but that's nothing food and some encouraging words can't fix. She's not broken, just banged up a bit.

He watches her on the playground. Her eyes follow the other children as they course around her. She stands perfectly still, looking for an opening in the boisterous crowd, a moment in which she can squeeze in on the game unnoticed. But she misses it over and over, misses the moment, and they pass in a shrieking mass of laughter. She wipes her hands on her overalls. She's not good at the interacting thing.

Sal couldn't care less. She listens well. Learns well. That's all he needs.

Finally Violet gives up on integrating into the children's game. She wanders deep into the park to a rusted maintenance shack. She fiddles with the lock. Slides her glittery hairpins out of her bangs and edges them around in the hole. Scrunches her face. It's the most emotion he's seen out of her yet. The moms—on the lookout for every child—correct her; no, not the rusty lock, the monkey bars! The seesaw! She nods and plays on them but ends up standing near the padlock again. When the moms aren't looking, she picks it a little more. After a half hour, Sal glances up from his book and checks her progress. The lock gapes open on the door. Violet sits, hugging her knees and watching it sway. He picks the girl up and twirls her.

"You're real talented, sweets." He laughs.

Violet doesn't get giddy like most children do with praise.

She lays her head in the crook of his neck and gives a little sigh instead—the sigh of a much older person. A heavy, guilty, dreaded thing. Sal's heart—hardened by the neon nonchalance of Vegas and the deaths of everyone he's ever loved—gives a flutter. A sad, touched spasm that he clamps off.

It is not always crime. It is not always training. He knows to balance the two with fun. She is his protégé, but she's still a child. To craft the perfect Erica, the perfect con artist, there must be balance.

He takes her to the Strip. A woman he used to know is performing in the Red Lounge as a magician's assistant. He buys Violet a Shirley Temple as they wait for the curtain to rise. Her eyes widen at the red fizzy drink, and the first sip has her smiling.

"You like it?"

She nods fervently. Nods until it seems like her head will fall off.

"Watch your neck." Sal laughs and looks at the menu. "All right, onion rings or chicken fingers? Your choice."

She makes a choice.

14: FEAR IT

I go grocery shopping with Marie. The store is the upscale, natural foods kind. Violet emerges; I'm not composed Erica as I steer the cart around, standing on the rung and using it like a scooter. Total casualties: one cartoon cutout display for oranges, the entire canned bean shelf, and a five-year-old's dropped Transformer action figure. My wheels chopped its head cleanly off.

I wince at the price tags—people can really afford to eat like this? The closest Sal and I got to organic was celery sticks, or frozen broccoli. But here everything is fresh, dark, leafy, vivid. I peek around the aisles. I get the feeling I'll see someone from school at any second. I slip in different snacks, ones neither Erica nor Violet have tried. When I drop a box of Popsicles in, Marie snaps.

"Don't slip any more in here. One dessert is enough!"

"Aw, Marie—"

"Ah." She zips her mouth. "One snack, *chiquita*."

I sigh and choose the cookies. In the checkout line, Marie glances at me over the checkbook.

"I know your mother doesn't want me bringing them up, but did your old parents feed you well? You look awfully skinny, even now."

I won't say I dieted for two years in preparation for being Erica. Lost fifteen pounds, every one of them painful. Sal fed me well enough when I was young—whatever was easy to chew or carry while running, in the car, on the train, the subway.

"We ate like normal people. Not much of this fancy organic free-range stuff."

Marie seems satisfied with that answer. The cashiers and baggers look harried. I spot a bagger at another checkout down the line, her dark hair in a ponytail. With the store apron on, she looks different. Taylor. She doesn't see me. She works here, too? I want to say hi, but she looks busy. I finger a few next-to-the-gum tabloids instead. My fingers hover over Brad Pitt's face before dropping down to a local magazine. My new face in all its blonde glory blares on the front page. My skin's too pale. I can see the stress zits starting on my hairline. They slapped on a picture of me and didn't even bother to airbrush it? In a Vegas magazine? For shame.

And then I realize it's the one of me in front of Club Riddler.

"Ohhh no," I groan-chant. "Oh no, no, no, *no*."

"What's wrong?" Marie asks. I briefly wonder if vomiting on the conveyor belt is an option (wouldn't it squish under the seam as it moves?) and then decide to spare the cashier from the cleanup. I quickly grab one magazine and add it to the pile of groceries. I take the other magazines and use them to cover the ones with my face. Thanks, Brad. You too, Angelina.

"This is you!" Marie exclaims, eyeing the magazine. "Why are you on the front page?"

Split second: pretend it's a hoax or admit to being there? Honesty gets points.

"Marie, you can't tell Mom. Please."

She quirks a brow. "Erica, you've been out clubbing? Why? Those places are dangerous—drugs, gangsters."

"I didn't do drugs, or drink. It was one night. Please, Marie. I just needed to breathe. I felt so trapped in that house."

"I will let you tell your mother on your own," she says coolly, hinting at a threat: she'll tell her if I don't. I roll the cart to the car. The air is warm again, little patches of blue peeking out from behind solid gray clouds. With the groceries in the trunk, I lean on the dashboard and read the magazine article.

MINOR VEGAS CELEBRITY Erica Silverman, seventeen, prodigal daughter of the Silverman fortune, returned to her family after living with a false one for thirteen years. A little pretty, a little privileged, and a lot of partying, Erica seems to be turning to the club scene to blow off traumatized steam.

At the age of four, Silverman was kidnapped by George and Kathleen Hastings of Dallas, Texas, but no ransom demand was put through. Psychologists think the couple was just cuckoo for a kid, and it raises the question: after a childhood spent with them, how will she cope with a life in the upper echelons? On top of it all, there have been two previous "Ericas," who've kept her name and case in the limelight. Police haven't commented on whether they believe this Erica to be the real one, but her mother certainly thinks so. Representatives of Mrs. Silverman say she and her daughter are rehabilitating together, trying to make "tragedy into normal everyday life."

"Are you kidding me?" I throw the magazine under my feet.

Marie sighs. "The sooner you tell your mother, the better. Let us hope she has not seen it first."

I puff. "The damage is already done."

"She'll forgive you. If you tell the truth, I'm sure she will forgive you."

Marie's answers are confident, assured. Violet couldn't give a rat's ass either way—she's so close to *La Surprise* that a little hiccup in the mother-daughter trust can be smoothed over. If Mr. White had shown them earlier, it would've been worse, but the foundation is strong. Erica flounders, fumbles, laments the stain on her social life. She doesn't want to be seen as a party girl, a bad girl. She wants to right all the wrongs. Violet laughs at her, at how much she cares. You're dead. Why should you care?

Erica snaps. She reaches down for the magazine and in a frenzy starts ripping pages, cracking the car window and throwing them out. Marie does a double take.

"Erica! What are you—"

"Stupid!" Erica's swears are comical, kid-like. "It's all so stupid!"

She rips up the page with her face on it into a dozen tiny pieces and throws them out the window like confetti. Marie gently works the magazine from her hand, a laugh in her words.

"Do you feel better?"

"Much."

I look at my shaking hands. That'd been Erica all on her own. Leaping out of my eyes like an untamable dog, my control a useless leash of dental floss. If it isn't Erica coming out, it's Violet. Where was my happy medium? My middle ground that was me, the ground I could stand on and not feel like an insane freak living a double life? The ground is eroding under my feet. It's falling away like sand, like earthquake-cracked cement.

Just a little more.

I just need to hold on a little more.

———

The house is dim and quiet.

It's not unusual, but that's only when no one is home. And Mrs. Silverman is home.

Marie shoots me a look, and while she's unloading groceries, I check upstairs.

"Mom?"

Her door is ajar, a low lamplight flooding through. I knock, two timid raps.

"Come in."

Her voice is sub-zero. The cold makes me suck in a breath. Something's wrong. I open the door. Mrs. Silverman's sitting at her vanity, dabbing on foundation. A few outfits are spread out on her bed for later tonight—a charity ball. On her bedside table is a magazine. *The* magazine. She sees me staring at it.

"Just ran its first publication today. A friend sent it to me in the mail."

"Mr. White," I say breathlessly.

"Ever-thoughtful man." Her words splinter with too-formal ice.

"Mom, let me explain—"

"There will be no explaining. At least not until he gets

here. You will wait in the living room with me for him to arrive. Situate yourself there. I will be down shortly."

What most would see as anger, I see as pain. She's feeling betrayed but trying hard to keep her composure. She wants to cry. Her lips quiver as I back out and shut the door. Marie doesn't look at me. I settle on the couch and press my hands between my knees.

Why would she invite Mr. White over? To confirm he saw me there? To clear the air once and for all? All of my training narrows down to this one moment. This confrontation. I have to get through it. I'm too close to the painting to be booted out like this.

All of my suffering, *all of everyone's suffering*, has to be for something.

I go through the modes in my head—martyr, victim, accuser. I can be all of them, but which one will work? A con artist's work is not preplanned—it's reactive, not proactive. I need to relax. Breathe. Deep breaths, just like Mrs. Silverman and I practiced. Just like we practiced together, calming down together, laughing together—

Erica's eyes water.

The tears drip on Violet's knees.

Focus. Focus harder on the edge of the coffee table. *Wipe your eyes on your sleeve and learn some composure, sweets.*

Mrs. Silverman comes in, moves stiffly. She sits beside me, too far away. The knock on the door shortly after mashes my heart into my throat. Marie answers it and ushers in Mr. White to the sitting room. He takes off his hat and settles across from us in an armchair.

"Mrs. Silverman. Thanks for having me."

"Thank you for coming on such short notice." She smiles.

"Would you like tea? Or perhaps coffee? With your long hours of work, caffeine must be your friend."

He chuckles. *Chuckles*. He doesn't even care that at the moment he's stress-aging me by a decade. He refuses any drinks, gaze flickering between us with almost-regret. Now he's having second thoughts? Or maybe he knows he's ruining me. Us.

"I'll get straight to business, Mr. White, to save us all valuable time." Mrs. Silverman folds her hands on her lap. "I wanted to ask you a few questions."

"Fire away." He nods.

"Why have you been following my daughter without my permission?"

Mr. White's eyes darken. Hesitates. "With all due respect, ma'am—"

"By following my daughter without my express order, you are showing a profound lack of respect for my family and me, Mr. White."

"I understand—"

"Do you? Do you really understand thirteen years of unending visceral nightmares? Of doubts? Of being questioned by the police who think you or your husband killed your own daughter?"

Mr. White keeps his mouth mercifully shut. Mrs. Silverman's face tinges red.

"I will not have you harassing my daughter like the police have harassed me. We have been through enough—"

"With all due respect, ma'am"—White raises his voice—"your daughter was seen at a club with the daughter of a notorious criminal defender with mob ties—"

"And that proves what, Mr. White?" Mrs. Silverman

interjects, her voice rising too. "That she's a teenager who sometimes makes poor choices? We all have. We all still do. You most of all."

"I can prove that she's been using a magazine to clandestinely communicate with—"

"You are speaking from your heart, Mr. White. Not your head." Her voice is a near-scream. It echoes in the huge house—the call of a dying hawk. I swallow hard and glance at Mr. White, his frown tightrope-tense. She knows about his attraction. I hadn't told her. Maybe she knew from the beginning.

"Erica," she says finally, "is there anything you'd like to say?"

"I'm sorry."

"I think we all deserve more than two words," she insists.

"I went to the club. It was fun. I didn't drink or do anything crazy. I promise. But Taylor, she got a little drunk, and I had to help her home. She lives on the edge, she has a weird dad, but she's not a bad person. She's just trying to live in her own way. Work things out in her own way."

"Why did you lie to me?" Mrs. Silverman asks softly.

"I felt so caged in. I love you, I love this house and everything you've given me, but after a while it just felt like . . . *stuff*. It felt like I was carrying it all around, like it was sitting on my chest. I had to get out. Try something different. Live. Try to be a normal"—I choke on the word, and it's not faked—"a normal teenager."

There's a beat before Mrs. Silverman stands. "You will not lie to me again. If you need that escape, that release, just tell me. Remember? We promised to be open with each other?"

"Sometimes"—I stand—"sometimes I just want to close down."

"And you can. If I'm too pushy, if I pressure you again, speak up. I'll give you space. You just have to communicate your needs with me."

Her understanding words are soothing harp chords on my tense brain. Unwind me note by note. Forgiveness. I expect a closet, no dinner. Some punishment. Mr. White stands as Mrs. Silverman draws me into her for a hug, and he makes for the door.

"Mr. White," she calls over my head. He turns. "Thank you. For your good intentions."

Mr. White and I lock eyes over Mrs. Silverman's shoulder for a split second. An acknowledgment. He nearly bested me. I nearly bested him.

A draw.

A courteous nod, and he's gone through the door, a mountain of a man who'd come the closest to busting the greatest teenage con artist this side of the Mississippi.

━━━

I still get grounded. My cell's taken away for a week, and I can't go anywhere with Cass or Merril. Taylor coming over is out of the question. Any plans I had of going to James's once-a-week band meetings to say sorry are kaput.

It takes one phone call to the lawyers to get the magazine's circulation to stop. I can only pray no one at school saw it or bought a copy. But my prayers haven't been known to do much. If the school sees it, they'll associate me with Taylor. While Violet doesn't care, it's not good for my Erica good-girl image.

Of course the school has seen it. The halls buzz with glances and whispers about Taylor and me. Cass shrugs and waves it off. Merril is angrier.

"How could you hang out with her like that? When Kerwin said you went, I didn't think you actually did it. Why Taylor? She's Commander Bitch."

"She's not so bad, Mer." I sigh.

"Really? Because this morning she drew a penis on my locker with red Sharpie and tried to trip Kerwin down the stairs. Do you know how dangerous stairs are? You can break your neck if you fall down too many. She could've killed him."

"She's a Goth, not a murderer." Cass laughs. "You over-react, Merril, seriously. Chill for once. I thought getting a boyfriend would *mellow* you out."

The rumors have even reached the faculty. Mr. Roth stops me as I pass his desk after class.

"Erica. A moment, please."

"Sure. What's up?"

"There's no easy way to say this, so I'll get right to it." He rubs his eyebrows. "I don't think you've been entirely honest with the office about your level of mathematical education. I feel as though you're holding yourself back. Many times, even on problems you get wrong, you take highly advanced shortcuts."

"Mr. Roth—"

"Please, Erica. This is not an argument. It pains me to see a brilliant student hold back her true potential just to fit in with her peers. I've seen the magazine like everyone else, and I won't grill you on it, but Taylor's is not the best example to follow."

"Yeah. Sorry. I guess I don't realize when I'm doing it."

"If you keep dumbing yourself down, you won't be able to reach for the bigger scholarships. Your talent will go unnoticed."

He cares. He cares about me. My "talent." He said I have a talent. A talent for something other than conning? The thought sends a spark through my heart and warms my blood. I'm good at something. Something other than being a liar.

"Thanks, Mr. Roth. I'll be sure to keep that in mind."

After school, on the way to the hospital, Mrs. Silverman drives calmly, merging into the next lane. The high of Mr. Roth's compliment is long gone. I'm back to reality now—conning. My life, my air, my blood. I need to take the next step in the con. I need more information on the code, and the zoo it pertains to.

"We went to the zoo," I say.

"When you were younger, yes. The zoo was your favorite place."

"Pandas," I murmur. "I remember them."

She breaks into a smile. "You were very scared of them."

"Scared? Of a two-tone teddy bear?" I quirk an eyebrow.

"Don't ask me why. Some children hate spiders; some don't like deep water. You didn't like pandas."

"They do smell bad."

She laughs. "We can go again if you'd like. Saturday's the day your grounding lets up. We'll go in the afternoon and avoid the lunch crowd."

I've brought a Polaroid camera I found in Erica's room. It's still loaded with a cartridge. Mr. Silverman must've gotten it for Erica—I found it tucked away in the closet with a *From Santa* still taped on the box. She was too small to use it, no doubt, but that didn't stop him from buying a bright pink skin with unicorns on it.

Mrs. Silverman shoots me a look.

"I thought it would jog his memory." I shrug. "It's worth a try, right?"

She sighs. "Anything is worth a try."

A stroke of luck—Nurse Rodriguez is nowhere to be seen. This is my opening. I have to act now. I steer Mrs. Silverman to ask the most harried-looking nurse around for access to Dad. Mrs. Silverman waits, like usual, by the vending machines. Instead of waiting for the nurse to bring Dad to me in the lobby, I meet them at his door.

"I can bring him to the table"—I glance at the woman's name tag—"Audrey."

"Would you do that?" Nurse Audrey sighs. "I've got a new admittance I need to see to."

I assure her it'll be fine. I wait until her heels disappear around the corner before I turn to Dad, lacing my arm through his.

"Can you show me your room?"

"No." He shakes his head. "Nobody sees it but me."

"But look!" I hold up the pink camera. "Do you remember this? You got me this. I never got to take pictures with it. I want to show my friends where my dad lives."

"I live in a bad place," he mutters.

My eyes glance around for Nurse Rodriguez. She could pop up at any moment.

"C'mon, Dad, please? You worked so hard on those beautiful walls. It would be a shame to never have a picture of them. What if the nurses paint over them? Erase them? You don't want them to disappear forever, do you?"

He nervously shifts from foot to foot. He finally makes a decision, and pushes the door open. Clears his throat.

"Only a few pictures."

"Thank you!" I dart in and snap away. Start with the top right corner, work my way down and up as I move in a circle. I air each picture out and line my coat pockets with them. Dad's head bobs in a few frames as he paces the room.

"Smile!" I call to him. He turns and makes a pained grin. Guilt. His listless smile sends dead bolt arrows of guilt to lodge in my stomach. I ignore them, smile back, and keep snapping.

The code.

That's all I need.

That's all I'm here for.

— — —

None of it makes any sense.

I'd managed to write the equations from the pictures into a notebook. Eight equations show up more than the others. I start dissecting them. I'm vivisecting the math beast Dad created. I solve them in a basic, sane manner, and come up with impossible decimals. I punch them into search engines, and piece together sections. They read like madman scrawl, but the amazing part is, they somehow *work*. Nothing is out of place. Everything is there for a reason, and the equations should come to a solid answer. Not a decimal like I'm getting. Not a four-letter hexadecimal after binary conversion. I need one number or one letter for each equation. I'm doing something wrong, but I don't know what.

Maybe I'm wrong. Maybe these eight repeating equations in his room mean nothing at all.

Sal pushed me especially hard in math. Now I think I know why. Mr. Silverman was an engineer. A professional mathematician. Habit is not easily broken, but it is easily traced. It's a scent the bloodhound in me is eager to follow, and the skills Sal honed can help me follow it further than anyone else. I'm the best person for this job. I've been *created* to be the best person for this job: Frankenstein in dirty blonde, elaborate lies, and cheerful smiles.

I'm looking at this the wrong way. I consider taking the problems to Mr. Roth. No, too risky. He'd know right away the equations weren't my work. He'd ask questions. Everything I do is under suspicion, and with Mr. White and Kerwin hanging around, I can't trust anybody.

Except one.

But I'm too chickenshit to call him. He's just as good as I am at math. He might have a fresh perspective, might see something I don't. But beyond morning pleasantries, I haven't talked to James since our date. Even Violet's hesitating, bravado sapped. This is for the code, Violet.

Learn some composure, sweets.

▬ ▬ ▬

I use the house phone to dial Taylor.

"What's up? It's Taylor. Leave a message or go away."

"Hi, Taylor. It's Erica. I just wanted to say hi. Sorry I haven't been talking to you much." I laugh nervously and go quiet. "You probably saw the magazine. I'm sorry. You know that I can't hang around with you when there's something like that out there. I'm supposed to be an angel, not a fantastic devil like you."

What else is there to say? You would get along better with my real self? Thank you for even trying to be my friend when I can't be honest or genuine with you? When I can't even say I like you out loud to the public.

"I'm sorry," I murmur. "I'm so fucked up."

I hang up. My words are slurring informally. I'm swearing. Go away, Violet. I'm so close. I'm almost there.

Taylor never calls me back. Friday passes. I pull a cardigan on and smooth my skirt. Mrs. Silverman wears a floral dress and a windbreaker. It's the warmest day in weeks. She holds my hand as we buy tickets. Families yell and cry and whine all around us. Mrs. Silverman stares at a baby in a stroller.

"You always wanted a brother or sister."

"Sister," I tease. "Who would want a brother? Sticky and smelly and annoying."

"But a sister would've stolen your toys to play with."

"Never mind. Brother, please."

She smiles and squeezes my hand. We watch the bright pink flamingos and wander through the African exhibit. The lions look cold and out of place lying across fake rocks. The hippos wade in murky water and drop poop. For a second I think Mrs. Silverman will wrinkle her nose or tactfully ignore them like a socialite might. But she laughs instead.

"Give him some privacy."

The giraffes look like mistakes—who could ever stand so tall on legs so thin? Tropical birds in all colors flit through artificial greenhouses. The elephants delicately slide hay into their gaping mouths.

"Their trunks have two points of dexterous contact. Imagine only having two fingers," I say. Mrs. Silverman holds up two in a peace sign. "No, more like only your index finger and thumb. You could still write like that. I wonder if elephants can write?"

"Probably," she muses. "Maybe those two points are like two thumbs."

"Elephants do paint." The zookeeper overhears us and walks up to the fence. She holds a hooked rod in her hand, probably for herding the elephants. "Though they generally need training. Just techniques and those sorts of things. The pictures they paint all come from their imagination."

"Do the pictures make sense?" Mrs. Silverman asks. The keeper shrugs.

"Sometimes. Not usually, unless they're guided by their handlers. They just scribble. But they're beautiful scribbles."

Paintings. I focus on the word. That's what I'm here for. I'm not supposed to be enjoying this outing as much as I am. I have to try to get the code from Mrs. Silverman too. Anything she says about the memory that the code is linked to will help. Delicacy is top priority.

The pandas sleep under a spray of golden bamboo that looks unnatural against the Nevada sky. This isn't foggy China. The pandas don't seem to care. Or maybe they've just given up wanting to go home. Maybe this *is* their home. Mrs. Silverman closes her eyes and smiles.

"When you were little, we came here. We watched the panda pair. You were afraid, so I bought us ice cream. Someone bumped into me, and I spilled my cone, so I bought another one. The sun was just setting, and you said—"

I hold my breath. She's deep in the memory. It must've been the one she clung to most when Erica was kidnapped. It may have even happened shortly before the kidnapping. That would explain why it's so vivid to her, why she uses it as a code. She looks to me.

"I said what?" I press.

She shakes her head. "Never mind."

"It must've been important. Or funny. For you to remember it for this long."

"We should go." The wind teases her blonde curls. "Marie wanted us home for dinner."

Pandas. Mr. Silverman talked about pandas in his delirium. The zoo. A memory Mrs. Silverman is reluctant to share. This has to be the code memory. What would a young girl say to her mom at a zoo after she'd spilled an ice cream? Was it something sappy? *I love you, I love Dad, I don't want us to be apart?* It if was any of those things, she would have told me. Those were simple and easy to understand. If she's reluctant to tell me, it's because Erica said something deep, profound, something that had a great and terrible impact on Mrs. Silverman's mind. We drive home in silence, but her hand shifts over and squeezes mine occasionally. She's trying to comfort herself. To make sure I'm still here with her.

I get my phone back when we get home, my grounding up. It has one message. Taylor.

"Fakey"—she coughs—*"sorry I missed your call. Don't worry about it, okay? Shit happens. Shit happens to people like us a whole helluva lot."*

I laugh, and her voice stops. It comes back with an inhale.

"Just . . . promise me. Wherever you go after this, after it's over, stay in touch, okay?"

"I will," I say to the recording. There's hope after all. She wants to be my friend even after I commit the crime. Even after I leave. Hope is sweet and cold and searing.

It's not so dark in here after all.

When Millicent offers tea, I take it this time. It tastes like grass, but the heat is soothing.

"Sometimes"—I clear my throat—"I feel like I'm two

people—past me and future me. I'm sure I'm not the only one to feel that way. But it's different when people have expectations for you, you know? They expect you to be polite. They expect you to be things. I guess that's true for everyone. I'm not anything special."

Millicent's eyes glitter as they always do when I say something she can dissect.

I go on. "Everyone has to figure out how to balance their opposites, you know? That's what living among others is all about. Some people compromise a lot and can get along with lots of people. Others stay true to themselves, and they might lose some friends, but I think they're content knowing they were honest."

I cross my legs. "You, for example. Thirtysomething, overweight your whole life. You've got pretty hair, though. I bet everyone compliments you on it. You don't have a husband. A boyfriend, though."

Her eyelids flicker, and she writes slower.

"He's not very honest with you. He says he likes your curves, but you think he's lying. You know he's lying. You're a psychiatrist, after all."

I wave my hands to the teas on the counter. "All these teas. You like herbal remedies. You've been trying them for a year now, hoping one of them'll help you lose weight. You're happy with your body, always have been, but he's not, and that makes you lose confidence. Resentment festers— resentment that he's the cause of your self-doubt. You never doubted before. You'd come to terms with yourself. But now you hate him sometimes."

She takes my words in with a small smile, nodding. Whether it's true, I can't tell. But it seems close.

"The point is," I press, "you don't really know who you

are, or what you're capable of, until you meet the right people. The people who bring those things out in you. Some people can be go-getters, but at the end of the day we're all reactive personalities. We just don't know it until we meet the right catalyst. Chemistry, and all that bullshit."

I look up at the clock, the hands moving so slowly, I can't see the motion. What's James doing right now? Is he thinking about me like I'm thinking about him? Is Taylor lonely? Does she, like Millicent, have resentment growing in her heart? What about Cass? Merril? Will they ever forgive me like Taylor? Or will they turn their backs when I reveal my true self?

Only the clock knows. The future knows. I breathe deep. "Time, and all that bullshit."

15: PLAY IT

I can't figure these numbers out.

I've asked Mr. Roth about portions of them, and he was eager to answer, but even with his clarifications, I feel confused. Nothing is working. It's like the equations themselves are incomplete. Did I miss the other half of the equations on the walls? Skip over them? I stare at the Polaroids until my eyes burn in protest, scouring the pictures for more numbers that might fit.

I'm doing something wrong, and I don't know what. I've tried reversing the numbers, mirroring them, making a matrix to try to break each down, but I end up with stupid decimal numbers and hexadecimals with more than two letters. I just need each of the eight equations to come to one whole number or one whole letter. Is that too much to ask?

I consider asking Sal about it in the magazine, but he wouldn't know. He wasn't the one who taught me—he got a brilliant dropout from MIT who'd turned to the seedy underbelly of Vegas to make it at the slots. Sal never graduated from high school, but he always wanted more for me. Wanted better for me, like a real parent.

He just wanted me to be the best to get this painting, is all.

I write the eight equations on a piece of paper and snap a

picture on my phone. Send it in a text to the one number I'm afraid of, along with the message

> Challenging myself. Can't solve them.

I wait. He's mad. Of course he's mad. I act like an idiot on our date and then text him expecting help? The glimmer of the touch screen lights my face as I bury it in the pillow. Bury the expectation, the longing, the anger at myself. How dare I text him. How dare I even talk to him.

How dare I expect something normal.

His reply comes at eleven:

> Sorry. Family dinner. Phone was charging. Where did you get these equations?

I feel like I'm swallowing my heart.

> College book.

His reply is almost instant:

> I think they're couplets. One and three. Two and four, etc.

Oh my God. I throw the blankets off and grab my notebook, scribbling by the dim light of my phone. He's right. Why didn't I think of that? Instead of eight equations, I've got four long ones, and they fit perfectly into each other. Now they make a little more sense. I still need to painstakingly solve all of them, apply the hexadecimal conversion where necessary, and then correlate them with each other, but for now it's a step in any direction. And I'm grateful.

My text is probably too enthusiastic. I hover over the exclamation mark. I should delete it. I should play it cool. But I can't. I'm happy—too happy. More happy that he texted me back than the fact the code is in my grasp.

Get ahold of your priorities, sweets.

I keep the exclamation mark.

He texts back:

Sleep well.

And with those words shining on the screen, I fall asleep with the phone under my pillow.

For this night, for *one* night, I'm like every other teenage girl in the world.

———

3c2p6pm.

The four equations equal those digits, in that exact order. *6pm* is obviously "six o'clock," for the time Mrs. Silverman and Erica visited the zoo. *2p* could be anything—but I'm willing to bet it meant the pair of pandas in the enclosure. *3c* was trickier, but I figured it out—"three cones," for the ice cream Mrs. Silverman spilled and Erica ate.

But there's still one digit missing. One last digit that relates to that memory. It's what Mrs. Silverman was reluctant to say. It relates to something little Erica said to her. It plagues me constantly, an empty space in my brain that yearns to be filled, to be known. It's all that's keeping me from completing this con—this *life*. The Erica in me giggles coyly when I ask her to reveal it. She's useless. She's enjoying watching me struggle, squirm.

Or she just wants me to stay.

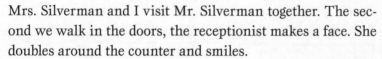

Mrs. Silverman and I visit Mr. Silverman together. The second we walk in the doors, the receptionist makes a face. She doubles around the counter and smiles.

"I'm sorry, Mrs. Silverman. I'm afraid you can't visit your husband today."

"Why not?"

"He's not doing so well." The receptionist pauses, as if listening. I can hear faint shouts.

"What's going on with him?" Mrs. Silverman strides down the hall. "Brandon? Brandon, are you all right?"

"Mrs. Silverman, please—" The receptionist dashes after us.

Nurses are gathered around a room, a male nurse trying to work the door open.

"What's going on here?" Mrs. Silverman's voice is shrill. One of the nurses turns to her.

"I'm sorry, Mrs. Silverman. He's having some sort of breakdown—he's jammed a chair in front of the door. We've called Dr. Polteski down. He'll be here shortly to talk him through it."

"Brandon!" Mrs. Silverman calls. "Brandon, please. It's me! I have Erica here. We came to visit you. Please, come out."

"No!" Mr. Silverman's screams resound through the door. "No, go away!"

A man in a white coat strides up. "Mrs. Silverman, please wait in reception while we clear this up—"

"No! He's obviously having a difficult time—"

"Which will be made more difficult by the presence of so many people," Dr. Polteski interrupts. "I want everyone to leave except Nurse Rodriguez and Nurse Gray. Now, please."

The nurses lead us to the lobby, easing us onto the couch. Mrs. Silverman buries her face in her hands, and I wrap my arms around her shoulders.

"It's okay." I use a comforting voice. Dad's every shout makes her flinch like she's being stabbed. "He's just having a bad day. Everybody has bad days."

The shouts grow louder. I can hear *Erica* laced through them. The doctor comes in and motions for me.

"I think it would be best if you spoke with him."

Mrs. Silverman gets up with me, but Dr. Polteski grunts. "Alone, Erica."

I smile at her. "I'll get him out. Don't worry."

The male nurse makes way for me at the door. I lean against it, the metal cool against my forehead.

"Dad, it's me."

"I don't want to go." He sobs.

"You don't have to go. You can stay here as long as you need to."

"You promised," he slurs. "You promised, Erica."

My fists clench. "What did I promise?"

"You said you'd come back. You said it. You said if I waited, you'd come back home to us, no matter what. Home. No matter what, you'd come home."

There's an immense quiet. My nails bite into my palms. The metal door is damp with something. Tears. My tears. No, not mine. Not really. Erica bites them back, gnaws on her lip, and lets the words explode from her.

"I'm sorry."

"Home!" Mr. Silverman shouts, ragged.

"I'm so sorry."

"Home! *Home!*"

"I can't!"

"You promised! You promised me and your mom. You promised everyone!"

"I c-can't." I sink down against the door, hiding my face in the metal from the onlooking nurses. I'm dead, Dad. I'm never going to come home. But I can't tell you that. I tried to tell you, but you wouldn't listen. You're the only one I tried to tell, and you refuse to understand. To hear me. Hear me: *I'm dead.* Feel it through this door that separates us: *I'm dead.* Listen to the sobs that wrack my ribs: *I'm dead.*

I'm— She's *dead.*

The ride home is silent. The house is silent. Dinner is silent.

Only when I crawl into Mrs. Silverman's bed does she try to hug me. Touch me. Comfort me. She let me have space for once. Instead of forcing her love, letting it overflow. Now I ask for it.

I sniff, the last tears drying on the collar of her robe. "Sorry."

"Don't be sorry," she murmurs. "There's nothing to be sorry for. You did your best."

Somewhere between my cold room and this warm nest of blankets, it hit me. Violet, drowned in tears that aren't hers, puts it together. Mr. Silverman said Erica promised to come home. He could be making it up, but the man's ramblings are based in truth—I'd seen that much with our zoo conversation. Nonsensical at first, it made sense later. It's worth a try.

The thing Erica said to Mrs. Silverman at the zoo disturbed her. That same thing no doubt relates to the final digit of the code. What Mr. Silverman said, that Erica told him she knew she was going away, but would come home, disturbs *Violet*. If the zoo thing happened a few days before the kidnapping, then Erica's promise would ring eerily, and coincidentally.

Violet knows there's no such thing as coincidence.

"When I go away, I promise I'll come home."

The words cut through the night air. Mrs. Silverman's hand freezes as it pets my head.

"That's what I said at the zoo. It scared you. I scared you, because a few weeks later, I really did go away. I don't remember it, but Dad kept shouting that at me today."

She exhales. "I lost you in the crowd for a moment at the zoo. Near the panda enclosure. You were hiding behind a bush, playing with ladybugs. When I found you, I lost my cool. Scared you. When you stopped crying, you said you would come home. You said even if you got lost, you'd come home."

"And like I promised, I came back. I came home . . ." I start.

Erica hasn't come back. The Erica that Mrs. Silverman clutches is not the real Erica. The real Erica's promise is dead—never to be fulfilled. An empty promise. I thought Erica had no tears left, but still they spill. Who's crying? Not Violet. Violet is somber, watching from the sidelines as Erica and her mother cling to each other in a bedroom filled with the smell of roses and sorrow.

"You're home," she says, and hiccups. "You're home, and it's all right now."

Home.

But it's not all right, is it? You keep crying. Something is not right. You can't put your finger on it. The other two didn't come this close to feeling right. Third time's the charm. You're telling yourself it's PTSD, Stockholm syndrome, something, anything. She's not damaged forever. She's not changed; you have not missed all her formative years. They made her into someone different. Change is normal. You convince yourself change is inevitable but you still shake with this fear.

You're so afraid, afraid that tiny wrong feeling will stay forever. You sense the suppressed Violet in me. You'll do anything to believe I'll get better, become more like the Erica you knew before. Love. Food. Clothes. Time. No meds yet, no doctors yet. But you'd pay for it all if it meant bringing your baby home. Your real baby.

I visit Mr. Silverman on my own. His gray hue isn't promising, and he isn't as enthusiastic as he normally is to play checkers. At least he's out of the room. He moves his pieces listlessly. I write the code down on a piece of paper and show it to him. Mr. Silverman's eyes widen. I lean in.

"This is the code, isn't it? For the thing behind *Robinson Crusoe*. You hid it, but I found it."

His hazel eyes bore into mine—an animal on point. A rat pausing to sniff the air for danger. After a beat he shakes his head, points to the *2p* and *6pm*. "Reverse."

I take a pen out and switch the two. Mr. Silverman touches the new code, and lingers on the tiny *h*. The last digit.

"Home," he says wistfully.

I smile and move my black piece. I feel like celebrating.

Even if he is crazy, the confirmation means something. Means everything. I've gotten a code with a very good chance of being the right one. I'm that much closer. One step closer to getting out of this place. Violet wants to dance. Erica wants to comfort the pitiful shell of the man who was her father.

"Why don't we do something different for once? Do you, I dunno, like to dance?" I start.

"Dance," he repeats dully.

I stand from the table and pull him up by the hand. I tap on my phone and bring up a default song—something classic and orchestra-y. Something James might play. Mr. Silverman looks wary at first, but when the nurses don't come screaming to reprimand us, he twirls me around and we do a sort of shuffle-jig facing each other. He's dancing something from an era before my inception, and I'm making it up as I go, flailing hands and schizophrenic feet. Violet misses showing her true emotions like this. The other visitors are staring. Some patients get up from their stools and clap. An old woman holding a child's toy squeaks it in time to the music. A tattooed menace of a young man dances in his chair and whoops.

The orderlies are not amused.

Violet has never seen Mr. Silverman smile like he means it until this moment.

Erica tried to imagine that same smile, tried to hide in the memory of it, when Gerald's hands were slitting her wrists.

Michelle Painchaud

16: HIDE IT

Sal never made a habit of keeping guns around.

The only gun I'd seen before going into Taylor's TV room was the revolver Sal kept for emergencies. He'd never fired it. It's unsettling to see so many guns in one place: mounted on the walls, under glass cases. The type of man to hoard this many guns is a hunter or a fanatic collector. No stuffed heads or photos of kills, so Taylor's dad is the latter. A collector of guns who doesn't actually use them. This says oodles about his character: focuses on details, a little pompous. The guns are in plain sight. He likes intimidating people or showing off.

The best con artist knows it's dangerous to have hobbies and quirks. They give away personality. Giving away personality is giving the opponent an advantage. Knowledge is everything. A con artist's job is to manipulate, not be manipulated. Violet's only vice is a good hamburger.

And a witty boy.

I shake my head to get rid of that thought. Taylor walks in bearing two cans of soda and a bag of popcorn. She hands me a can.

"Thanks. For inviting me too."

"Don't thank me." She snorts and pops her can open.

"Consider it a sorry-I-was-a-jerkass-all-this-time-so-here's-some-popcorn night. Sleepover makes it sound so kiddish."

"I'll do your hair like normal girls do. Give you a Mohawk." I smirk over my soda. Her hair's down to her back. "It'd be a lot of hair gel. But worth it."

"So you can take pictures and blackmail me? I don't think so." She snorts again.

"You're such a suspicious individual." I pretend to act shocked.

"So are you, Fakey. You just act all smiley about it."

Taylor's fighting bruises are healing slowly but surely, faint rings of purple and green. She doesn't wear as much caked foundation to hide them anymore. She flips through the movies on Netflix. Her queue is full of horror and thrillers. Crime thrillers.

"You like guessing who the murderer is?" I ask.

Taylor shrugs. "Yeah. But TV is too predictable—it's always the best-known actors. British TV is a little harder to guess."

A woman strides by us, legs long, wearing little more than a towel. I nearly jump, but Taylor's expression is dully unsurprised.

"Taylor, do you know where the extra shampoo is? Charlotte used it all."

"Bottom drawer on the right," Taylor says.

The woman's face lights up. "Thanks!"

I wait until she's gone to speak. "I saw you at Green Foods. You work at a lot of places, right? To get out of the house. Because your dad lets these girls practically live here, and it annoys you. Makes you feel caged in."

She grunts again and sinks into the couch. Her house isn't so different from Erica's. It's smaller, but just as chic and filled with expensive things—stainless-steel refrigerator, art on the walls, leather couches. She doesn't find solace in the rich things like Violet does. Even if it's fancy, it's not a home to her.

"Where's your mom?" I ask.

"New York. I spend summers there."

"You can't live with her instead?"

"The only things Mom loves are herself and her art." Taylor shrugs. "I'd just cramp her style and ruin her idiotic bohemian parties."

My stomach clenches. She fishes her cigarettes out.

"S'fine. I'll be gone in a year to college, anyway. They can fuck up their lives without me stopping them. I bet they'll be thrilled."

"That's not true. They love you," I try.

"Yeah." She chuckles and takes the first drag. "Sure."

Taylor offers me a cigarette. I've never smoked in my life. Violet thinks it's nasty. Erica wants to try everything at least once, before she has to go away for good. I choke, and Taylor pounds me on the back.

"Shoulda known you wouldn't know how. Look"—she puts her hand on her chest—"put the cigarette to your lips. Breathe in once, hold it in your mouth, and then breathe in again so it goes in lower. And now let it out."

I exhale. Smoke spirals toward the ceiling. I wrinkle my nose.

She takes her own drag and checks her phone. "You wanna go somewhere?"

"I'm up for whatever you are."

She doesn't drive, so we head to the bus stop. I don't ask where we're going—it's just nice to be going somewhere, period. An older woman watches Taylor suspiciously from a bench.

"Black jacket and leather pants make you an automatic bad girl," Taylor mumbles. "Or it's the contrast. Angelic you standing next to grungy me."

"Like chocolate and vanilla," I offer.

"*Harold and Maude,*" she counters.

"Hamburgers and French fries."

"Why are all yours food? Are you hungry?" She laughs. I rub my stomach as the bus rolls up. She uses her pass and pays for me, and we sit across from a sleeping hobo.

"Don't worry." Taylor removes her jacket, tank top showing off her arms. "Where we're going, there's plenty of free food. The good, fancy stuff too. Salmon, pesto, salad."

The bus takes us to another suburb, one farther from the city. It stops in front of a sprawling golf course, a huge white building with a waiting roundabout. BLUEWELL COUNTRY CLUB, the sign blares. Taylor jumps off the last bus step and breathes in.

"Ah, fake grass and arrogance. My favorite smells. Oh, and a hint of—could it be—Botox?" A group of overtanned women in golf gear rivet their heads toward her at the word. Taylor waves. "Afternoon, ladies."

"What's so special about this place? Other than the prime snob-watching?" I ask.

"Look who's talking." She elbows me. "Your mom's one of these snobs, I'm sure. You, Fakey, are destined to become one of 'em too. If you stick around."

"Me and destiny aren't on speaking terms."

"Country clubs!" She throws up her arms. "Home of Rolexes, inane conversation, and who-knows-who-is-who. And recitals." She opens the front doors for me. The lobby isn't big, but it's swarming with people. My stomach sinks.

Moths beat their wings against the lining. Recitals. She can't mean—

"Excuse me, ladies." A man at a podium in a suit clears his throat. "What are your member numbers?"

"We're here for the recital, Chumley. Friends of James." Taylor smiles.

"I'm sorry, you're going to need an invitation in order to—"

"Calvin!" a voice booms.

A man in a neat vest walks up. I'd recognize that face anywhere—

"I'd recognize that face anywhere!" The man smiles at me. "Erica Silverman, right?"

I nod. Calvin the concierge fumbles. "Sir, I certainly—"

"Let them in, will you?" The man thumps Calvin on the back. "They're friends of James, and one of them's a minor celebrity. What more could you ask for?"

"Not much, sir," Calvin grits out, and waves us through. Taylor mock-salutes as we pass.

"I've seen you on the news, Erica." The man adjusts his vest. "Terrible tragedy, but at least you're back now, eh? What doesn't kill you and all that?"

"Yes." I nod. "I'm sorry. I didn't catch your name?"

He smacks his forehead and extends a hand. "I apologize. I've been all over the place today. I'm Michael Anders, James's father."

I knew it. His face is a lot like James's—placid, mild. An everyman's face. He shakes my hand vigorously.

"I'm Taylor." She offers her hand.

He just smiles at it and adjusts his collar. "Pleasure. Let's get you some good seats, shall we?"

Mr. Anders puts his hand on the small of my back and steers me toward a ballroom. Taylor stalks after us, clearly pissed at being slighted. The tables are crowded with people. At the front is a grand piano, gleaming midnight on the small platform. At the sides are buffets of cold meats, salad fixings, and finger sandwiches. Taylor heaps a plate and leaves me to be corralled around by overeager Michael.

"So how are you liking Saint Peter's?" he asks, and pulls out a chair for me at a front table. This isn't good. James'll definitely be able to see me as soon as he walks in.

"I like it." I put on my best smile. "Everyone's been so nice to me. I was expecting something more showy when the police said my real home was in Vegas."

Michael nods. "It's a place built on show business. Once you get used to it, that mentality starts to leak into your life-style. It's a fantastic mind-set—positive energy covering up all the negative stuff."

"To be honest, I like the nonglitzy parts best. Much less shallow."

"Of course you do." He smiles dismissively and motions to a few people. "Ann! Simon! Come over here for a sec. Got someone you'll want to meet!"

I glance around for Taylor, but she's still stuffing her plate. Am I supposed to be here? Would James hate me being here? Why did Taylor even bring me? They're the ones who should date eventually. Does she still think I like him? Am I that obvious?

"Ann, Simon, this is Erica Silverman," Michael says.

"I've been following your case since day one, dear," Ann assures me, horse face creased with concern.

"She's even written letters to the governor calling for

harsher sentencing on your kidnappers." Simon laughs, his bald spot showing.

"Thank you?" I don't sound convinced.

"Oh, it's nothing big, really." Ann smiles. "I'm just doing what any Good Samaritan would."

"That's my little activist." Simon laughs again. Michael laughs with him.

Simon looks to me. "So, I heard you and James go to the same school. Do you know him well?"

"Sort of." I smile.

"He's a nice kid. Been coming here since he was little. Though I bet his dad wishes he was a bit more music-superstar material. Don't you, Mike?"

Michael shrugs. "He'll get there one day. You should see him play now; he's got that stage fright thing mastered."

"So I've heard." Ann nods. "How did he do it?"

"Eight-hour practice days on the weekends, and four-hour sessions on the weekdays in front of minor crowds. Just family, mostly. Friends of family. Stick him in the middle of the living room while we're having a party and make him play. It really works wonders for his performance anxiety."

I furrow my brows. That sounds intense. Eight hours every weekend? And four every weekday? What kind of life could you have like that? It's a miracle we'd gotten to go on a date at all.

Michael keeps on.

"I've been talking to my old professor at Julliard, says application season is hideous, but it's only the top three percent that they really consider, you know?" Ann and Simon nod. "So I said to James: 'You're already in the three percent; just get a little better than the other two point nine!'"

As if on cue, they all burst into laughter. I don't get the joke.

"What's he playing today?" Ann asks.

"Oh, something surefire. Beethoven."

"He should play one of your pieces, Mike," Simon insists.

Michael waves his hand. "Someday. Right now it's all about the old masters and developing technique."

"Doesn't he play guitar, too?" I ask.

Michael looks at me, startled. "We're focusing on piano, as we've done since he was a child. There's no room for that sort of thing right now, especially with Julliard so close."

"What if he doesn't want to do piano?" I shoot back.

Violet's being too blunt. Ann and Simon both tense up. Michael looks as if I'd slapped him.

"He loves piano. Ever since he was—"

"What if he loves music? All music. Not just piano."

Michael stares at me, his blue eyes near mirror images of James's. But James's are kinder. Michael finally breaks into a nervous laugh.

"Of course he loves music. That's in the blood."

Simon and Ann laugh with him. I roll my eyes and fix them on Taylor. She trots over and sits by me, spooning potato salad into her mouth.

"Why'd you bring me here?" I ask her.

She swallows her mouthful. "Because you like James."

"Tay—"

"You realize"—she stabs a bit of salmon—"that in all the seventeen years I've known him, I've never ever seen him so happy. Upbeat. Fuckin' positive instead of dreary and prissy! When he's with you, he loses his wavy-haired head."

"Look, I can't date anyone right now. You know why—"

"You can date if you want. Don't kid yourself, Fakey. You want to. I'm sick of seeing you mope around about it. Let's settle this." She takes out a coin and smirks. "Vegas style. Heads, you go out with him. Tails, you don't."

I pick at my jeans. She smiles.

"This is fair, right? A coin is fifty-fifty, nice and even and clean. Nothing personal. It's the best judge."

"I'm just going to hurt him, Taylor."

"You never drop that dumb people-pleasing smile. So what if you hurt him? He'll hurt you. You'll hurt each other. That's what love is about, right? You can't know what'll happen till you actually try it. Don't try to make excuses like you're protecting him."

"I'm not making excuses!" I hiss. "This is how it has to be. He can't go out with me. I can't go out with him. I'm not a good person."

"You wanna blame it on being *bad*?" She laughs. "Fine. Be my guest. But we both know that's not it. You just don't want to make your own choices."

"That's not true!"

"You like James, but you're scared of choosing him for real, making a commitment, so you refuse to even try. Me and the populars, you waver between us. You like me. Even though they're dumb airheads, you like them. You're just standing on the middle ground and throwing around bull-shit so you can delay choosing between us because you don't know how to choose. Because you've never had to make your own choices. It's always just been someone ordering you around, hasn't it?"

Of course I take orders. I have to. What would you know about living your whole life for one con? Throwing yourself away to become another girl entirely? I never had a choice. This is what I was raised for. I can't go against that. There's always been a plan. Every breath, every month, every laugh or flu or Barbie doll has all been part of the plan. I've spent my life digging myself into this grave. I can't dig myself out.

That's what I tell myself every day.

Taylor tosses the coin up. It spirals then clangs against the tabletop. Taylor slams her hand over it. I faintly hear an announcer talking, the crowd cheering, but my eyes are fixed on the flash of silver between her fingers. It's just a coin. I'm not serious about this insane bet, not like Taylor is. Her brown eyes are filled with something I can't discern, and it scares me. She pulls her hand away. Heads.

"There we have it." Taylor smiles and claps me on the back.

"This is childish, Tay."

"We're legally children, dork. For one more year, anyway." She slings an arm around my neck. "Look at it this way—you go out with Beethoven, or I'll spill your secret to the whole school. How does that sound?"

"You wouldn't." I glare at her.

"Oh, I would. If it meant getting you two together." She smiles and glances behind me. "Speak of the devil."

Applause ricochets around the room as James walks up to the piano. He's in a black shirt; he gives little bows to the crowd. The announcer says something about his dad and piano teacher, and they stand and wave too. There are other nervous kids waiting their turns to perform after him. James's mouth crimps, his hands clench and unclench. He hates this pomp and ceremony. He hates this. Why? Why does he keep going up there to perform for these people?

We lock eyes. Taylor snickers, but I barely hear it. It's just me and him now. My eyes and his. That kind face I thought was so forgettable at first has now become unforgettable. I can't tell if he's angry at me for how I acted at the pizza place, how I've ignored him, how I've put off making my own decision about him. I can't read his face. And I'm Violet. I can read every face.

He breaks the moment and sits at the piano. A hush falls over the dining room. He cracks his knuckles, nods to himself, and starts playing. With barely the first minute of haunting music out, Taylor gets up and leaves. Retreats. She looks back once, giving me a tiny smile. Leans on the doorway and watches James from there. Michael's face has changed from smug satisfaction to abject terror, only getting fiercer the longer James plays. His friends at our table whisper to him.

"What is he playing, Mike?"

"This certainly doesn't sound like Beethoven."

The music started off calm enough, but now it's a complicated, seemingly off-key-sounding medley. Despair. All I can hear in it is two needs clashing—order and chaos. Neat clean expectations and rampant fetid desires. Michael's face is white.

"Prokofiev's eighth sonata. B-flat. We've never practiced this. He's not ready for this."

"Sounds ready to me," I murmur.

The music is so strange, stranger than any piano music I've heard before. I can tell from Michael's face that it's not an easy piece to play. The notes are lilting and quiet, like the voice of a tiny girl, and in another second, they boom, a full-grown man yelling into a canyon. And then the notes break my heart—two chords that sound so timid, tiny, unsure of themselves. James runs his fingers up the keys, two flesh spiders dancing.

James's piano teacher leans over to Michael. "I had no idea

he decided on Prokofiev. Isn't that the same piece you played for your Julliard application?"

"He's not ready for this," Michael hisses.

The teacher pats his back. "What's wrong, Mike? You should be proud. He's doing a damn good job."

James's playing acidic, intense chords, but his face remains calm. I watch Michael's. I see it then—fear. Michael's afraid. He's controlled James all his life through piano. He's related to James through piano. It's a means for them to communicate, for Michael to teach and guide. He did it because he's a piano genius who maybe doesn't know how to relate to people, let alone his child, otherwise. It's all he knows. James playing an obviously complicated piece like this shows he doesn't need guidance anymore. That maybe the time for student and mentor has left, and the time for father and son has arrived. Michael has to let go of James, and that thought terrifies him.

I'd tried to let go of James. Taylor made sure it didn't work.

The music trills out; James gently rolls his fingers across the keys and lets the sound drip into silence. The crowd's applause is a storm, getting louder as James stands, grabs the sheet music, and takes a bow. He's smiling now. He stands taller now. A weight is gone. James waits for the applause to die before looking at his father.

"I'm quitting piano, Dad."

It's four words. Four tiny words that make Michael go still. They hang in the huge silence of the dining room. No one moves. One voice dares to ring—Taylor.

"Man, you people are so melodramatic."

I look back just in time to see her pull the fire alarm on the wall. The high siren whines. The sprinklers flood the air with cones of water, drenching tablecloths, weighing down bouquets of flowers, and making shirts translucent and screams erupt from startled mouths. People rush out of the dining room in panic. The waiting pianists throw a table-cloth over the piano, shriek, and duck backstage. I cover my head with my jacket—futile. The water soaks it in seconds. Michael continues to stand still for a moment, the water waking him from his shell shock. James watches him leave, the sodden sheet of music in his hand dripping on the floor. He shakes his hair—stringy around his face—and laughs.

"Oy, Beethoven!"

Taylor. Her dark hair plasters to her forehead as she grabs a cupcake from someone's plate and lobs it at James. He ducks, but the frosting grazes his cheek. A laugh bursts from me just as I feel something wet hit the top of my head—another cupcake.

"Taylor! You asshole!"

Taylor snickers and ducks a half-eaten sandwich. James stands by my side and eases his arm down from its throw as he looks at me.

"What's a smart girl like you doing here?"

I pull the cupcake from my hair and smack it against his cheek. "Being really, really dumb."

He grins, frosting indenting his smile lines. "Oh, you're so dead for that. Or frosted. Whichever you prefer."

"Dead is permanent. Frosting is sweet. Not much of a choice."

James grabs my hand. I feel so hot and cold all at the same time. I pull away.

"You're not mad," I say.

"No." His smile just gets bigger.

"I'm sorry. About everything. You're really not mad?"

"I was. Then I got over it."

My heart spasms. "You can't like me."

"Too late."

Before, exposure to the friends and family weakened Erica and made Violet strong. Now, my two sides are in agreement. The scale is in a perfect still balance. We both want to kiss him. He's close, chest almost touching mine. The sprinklers stop, the sirens die. Water drips off the end of his nose and eyelashes. I stand on my toes and he wraps an arm around me, heat radiating from under his wet shirt. Pulls me close. We can't get any closer. His lips are intimidating. Violet has no idea what to do with them. Erica is equally inexperienced, and she's on the edge of losing it. So much stimulation, so much skin and longing in his gaze. Violet smirks and licks frosting off his cheek instead.

"It's sweet." She tries to pull away and make a joke, but the arm tightens around her back, crushing her into him. It's soft and insistent, hesitant and burning at the same time.

Every thought in my head is obliterated by a nuclear fire spreading from my heart. My lips tingle where his touch. He pulls away, gasping to breathe.

"Wanted to do that for a long time. That's all I wanted. You can go back to ignoring me, now."

"No." I shake my head. "No running away anymore."

"Who were you running from?" He tilts his head. "Me? I *am* pretty scary—"

I say one word. "Erica."

He goes quiet. I slip my hand in his and squeeze. Taylor wolf whistles when we come out of the dining room. Security has her against a wall, questioning her.

"She didn't do anything, officers," James insists. They open their mouths to answer when Taylor waves us off.

"My dad will be here soon. Don't worry. Taylor Mansfield

doesn't get criminal charges. I'll see you two on Monday. Sorry, Fakey. Sleepover postponed. We'll reschedule."

"Thank you—"

"Don't thank me. It was the coin. Lady Luck, or whatever." She laughs. I turn it over in my hand as James and I walk away, the metal smooth.

"What was she talking about?" he asks.

I flip the coin over. Both sides are identical. Both sides are heads. She used a double-sided coin guaranteed to give me heads. She knew full well it would land on the go-out side. She's a conniving bitch. But then again, so am I.

"I have no idea." Erica leans in to James's shoulder and kisses him on his frosting-covered cheek.

This is her first boyfriend. Her last boyfriend, the boyfriend who never was and never will be. She memorizes the taste, the feel of his skin under her lips, and hopes they will follow her into death.

17: DEFEND IT

Sal slides a bowl of Cheerios over to seven-year-old Violet. The girl puts her pigtails over her shoulders so she won't drip them into the milk. Sal settles at the table, lights a cigarette, and watches his daughter eat.

"Vi?"

The little girl doesn't look up. Sal knows she's listening by the way her eyes flicker.

"When I adopted you, you said you wanted to be like me. Why do you want to be like me, Vi? I'm not a nice person."

"I want to be with you," Violet murmurs.

"Why do you want to be with me?"

"Because I don't wanna be alone."

Sometimes Sal leaves on "business trips." He leaves Violet with a man and woman who live in a nice condo with nice dogs and nice art. Sal says they're "fences," but Violet is confused because they are people, not wood planks painted white and surrounding a yard.

She likes them fine. They feed her, but they don't look at her.

Violet puts on lipstick in the mirror. She adjusts the cropped black T-shirt and tiny skirt she's wearing. Pulls it up higher. She's done this scam with Sal a hundred times before. He just needs to pick an honest John. Everything goes smoothly with an honest John. She pulls her black hoodie around her. It's November. Too cold to stand on a curb and pretend to be a hooker without a jacket.

Sal walks in from the bathroom; he's wearing a tracksuit. "You ready, Vi?"

"Always."

He watches her and pats her head. "We're closer. You know that, right? Every year, we get closer to the big one. Two years, three years from now, I'll be on some beach and you'll be traveling the world with your big brains and your big beauty. You'll conquer hearts and minds, sweets. Hearts and minds."

"Yeah." Her lips are blood-red crescents.

"It's just us. Just a little more. Just us against the world."

It's always them against the world.

He pulls the door open and leaves. Violet sits on the bed and waits for his phone call to start the sting. She listens to the ambulances wail outside, watches the wallpaper grow ever more brown and molded, and scratches absently at her skin—a mosquito bite, a sore, something pressing through that her nails try to free.

The desert of Nevada is hot, dry, and empty. Violet watches the sky the most. Reading in the car makes her sick. She spends the hours watching time paint the sky. It's blue in the day—blue skies, blue reflections off the hot sand, blue cars and signs. At sunset it is a burning fire-red scarlet.

There is a moment when the two times meet—dusk. Blue and red meld together into a last soft lavender that deepens as night encroaches. The lavender turns to periwinkle, periwinkle to a sable purple with an opal moon pendant. And finally, just before darkness consumes the world, there is violet.

18: RUN IT

Sal took me to the salon once or twice, when I needed a fancy hairdo as a disguise for a con, but those had been penny places—cheap perfume clouding the air and tacky neon signs in the windows. Mrs. Silverman's salon is on the fortieth floor of a building downtown, with glass windows the size of walls, and leather couches and air smelling like exotic flowers. They give you aprons and free coffee and tea and pastries. I stuff a cherry Danish into my mouth. Mrs. Silverman sighs.

"Erica, please. Small bites."

I swallow. "Sorry. They just look like something out of a magazine. This whole place does."

"I'm glad you like it." Mrs. Silverman settles onto the couch, coffee in hand. "I'll be getting a trim. I signed you up for the complete package. I want you glowing when you go off to prom."

"Complete package?" My voice pitches up nervously. "Like, the whole hot-wax-razor-blades-general-instruments-of-torture package?"

"Beauty is pain. But mostly it's beautiful," she singsongs, and flips through a magazine. They call my name, and Mrs. Silverman flashes a smile. "Good luck."

I follow the impossibly chic-looking lady. She washes my hair and trims the dead ends. The next lady gives me a manicure and pedicure that goes terribly wrong with my ticklish feet—I laugh and nearly kick her in the face. The next woman leads me to a private room with a table.

"Uh, what's this for?" I ask.

"Bikini wax, as ordered." She smiles.

"Are you kidding me?" I leap off the table.

"Ms. Silverman, please. Lie down."

"Aren't you going to give me painkillers at least? Morphine?"

"Please, lie down."

"Booze?"

She wordlessly starts the hot wax pot.

"Do I have to take my underwear off?"

I see her do a tiny eye roll, but her smile covers it. "That would be nice. Please relax. It will go by faster that way."

I flinch as the hot wax slathers on. "I'm not even going to have sex there, you know. It's just prom. I'm just going to dance."

"You never know. Best to be prepared for everything." Her smile gets sweeter just as she rips the cloth away.

"Jesus fucking—!" I scream.

"Is that your phone ringing?" the woman asks lightly as she applies more wax. I ignore the throbbing. I motion to my bag, and she hands me my cell.

"H-hello?"

"Sup?"

Taylor.

"What's wrong? You sound like you're crying."

"I'm at the—fuck!—salon."

"Are they torturing you?"

"Wax," I murmur. "Holy shit! Can you go a little slower?" I ask the woman.

She nods. "If you'd like. But it'll only prolong the pain."

I groan and lean my head back.

Taylor laughs. "You're really going all out for this prom crap, aren't you?"

"You're coming, right?"

"Why? So I can make fun of your bimbo friends and stuff my face? Sorry, but that's pretty much every day for me. Prom isn't anything special."

"What were you going to do instead?"

"Go to Riddler again. Get trashed."

I bite my lip. I don't want her to go there without me. She might get into serious trouble.

"Come with us to prom," I say. "Cass doesn't really mind you. Merril will be okay if I talk her through it."

"And what do I for a date? Boys generally stay away from bitches like me."

"You don't need a date. Just come with James and me. It'll be fun with the three of us."

There's a beat on her end.

"Damn it, I have to buy a dress now, don't I?"

"Something black." I smirk.

"I'm fucking tired of black."

Marie's face looks anxious when we come home. "Erica, there's someone in the kitchen for you. A friend."

My heart leaps, but then I realize she doesn't name James. It's not him. Who, then? Mrs. Silverman shoots me a questioning look but tactfully stays out of the kitchen to give me privacy. There, sitting at the island, is a broad-shouldered, dark-haired boy. Kerwin.

"What are you doing here?" I sniff.

He turns on the stool and smirks. "Erica. You look fresh and primped."

"Just got back from the salon. You didn't answer my question."

"I heard you and James started going out. What do you see in him, by the way? Just a friendly inquiry."

"Nothing about you is friendly, Kerwin. Why are you here?"

"That's a complicated question. It mostly has to do with what you're hiding."

My hands tighten into fists. "What am I hiding? Please, tell me."

"You're not Erica." His eyes are voracious, his smile never faltering.

"I've had three people say that to me since I've been back. And dozens more imply it. So if you think that's going to scare me—"

"I brought some flowers for you."

He produces a bouquet he's been holding behind his back, a spray of deep purple blossoms with thin petals. Violets. I stare at them, trying to interpret the possibilities. No such thing as a coincidence. He knows my real name is Violet.

Kerwin stands and stretches leisurely. He goes into the hall and leaves through the front door without a word.

Marie peeks in from the living room. "Flowers? Do you have another admirer besides James?"

Mrs. Silverman laughs as she enters the kitchen. "Another boy? Goodness. I knew she'd be a heartbreaker, but not so many so quickly." A pause. "Erica? Is something wrong?"

I look up and smile. "No. I just don't think he's my type."

I talk through dinner about the weather or Marie's grandson or Mrs. Silverman's new haircut, but between the clanging of forks, my mind is doing laps around itself. He knows my name. I know he's up to no good. How did he find it out? Does he have contacts? No one is supposed to know my real name. Sal made sure of that. No friends. No acquaintances. If I met anyone, it was always under a pseudonym. If we went anywhere, Sal called me by something else. My real name was used by Sal only, and in private.

Sal.

He's the only one who knows my name is Violet.

They say what's most obvious is the truth. The most obvious explanation is that Kerwin knows Sal. Kerwin hasn't tried to lob evidence against me like Mr. White has. He came to my house and told me he knows my name for some reason. There is no such thing as coincidence. If he's Sal's friend, in any form, then he's stationed at the school because of me.

To watch me.

But why? Sal wouldn't do that to me. He trusts me, right? He's sent watchdogs after other con men; I've seen him do it. But not me. Never me. He said he trusted me, that it was us against the world. He never once sent someone to tail me when I was pulling off cons. Why now?

Because this con means everything, that's why. I quash the little voice in my head. I'd been raised to do this, and Sal still didn't trust me enough to let me pull it off. Kerwin's been following me, has tried to date me to get closer to me, and went out with Merril when he couldn't go out with me. Merril is close to me. He's close to her. He used her as an excuse.

Someone told Kerwin to get as close to me as possible. To watch me as closely as possible.

Sal.

If Kerwin is working for Sal, giving me these flowers is undoubtedly an order from Sal. Kerwin wouldn't give me them on his own. Why would he? Revealing that he knew my name holds no advantage for him. The flower is a message from Sal. An I'm-behind-you-all-the-way message. A you're-doing-great-you're-almost-there message.

Why is Kerwin working for Sal? If Sal hired a young kid to enroll in this school too, planted him here before I came, then that kid must be desperate for money. But Kerwin's been subtle and sharp. He's no off-the-streets informant. I hadn't noticed him following me until he told me himself, and I notice everyone, especially if they're following me. Kerwin hides himself better than Mr. White does. He knows what he's doing. This kind of subtlety is a pro's work. I'd only seen it among guys of Sal's caliber, and after years of training. Lifetimes.

Sal . . . ? No. That's impossible. Sal was with me my whole childhood. The little niggling worm-whisper in my mind can't be right. Kerwin is not like me. Sal did not raise Kerwin; he had no time. Sal was with me practically every day. But that's not all true—he would take "business trips," leave me to be watched by his friends for weeks on end, but I never thought much about it.

He was with Kerwin.

No, that's impossible.

Highly trained con artists raised from a young age to be perfect criminals. It's not true, but if it were, how many more kids are there like us? More puppets for Sal to pull the strings of? How many more have come before us and are being groomed to come after us?

Sal is greedy. Always has been. Settling for just one—just Violet—isn't his style. He's had his fingers in every pie at all times, even if the pie's innards scorch his skin. Just the faint possibility that I'm not the only "Sal kid" makes me want to puke my broccoli all over the table. I clutch at the tablecloth and smile when Mrs. Silverman asks if I want dessert.

"Sure."

I can barely keep the flan down. I make an excuse about homework and go upstairs. Turn my stereo on, the music blaring loudly. Vomit everything into the toilet until my stomach is a shriveled ember. Even with the music all the way up, Mrs. Silverman knows something's wrong. She knocks. I wipe my mouth and open the door.

"Are you all right? Or is this one of those times I should leave you alone?"

Her face is so sincere. More sincere than I could ever fake. I shake my head. "I'm sorry. I'm just nervous. About prom. James. Everything."

We're quiet. The loud music grates on me. I reach for the remote and turn it off.

"Come with me." Mrs. Silverman takes my hand. "I want to show you something."

She leads me into the library, and over to the shelf. *The* shelf. She turns to the wall by it and pushes down on a section. It pops open, the wallpaper lifting to reveal a button. She pushes it, and the bookshelf shifts slowly to the side, leaving a safe built into the wall.

"I know what you must be thinking: James Bond much?" She smiles. "But your father wanted it. He wanted it to open by pulling out certain books, but even I wouldn't agree to something that ridiculous."

"What's in the safe?" I ask. I know exactly what's in the

safe. The fact she's showing it to me has my heart beating and my mouth dry. Does she trust me now? Is she showing it to test me?

"It's just some old painting. It's not worth much, but someday it might be, so your father and I decided to keep it in a secure place. We wanted it to be yours. When we're gone and you're grown with children of your own, it'll be a good investment."

I watch her fingers dance on the keypad of the safe: *2p6pm3ch*. I was right. I guessed right, but the surge of pride I feel is sour and heavy. The safe door swings open, and she slides out the painting, framed in old wood and shrouded by a glass case.

I'd seen the image on the Internet. I'd stared at it sometimes, wondering how such a simple painting could be worth so much. But now I get it. Staring at it in real life, seeing every brushstroke, I finally feel the emotion behind it. Or maybe I'm a different person now, one who can appreciate it. Under a twilight-blush sky sit three people on a bench—a court musician with a ruffled collar and a lute, and a couple. The musician is staring at the couple, hand still poised over the lute as if he's paused to look at them. I can almost hear the final chords of his music petering out into the garden air. The couple kisses, the man drawing the woman into his arms, and the woman presses against him, all balance lost, his arms the only thing holding her up. They're ignoring the musician— ignoring everything around them save for each other and the sudden passion between their lips. A little dog studies the musician in turn, looking lost, or maybe he's pitying the musician and his lack of love.

Michelle Painchaud

"Funny, isn't it? Looking at it always makes me indescribably happy." Mrs. Silverman sighs.

"It's sad."

"But they're kissing! And look at the funny dog!" she protests.

"Yeah." I nod. "But there's a whole world around them, and they're forgetting it."

"It's romantic."

"It feels sad to me. Is their love the only good thing in their lives? Is that why they're throwing themselves at each other so desperately? Maybe they know they don't have long to be together. And the musician—you can see it in his face. He's wondering why he's never had that kind of love. But it's more than that. It's like he knows he'll never have it. Like he's resigned himself to playing romantic music for every other couple in the world, and never for himself."

Mrs. Silverman watches my face, then the painting. She finally smiles.

"I'm glad it moves you so." She returns the painting to the safe and closes the door. She presses the wall button again, and the bookshelf slides back into place.

The night bathes the house in velvet indigo. As I brush my teeth, Marie leans in the doorway.

"That boy Kerwin seemed very familiar."

My hand freezes. I force it to keep moving, and spit the froth into the sink.

"What are you talking about, Marie?"

"I have very sharp hearing." She wipes a bit of stray dust

from the counter. "And a nose for trouble. He is no good. Whatever he said to you, it was no good."

I gargle water to give myself time to answer, but she keeps talking. "You are not Erica."

My stomach flip-flops.

Marie's dark eyes smile, even if her mouth doesn't. "But I know that only in my heart. I prayed to God for answers many years ago. God told me she is dead. You don't have the blood in you, but you bring Mrs. Silverman joy in ways the other girls could not."

I look into the hallway for Mrs. Silverman, but Marie laughs.

"She is asleep. Do not worry."

"Marie, please—"

"I will keep it to myself. You have Erica's spirit. Perhaps it came into you when she died. All I know is that you will not hurt Mrs. Silverman."

I will rip her heart out.

She will hate me for ripping her heart out like all the others.

I close my eyes and let the world spin around me. I stumble, the weakness sudden. Marie leads me to my bed and puts me under the covers. The dolls stare, but it's a sad stare this time. The faint light from the hallway glints in their glass eyes like tears, glass laminating lament. They know. They've always known, have always cried with the knowledge.

Sal,

Confirmed code. Ready for extraction. Prom on Saturday the twenty-third. It's the perfect cover—I leave early and go back to the house, take the surprise.

Michelle Painchaud

You pick me up. We'd be gone in thirty minutes.

I held on. It was hard. But I did it.

Violet,

Will be few blocks from house that night. Cable company van.

Couldn't have done it without you. You'll be the best con artist Vegas's ever seen. Bring passport—London is far. Couldn't get something closer. Ricebowl wanted handover there.

Take your time saying good-bye. I know you've grown to like those people.

You've got a big heart, that's why.

19: SING IT

"What should we talk about today, Erica?" Millicent smiles. I sip my tea. It doesn't taste so bad anymore. "Honesty."

> Sal,
>
> Wanna give Mrs. Silverman note night I leave. For closure. Where's Erica buried?
>
> Vi,
>
> Mile marker twelve on Kalstead Road. Walk two hundred paces till burned barn, a hundred west from there. Under an acacia. Purple blossoms.

Violet screams a lot.
   What are you doing what are you doing what in the hell do you think you're doing
   Erica sings in a tiny voice.
   Home home home, home home, finally home
   I make a choice.

20: CHOOSE IT

Mrs. Silverman does my makeup, fingers sweeping over my eyelids with pale blue powder. She dabs pink gloss over my matte lipstick and rubs just a bit of blush on the apples of my cheeks. She's used to makeup—good at it. When she's done, I'm a different girl, a pretty, honest girl with accented eyes and a healthy glow. She brushes my hair, a hundred strokes, and leaves it hanging around my shoulders with a bit of product rubbed in.

"I feel like a kid's doll."

"You're prettier than a doll," she offers. "Now, let's you get in that dress before James gets here, shall we?"

I squeeze into my dress and she zips it up. I step into heels and her chest swells.

"You're stunning."

"It's obviously not Dad's genes—no five-o'clock shadow."

She laughs. "Wait here. I'll be right back."

I sit on the bed and twist my hands around each other. James. I'm suddenly nervous thinking about him. He's probably dressed up too. Does he like blue? Does he like girls with long hair like this? I never bothered to ask him. Are girlfriends even supposed to ask? I'm so out of my element.

Not for long, though. I'll be back in my element soon, him in my proverbial dust with that wounded-dog look, tearing at my heart, my mind, my every memory of his soft lips and kind eyes—

Mrs. Silverman comes back. She hands me a blue clutch with delicate gold stitching.

"It's amazing." I gape.

"Look inside," she urges.

I open it. Inside is my wallet, a pen, some makeup for touch-ups, and a condom.

"Mom!" I flush.

"It's just in case," she says sternly. "But look under all that."

I shuffle through it, feeling embarrassed about touching the foil of the wrapped condom. Underneath it all, a string of gold glints up at me. I pull, and a necklace with a multifaceted deep blue sapphire pendant spills out.

"Oh my—"

"It was your grandmother's." She smiles.

"I can't wear this."

"You can and you will. It was never meant for me. Your grandmother left it to you in her will. Try not to lose it tonight."

"I don't know what to say."

"Don't say anything. Just bask in the beauty." She pats my back. "Now, let's get you downstairs. That limo should be here any minute. Marie? Have you seen my camera?"

Why am I so nervous? It's just prom. Erica's never been to prom. Violet can't even imagine what one is like. She's assumed it's dancing and food and making out, but that can't be it. There has to be more, with the way people talk about it. The sapphire is cool against my collarbone. It's so heavy. I'm no gem expert, but it has to be worth more than fifty thousand. It's not really mine. It's Erica's. This whole night is her night.

This is the last night.

I watch Marie show Mrs. Silverman how to adjust the settings on her digital camera. Marie sees me staring and smiles, waving.

"You look very hot."

"Thanks." I laugh.

"Erica!" Mrs. Silverman calls from the front door. "They're here!"

"Tell them I'll be right down." I take the stairs two at a time, which is killer in heels. I get my toothbrush from the bathroom and fish my fake passport from the drawer of my desk. I'm ready.

I am Violet Sanders, Sal Sanders's protégé.

I am the best teenage con artist this side of the Mississippi.

I glance out the window—two headlights blare against the twilight. A long white limo stretches up the driveway, and a crowd piles out. Taylor's in a bright purple dress, a sleek ponytail making her look even taller. Cass's hair piles on top of her head in gentle curls, her gold dress blushingly short. Merril wears red, with ruffles, and her hair is pinned back in a bun. Alex, Cass's boyfriend, looks a lot older than he already is in his dark tux. Kerwin stands behind Merril, eyes laughing at me. I'm determined to ignore him tonight.

And then James gets out.

He's obviously still uncomfortable around so many people, but he tries. He stands with them as Mom sweeps out of the house and starts taking pictures. His tuxedo makes his height more dignified. His hair is combed and pulled back in a little ponytail. He smiles nervously when Mrs. Silverman talks to him.

"They're waiting for you." Marie walks up and nods as if to comfort me. "It'll be one of the best nights of your life."

It'll be the last night of Erica's life.

"Take care of her." I hold Marie's hand. "Please."

"Are you going somewhere?" she asks lightly.

"No. Of course not." I squeeze her hand before I walk down to join everyone else. Cass flutters around me, cooing at my dress and necklace. Merril can't take her eyes off my necklace. Taylor whoops appreciatively and slaps James on the back, and he looks lost for words. His mouth opens, then closes, then opens again.

"Oy, quit with the fish act." Taylor laughs. "Just say she looks pretty."

"You look beautiful," he finally manages.

Cass and Merril do an *oh-how-romantic* sigh.

I glance my hand over his ponytail. "Like the hairstyle."

"I was going to cut it, but that seemed like a compromise." He smirks.

"Makes you look like an eighteenth-century dandy."

"Even better." He motions to his pants. "Do you like my pantaloons, madam? Or how about my beauty mark?" He gestures to an invisible dot on his cheek, and I laugh and lean up to kiss him there instead.

Mrs. Silverman's smile is so big, I feel like it'll fall off her face. "All right, everyone squeeze in together. I want one good picture of you and the sunset."

Then, after an onslaught of solo pictures, Mrs. Silverman hugs me one last time.

"Have fun."

"I will."

"Come home safely."

"I will." I smile. I lie.

She pulls me in for another long tight hug, this one wordless. I breathe in her scent, watch the sparkle of the tiny tears that squeeze out of her eyes. Her heartbeat thuds against my chest. It's slow, heavy. With every beat I feel the brunt of her emotions, all mixed together, collapsing on me, absorbing through my skin.

She doesn't want to let go. But she's so happy—blindly happy—that I'm alive to enjoy this night. She feels that if she lets go, I'll be gone for good. She's had that fear every time she's hugged me. Every time she's hugged every fake Erica.

"I love you," I murmur. *That* is not a lie.

"I love you, Erica Jane Silverman." She hiccups, then urges me toward the limo. We pile in and choose our seats on the expansive leather, and Marie and Mrs. Silverman wave until we leave the driveway.

"Nice wheels." I take in the ambient LED lighting—it's a soft green, but the lights cycle through the rainbow slowly.

"Minibar." Alex gestures to the side, near the radio controls. "What'll you be having?"

"Um, Shirley Temple?" I try.

"Yeah, fuck that, gimme one of those little airplane booze bottles." Taylor points. Alex passes her one, and we watch as she downs it in one fell gulp. "What're you looking at?"

"They do breath tests if you look hammered, I'm sure." Cass frowns.

"It's just a bottle. Don't worry." Taylor waves. "I can always sneak in the back. 'S not like I haven't crashed the country club before."

Kerwin looks perturbed. Merril pats his knee. "Don't worry. She's just the resident badass."

"Was that a compliment, Whiny?" Taylor quirks a brow.

"One-time deal, only good for tonight," Merril snaps.

"Give me orange juice and vodka," Cass orders Alex, and looks to James. "What do you want?"

"I'm okay. Don't really drink that much."

"It's prom!" she insists. "It's the one time you actually should be drinking."

"Someone's gotta play sober for you guys." He shrugs.

I rest my head on his shoulder. "I won't drink either. Long night. I want to remember all of it."

"Oh!" Cass nearly slops her drink as she puts it in the cup holder. "Did you give her the corsage, James?"

"Right." He pulls something from his breast pocket: a spray of light pink blossoms attached with ribbon and lace.

"Wow. For me?"

He nods and takes my wrist. His fingers are warm, and I can see a faint blush on his face as he wraps the ribbon around my wrist and ties it.

"How many Cabbage Patch Kids did you kill to get this?" I smirk.

His nervous blush fades. "Only four."

"Only four." I try to sound impressed. "Thank you. It's beautiful."

"I got one for you, too, Taylor." He leans over and takes out a red flower bunch, tying it to her wrist. Taylor's face matches the flowers' hue.

"Are you . . . *blushing*?" Merril peeks at Taylor.

"No! Shut up!" She rips her hand away and tightens the corsage herself. "Thanks, man. It's nice."

"How come he gets to bring two chicks to prom and I only get one?" Alex laments. Cass elbows him—hard—and he clears his throat. "I mean, you're the best, baby. You're, like, two completely different girls in one."

Even Taylor barks a laugh.

The limo speeds down the highway. We pull off, the exit ramp flashing by in cement. Above it are the lights of the Strip, glowing with exuberance, hundreds of neon shades blending in a dizzying haze. Hotels tower as boxes of gold, triangles of purple, and fountains throw up water and sparkling lights. Somewhere, in a run-down apartment not far from the Strip, Sal is putting on a disguise for the millionth time. For the millionth trip. Millionth *escape*.

"You look even better." James's low voice yanks me into the present. "You look even better with that little smile."

"I'm starting to think you're buttering me up to get something later," I tease.

He's blushing again. "N-no. Not that. Not yet. It's too soon."

"Virgin." Taylor coughs the word between sips of a second mini bottle of vodka.

"Some conversations are meant to be private," James says, mortified.

"Man, c'mere and quit being stubborn. I'll give you some tips." She pulls him forward.

"I don't want any of your tips!"

While Taylor wrestles with him, Cass leans over and plants a kiss on my cheek.

"I'm so glad you're here, Erica. I never thought . . . well, you know. You being here is a big surprise. A great surprise. Stay with your old parents a month longer and you would've missed prom. What a coincidence."

"Coincidences are for schmucks."

She laughs and sips her drink. "And everybody's a schmuck."

Outside my window, the Strip fades into the distance as we head to the country club. I understand it now—why Sal keeps coming back, why he pines for Vegas when we leave. He's a moth, a great gray moth that dominates the night, makes it his own. The darkness is his world, but the lights of the Strip are his fascination, his ideal, his hope for the future. Everything bright. Everything rich and full of good things, like the brochures promise.

"Hey," James murmurs. His voice is in my ear, and I start, smiling.

"Hi."

"I lost you for a second there," he says breathlessly.

Did you? Have you even really found me to begin with? I force my smile wider and press my lips to his, hard. He's so nervous—his bottom lip trembles, and I bite to still it. He sucks in a breath and weaves his fingers through my hair. I can hear jeers, faintly. But it doesn't matter. Only this second matters. Only his lips, his smell, his taste.

There can only be this kiss. This moment. There is no future. There will be a good-bye, as good a farewell as I can give him. I need to disappear from his life—a clean quiet cut. He needs to stay here, graduate, start his band, add more members, get a CD out, go on tour, go to college, and meet a nice girl. An honest girl, a truly kind girl.

He does not need to love the girl who never was.

"You'll never lose me," I murmur as we part, my lips sore, his bitten red. His blue eyes are dark. He tenses—the muscles in his arms flexing. He wants to say something.

"Say it," I whisper. "Say what you want to."

He just pulls me in for another kiss.

Bluewell Country Club glimmers with warm windows and thrumming music filtering from the open doors. A banner above the entrance hall reads, WELCOME ST. PETER'S PROM CLASS OF 2013! Chaperone teachers are dressed in black-tie attire, taking invitations and checking off names from clipboard lists. Our class pulses around us as one mass of fancy dresses and waves of clashing cologne and perfume. Lavender, jasmine, vanilla, spice. Sweat, too, the heavy scent perfume tries so hard to hide. Couples hold hands, groups of girls huddle together and groups of boys shift awkwardly in their suits and mock each other for it.

Kerwin looks downright dashing in his suit. Every girl, with a date or dateless, is calling to him and waving. Merril bristles and pulls him to her side. He locks eyes with me and then looks away. Cheerily. Happily. Like nothing ever happened. Like he didn't give me those flowers to let me know he's onto me.

"Why is he even bothering?" Taylor sneers.

But he can't hurt me anymore—tonight I'm invincible, because tomorrow I'm gone.

The buffet tables are laden with salads and soups, sweet-and-sour pork, roast beef and mushroom Alfredo. Taylor takes an entire plate of just garlic bread as her appetizer, and Merril snorts something about "breath" and "won't make much of a difference." Taylor flips her off and adds Tabasco sauce on a slice. We have our own table, near the DJ. We watch him set up, cables and laptops and earphones. I smirk and lean in to James.

"Ever think about being a DJ?"

He takes a sip of water and snorts. "You have to know how to work a crowd."

"What'd you call the recital then? Making that dramatic exit and all?" Cass asks. "My mom's friends were there—talked about it for a full week."

"They were talking about the sprinklers, Cass," Merril corrects. "Someone pulled the fire alarm. An emergency trumps a dumb piano recital." She glances at James. "No offense."

He laughs. "None taken."

Taylor's smug smile lasts until dessert rolls around. She takes two forks and piles them with cheesecake before turning to us.

"Open up, you two."

"Why?" James dodges a creamy fork.

"You're both skeletons. I'm trying to help you put some meat on."

I laugh and take both bites off the forks, relishing the taste. I'd eaten all the roast beef I could handle, and the richest desserts. Violet is rolling in euphoria, and Erica is fretting over how the calories will mess with her waist. Their voices are faint. Fainter than they were when I first started this con. Is it the dark static trance music wafting from the speakers as the DJ gears up? Is it the way James's hand interweaves with mine under the white tablecloth, sending spirals of warmth through my veins? Or is it the bitter cold in my stomach, the dense pit of nothingness, a black hole hungering for anything happy? Is it the dread circling me like a scavenger, waiting for the corpse to perish?

This is my last night of living like a normal person.

I smile and pull James to his feet the moment the music starts. The dance floor, a wide polished space near the tables, is completely empty. A few people edge around it, waiting for someone to be the first to take the plunge and dance.

James is hesitant. "I dance like crap."

"We all do." I smirk and put my arms around his neck. "There's a trick to it."

"And that is?"

I relax against his chest, the tempo of the beat too fast for slow dancing. But I'll do what I want. This is my night.

"You just have to pretend. Pretend you're someone else—a pro dancer. A guy who frequents clubs. Get in the mind-set, think like he might think."

"And then what?" He raises a brow.

"Your body will follow your mind's lead."

"What about the heart?"

"Hearts don't matter." I smile. More people filter onto the dance floor, and our slow dance looks out of place. James sighs and presses his forehead to mine.

"Hearts matter. You know that."

I just smile wider and make space between us. I spin out and back into him and dance like I've seen pretty girls in clubs do—arms in the air, moving sensuously and slowly to the beat. He stands there, then finally puts his hands on my hips, turning me, guiding me, doing nothing but swaying with me and burying his face in the crook of my neck.

"I knew," he murmurs. I can hear him over the music only because he says it right in my ear. "Right after we talked in the mall, I knew."

"Knew what?"

"That you were going to be the first girl to break my heart."

My breath catches. I force the smile now. "I haven't broken anything yet, right?"

"You will. Someday. But everybody breaks everything.

For now we're fantastic. It's just, the better we get, the harder I realize the fall will be."

You've already broken my heart, James. Or I've broken it because of you. To make this pain less. To make this night, this parting, hurt less. That coin flip made me happy and ragged all at once—sealed my fate like a cement block over an open casket. I would love you. I fought it, and it still won in the end. It's the one thing I can't fake.

Who does he like more? I wonder. *Violet or Erica?*

It won't matter after tonight, Violet shrugs.

But the question will haunt you until you die, Erica whispers.

Neither of them knows I've already made up my mind. I keep it to myself and peck James on the cheek.

"Need something to drink."

"I'm not dancing if you're not here." He frowns.

"I'll get Taylor to come join you." I wink, and before he can protest, I elbow through the dancing crowd. Taylor's not hard to miss—her jet black ponytail standing out over the blonds and brunettes.

"Hey." I grab her arm.

She turns, two cups of punch in hand, and passes me one. "Drink up, Fakey. Long night ahead of us."

I down the punch gratefully, the slight burning aftertaste a dead giveaway. "You spiked it?"

She snickers and tucks an empty mini bottle of vodka into her clutch. My stomach twists—I need to be level-headed. Alcohol isn't going to help my thinking, and this is the one night I need to think. I consider going into the bathroom to throw it up, but I quash that thought. Alcohol moves fast, hits faster. I clutch at her arm.

"James is over there. Dancing alone." I point.

Her brow wrinkles. "Whaddya want me to do about it?"

"Entertain him." I smirk. "Do that hard-to-get-bitch thing you do so well."

"I can't dance."

"I can't either."

She snorts. "I'm not the happy-joy-joy type who can fake it like you."

"Fake it," I repeat softly. "Look, please? Just dance with him or talk with him for a bit. I have to go do something."

She heaves a sigh and pats me on the shoulder. "Fine. But just this one time, and just for you."

I watch her shove dancers out of her way to get to James. I feel a familiar viselike grip on my arm. Merril laughs and leans in to me.

"My feet are freakin' killing me already!"

"Mine too," I lament. "But you looked good out there."

"Are you kidding? You and James totally stole the spotlight." She giggles.

"I've gotta go the bathroom."

"Oh! I'll come with you!"

"And by bathroom, I mean 'the curb outside for fresh air.'"

She leads me through the doors and away from the thumping music. I look back once, Taylor awkwardly leading James to the table. A sardonic half argument plays at their lips, and seeing it makes me smile.

Everything is back to normal. Revert.

People linger on the sidewalk, taking in the cold air. Older kids smoke a good ways away. Merril leads me to a bench near the golf course and we sit. I take deep breaths, and Merril adjusts her bodice, wincing.

"How's Kerwin?" I ask. "Dance-wise, I mean."

A grimace. "He's okay. I mean, nothing special."

I quirk an eyebrow and smirk. "A month ago you would've

shouted that he was a dancing god, and then rolled out a red carpet for him."

"Hey, I can grow up too, you know. I totally got out of that phase. We're more down-to-earth now."

If my hunch about him is right, he'll leave when I do. Tonight.

She wrinkles her nose. "You think you and James are going to last?"

"Nothing lasts, Mer."

She sighs and lays her head on my shoulder. "I know. But you don't have to say it. Saying it makes it too real."

We enjoy the silence for a moment longer before a shriek of laughter and the rustling of a nearby bush makes us look. In the faint light from the streetlamp, I barely make out girl's and boy's legs sticking out from the bushes. I clear my throat. A squeak resounds, and the legs disappear to be replaced by heads.

"Cass?" Merril's eyes widen.

Cass smiles, hair riddled with leaves. Below her, Alex sits up quickly.

"Fancy meeting you here." Cass stands, adjusting her skirt as she frees herself from the bush. "Alex, are you just gonna lie there?"

"Yes." His voice reverberates from the bush. "Come back in when you're done talking."

Merril and I shoot each other a look. Cass fluffs her hair out. "Well? What are you two doing out here?"

"Too stuffy in there." Merril sighs. "And they were playing Lil Jon. Ew."

Cass laughs and sits on my right side, leaning her head onto my shoulder. Now both shoulders are occupied by tired prom-girl heads.

"I'm feeling a little sick," I say, moaning. "And I forgot my birth control."

It's a lie, but it gets both of their attention.

"Really?" Cass's eyes widen. "I didn't know you and James were so far already."

"There're taxis just down the road." Merril points. "I mean, teachers won't let us off the grounds, but it's just a few yards. We could sneak to Safeway, buy some stuff."

"Safeway? In our prom dresses?" Cass laughs. "We'd be so out of place. We can get all that stuff at the hotel. Besides, Erica can't leave yet. They're going to announce prom queen."

"You're kidding, right?" I fidget with my clutch. "There's no way I can be queen."

"Erica, get real. You're the prodigal returned daughter or whatever. We grew up with you missing. Now that you're back, it's a dead giveaway you'll be prom queen."

"I don't deserve it. You do, Cass. Or you, Merril."

"I would have a heart attack and die of joy if I were queen." Merril purses her lips and pats on some lip balm. "I don't wanna die this young."

Cass smiles and helps me up. "You two, go inside. Get crowned, dance, get crazy. The night's really young."

"And you?"

"I've got some unfinished business." She winks and nods at the bush. "But I'll be in to see you crowned."

Merril rolls her eyes as we get up.

Me? Prom queen? I shake my head to clear it. That's wrong. Revert. It all needs to revert, as if I were never here. I rummage in my purse and take out a piece of paper and a tiny pen. I scribble:

I hereby officially give the crown of St. Peter's prom queen to Merril Breton.

Erica Silverman

Merril looks at me, then at the paper. Those huge eyes of hers get even bigger. "Rica, what are you playing at?"

I put on my best smile. "I really do have to go. I'm not feeling well."

"I'll come with you! You don't need to do this! We'll get medicine and then come back in time—"

"That crown isn't mine, Merril. My time to shine is over. I've taken up the attention of this town for years. I'm stepping down. It's your turn. Your moment."

"Rica, what's going on? Why are you being like this?"

"You don't want to be prom queen?"

"I do!" she answers immediately, too quickly. Her desire is palpable, sweet desperation in her words. "But, if it's yours first—"

I clasp at my sapphire necklace. "Mom gave me this tonight. It was my grandma's. She left it in her will for me. So it was never Mom's to begin with. This crown, queen thing, is the same. You get that, right?"

She scrunches her face, an argument on the tip of her tongue.

"I'll be right back. Just going to get some Tylenol. I'll be back before you know it."

Merril nods reluctantly. I push her toward the open doors.

"Go on. You've gotta give Kerwin at least one more dance."

And distract him while I make my getaway.

Her smile finally feels real, and she walks into the music and the lights. I take a breath and turn to the darkness. They might not accept the note, but when they find out I'm gone and Merril shows it to them, they'll have no choice but to crown her, as per my wish. I'm the kidnapped girl. They'll do it for me. The teachers are watching me. I wait. Mrs. Anderson is too old to stand long in one place, and Mr. Gregory is too hungry-looking, chewing on his toothpick like it's gum. They'll go in and switch shifts very soon.

Five minutes, and they both walk in together. Sometimes I love my gut feelings.

I get up and start down the sidewalk, to the darkness and clamor of the main street.

"Rica!"

I turn. Cass peeks her head from the bushes, a bright hickey just beginning to solidify on her neck, her cheeks flushed.

"It was nice. Getting to know you."

The choice of words is so final. Her eyes glint, a little wet. She knows I'm leaving, and not temporarily. She's sharper than she lets on. Neither of us is skilled at good-byes. I smile.

"You too."

She ducks back into the bushes, and I turn on my heel and stride behind a hedge. A cab waits just outside the mall, scouring for late-night stragglers. I tap on the window and slide in.

"Home Depot, please."

The cab driver puts out his cigarette and chuckles. "And what is a fancy-dressed girl like you going to buy there?"

"I need gloves, a pickax, a shovel, a flashlight, and twenty glow sticks. Let's get on with it. The night is only so young for so long."

Home Depot's parking lot has fewer eyes watching it than prom.

When I was thirteen, Sal taught me how to break in to and hot-wire any car made earlier than 2006, using a nail file, the heel of a shoe, and gum.

The road goes on forever.

I know that's not true. It has to stop somewhere: the edge of a sea cliff, a gravel dead end in a peaceful neighborhood, or the cracked fissure of a canyon leading down into the earth itself. I tap my fingers on the wheel of the stolen Range Rover and pull onto Kalstead Road. A hula girl doll sways her hips on the dashboard.

I slow at mile marker twelve and pull over. The road is dead. I lace the bag with the pickax and glow sticks over my arm and grab the shovel in my right hand and the flashlight in my left.

I'm being followed.

I wait fourteen seconds. The glimmer of headlights in the distance is from the same direction I came from, but they cut out when they crest the hill.

"Should've turned the lights off earlier, Kerwin," I sing-song to no one, and start into the darkness.

The moon is full, shining like a cold sun on the scrub trees and brush. Every few feet I crack a glow stick and drop it on the ground. A trail. Hansel uses fluorescent green in our world, our time. Hansel is going to dig up Gretel.

The shovel slows me down. The damn dress slows me down. I'd traded the high heels for gardening galoshes, but the new pleather rubs blisters on my feet. Just one mile and a third. Push through the pain. Push through it just like you've pushed through time, life, people. Blowing holes in them, passing them off to others, deflecting their attempts at real friendships—

I trip. The sparse grasses give way to broken fence. Rusting barbwire clings like vines to the posts. Beyond is the burned barn Sal mentioned. The outside is charred black, blistering where fire consumed it. The roof is a half fang, standing proud and stabbing at the moon. I turn west, the direction the moon is setting in. Follow the moon. I would be afraid. Trekking through darkness makes people afraid. But it's never really dark here. The lights from the Strip might be faint, but I can see the glow on the horizon. I'm not really alone.

Shards of cow skull mark a coyote's den. A mother grouse leads her babies across the cool hard-packed sand, clucking comforting things. They scatter when they hear me coming. I look at the ground, watching for scorpions and keeping my ears open for the faint hiss of any snake.

My eyes strain against the darkness until the spindly branches of my goal poke my vision. The acacia isn't blooming anymore, a great blanket of molding flowers spreading beneath its twisted roots. Purple shows faintly through the browns and greens of decomposition. It's an old tree, three times my height. Abandoned ravens' nests cling to the naked branches, the trunk hollowed by owl holes and bug pits. Everyone has taken advantage of the tree. I put my bag and shovel down, and hike my dress up.

Thirteen years ago, Gerald carried a little girl's dead body here.

I hate it, but I slide into his mind-set—where would I bury the body if I were him? On the west side of the tree? No, the sand is packed too hard there. Definitely not the south; a huge root blocks most of that area. The softest patch of dirt, easiest to dig in, and with the least roots in the way. Northeast.

I double around, shake Gerald out of my head, and grip the pickax. The first strike is hard, the iron spike puncturing the dirt crust. The clink of the pickax against sand and roots is the only sound in the wasteland. The wind whistles faintly, snaking around cacti and through the brush. This is the land of the dead—I'm the only one here. The Strip, Vegas, is just a few miles away, and yet I'm the only one out here. I am alone and surrounded by people all at the same time.

My phone rings, the orchestra ringtone I picked for James piercing my brain. No. Not now. Not anymore. I wipe dirt off my face with my shoulder and reach for the shovel. Again, the orchestra rings. Stop, James. I'm not her anymore. She's below me, just below me in sand and mud—

He rings five times, a tired silence settling after the last ring. I break into the torn-up dirt, shoveling the excess over my shoulder. Three inches. It's gotta be more than that, otherwise the coyotes would've gotten her. Four feet? Maybe the full six. I don't know if I can dig that far down. But I have to try.

I have to find her.

Someone has to bring her home.

Sand spills down my dress and itches my skin. Sweat smears my makeup as I get a foot down, two feet. Scorpions scatter, my shovel edge smeared with green guts and pieces of pincers. I'm sorry. I'm sorry, but I have to get down there. I'm sorry, move on to something better—

Taylor's ringtone resounds, a hard rock song. Once. Twice. Go away, Taylor. It's over now. I can't be Violet anymore either.

Water. I reach into the bag and gulp at the bottle greedily. It spills down my chest and washes away the sand, darkens the blue silk. This isn't my dress. I tear at it, the silk resilient. This isn't my dress; it's hers—

I grab the shovel and stab into the earth, bring it up, fling it into the air and make it fly. Merril's ringtone, the sound of bells. I squeeze my eyes shut and fling more sand. More sand. More dirt. Somewhere in this dirt is the one girl everyone's been looking for. Somewhere in this dirt is closure, Marie, *closure*—

The sapphire slides on my sweaty neck. I unclasp it and throw it into the bag. Too slow. More speed. More dirt. My arms cry burning tears, the shovel a blur as I push harder. I have to see her. Just once. I have to find her, bring her back to the people who want her, to the hole in the shape of her in each of their hearts—

James's orchestra rings.

"Stop! Leave me alone!"

Three feet. Too deep to reach down and shovel. Rocks. I throw rocks in the bottom, the biggest and heaviest I can find. Use them as a ladder, in and out. I'm not digging wide enough. I'm not digging fast enough, I'll never find her—

The airy ringtone I'd chosen for Mrs. Silverman pierces my panting.

"I don't want to talk!" I scream, the shovel biting into the dirt with more force. "I never liked any of you! I never liked you to begin with!"

A lie. Lies on top of lies, dirt on top of dirt—

"It was just a con!" I laugh, my breathing heavy, the shovel-fuls of dirt getting even heavier. "All of it was just a big fucking lie, and you all fell for it!"

Did they really . . .

"Every last one of them, blinded by the pretty face and the pretty clothes and the pretty memories; outside is all that counts, always. Just make your outside shine and they love you, they'll love you!"

Merril rings.

"You never liked me!"

Mrs. Silverman rings.

"You loved a dead girl!"

James.

"You never f-fucking loved me! I'm not real, none of it is, it's all a stupid lie—"

The shovel's too heavy. Too slow. Fingers scrape at the bottom, a mole, a rat in the maze, vultures, something disgusting—

Something hard, smooth. I sift the sand off. The moonlight shines down; a soft wind spirals into the hole and dries my tears. Two eyes peek out at me, two dark holes. The face skin is brown and leathery, dry and smooth despite the deep wrinkles. The mouth hangs open, a few baby teeth just barely wiggling loose. Fine, pale, angel-blonde hair laced with roots and dust falls around her wrinkled shoulders, the bones sharp. Little arms are crossed over each other, hands clasped together. On the leathery wrists, two deep cuts pry the skin apart, darkness inside.

She stares right through my shouted lies.

"Erica."

The desert sand has preserved her—a perfect mummy. She smiles that baby-tooth smile up at me, the same smile in the photo album: friends, Slip'n' Slides, pools, laughter, and dreams transform into a ballerina, a girl who can do anything, a girl who never, *ever* dies.

Michelle Painchaud

I scrabble to haul myself out of the pit and to my now-silent phone. Seventeen missed calls. I look in my phone book, for a certain number I'd stolen from Mrs. Silverman's phone.

It rings twice before a tired gruff voice picks up.

"Hello?"

"Mr. White." I wipe my eyes. "I found her."

"Found who? Who is this?"

"I found the girl you've been looking for all this time."

There's rustling as he gets out of bed. "Erica? Is that you?"

"Sure." I give a watery chuckle. "Both of us are here."

"What are you talking about? Where is 'here'?"

"Kalstead Road. Mile marker twelve. I left a trail of glow sticks."

"Erica—"

The world blurs, my eyes pour. "C-come and bring her home, M-Mr. White."

I hang up and look into the sky, trying to force the tears back into their ducts. I need clear vision and clearer thoughts. Deep breaths. Just like we practiced.

I put my tools away, brush sand off Erica's face to see her properly. My voice, though small, is eerily loud among the sands and cacti.

"Come out, Kerwin. I know you're there."

There's a crack in the brush. I don't turn around.

"Guess I wasn't as smooth as I could've been." He sighs.

"Tell me once and for all," I murmur, staring into Erica's hollow eyes. "Who are you?"

"Sal said you'd go for the body instead. I kept telling him: 'No way, not Violet. She's your best student. She'll definitely go for the painting before the girl.' Looks like I lost that bet."

"You've called him, then."

"Yeah." Kerwin yawns. "He'll be here. Even if you change your mind and go for the painting, he'll still be pissed."

I stand and brush sand off my dress. "Your real name?"

"Darren Morris. Nice to meet you."

"The accent was faked?"

He drops the accent. "Yeah. Accents are my forte, like math is yours."

"No wonder I couldn't find anything on you. Where did he raise you?"

"Colorado. Boulder."

"He teach you the Grover trick first?"

"Breadbasket version."

I scoff. "That's a hard one to pull off."

"He figured I could do it."

I face him and laugh, the sound bitter. "How many more of us are there?"

"I don't know. He never talked about any of them except you."

"So in a weird fucked-up way, you're like my brother."

"And you're like my little sister."

The desert wind blows, cold and biting. I hug myself and shiver.

"Did you have fun pretending to be normal?" I ask.

His eyes darken, voice softening. "Yeah. Too much."

"Look, I just want to go. I don't want to be a part of this shit anymore. Just let me go."

"I can't, Violet. You know that."

A figure cuts through the bushes, scraping thorns announcing his arrival. He always makes an entrance, and against the black sands and white moonlight, this is no exception. The stolen cable company uniform, the flashy rings, hair slicked back and slightly balding toward the front. His shoulders are broad, age wrinkling him with dignity around his blue eyes.

No one moves.

No one can move. Sal ingrained it into us that we stand straight, tall, and proud when he's around. That we look him in the eye and answer in clear concise words. Especially during a job.

He's *smiling.*

"It feels like ages since I've seen you, Vi."

"Three months," I say.

"That's, what, a fourth of a year?" He shrugs. "Can't be kept away from my star student for that long. It's cruel. Inhuman."

He walks closer. Circles me, the grave. Nods at Kerwin as he passes.

"Can I ask what you're doing out here, Vi?"

"As long as I get to ask a question afterward."

"Course." Sal smiles. "Fair is fair."

"I came to bring the body back to the family. They deserve closure. Erica deserves to go home."

Sal nods and motions for me to ask my question.

"Why didn't you tell me about Kerwin? Why didn't you trust me?"

"It looks like I didn't trust you with good reason." He points at Erica's body. "I understand living this con might've messed with your mind, your priorities. But I taught you better than this, didn't I? The job first. Everything else later."

"How many more kids were there before us?" I bark. Kerwin flinches at my tone. *I* flinch at my tone. I never talk to Sal like this. Never. Sal puts a finger to his lips, as if he's thinking, and then shrugs.

"Let's not talk about them. None of them are as good as

you, Vi. None of them had that inherent talent, that mystical potential people are born with once in a lifetime. You're the clear gem, and they are the costume jewelry fakes."

Kerwin shifts, a shadow passing over his face.

"We're here because you're not where you're supposed to be." Sal smiles at me.

"I'm not stealing the painting. I don't want it. No one should have it. It's Mrs. Silverman's, not ours."

"She's well-off already. She won't miss it."

"Don't try to persuade me, Sal. I've made up my mind. I'm not stealing that painting. I'm not doing anything for you anymore."

Sal's face doesn't change—a masterful control keeping it the same. A tendril of sand blows by. Kerwin clenches his fists.

"You'll give me the code, then," Sal says.

"I don't know it."

"You said you did."

"I was mistaken." I pour everything into the lie, but Sal still sees right through it, smile growing toothy.

"So this is your final decision?"

No more conning. No more lies. No more nothingness.

"Yes."

There's another silence. Sal paces, adjusts something in his pocket. Nods to himself. Mumbles. My eyes dart around for an exit, but Sal's too close. Kerwin's too close. I can't get away from both of them.

It hits me when Sal takes the gun out like one would take out a pen. Calmly. Without thought.

I'm not going to get away this time.

As Sal steps closer, barks at Kerwin to restrain me, I realize I knew, the moment I left prom, I wasn't going to come back from digging up this grave. The feeling uncoils, cold ribbons of acceptance. I'll never leave Sal. The con world. They won't let me leave alive. I've seen Sal do it a hundred times—call his "people" and tell them to clean up a "mess." Someone who knew too much would go missing in a matter of hours, never to be found.

I'll be one of them, buried in this unforgiving desert. Probably right next to Erica.

I kick at Kerwin, but he's so much taller and stronger. He holds my arms behind my back and forces me to my knees by kicking the back of them.

"Kerwin, please. You don't have to listen to him. You don't have to do this."

He kneels with me, mouth near my ear. "I'm not as brave as you."

Sal walks in front of me. Loads the gun—a revolver—one bullet at a time.

"In the days of the old West, they'd shoot thieves in the hands. Right through the palm. Murderers shot through once in the middle of the forehead. Execution-style," he says.

I can't stop the whimper that tears from me. Sal smiles at it.

"Vi, I'm not gonna kill you. You know I'd never kill you. I'm just not the killing type. But what I *am* gonna do"—the cold barrel of the gun rests against my kneecap—"is ask you politely, one last time, for the code."

I squirm, trying to get purchase on the sandy ground, but Kerwin has his leg on my feet. He's shaking too. I can hear him swallow as the gun presses harder into my knee.

"I've been shot a few times." Sal sighs. "And trust me when I say that the kneecap is the most painful. You'll never be able to walk right again. Where do you think I got this little limp?"

The tears start. "S-Sal, please—"

"Ah-ah." He puts a finger up to my lips. "No begging. I never taught you to beg. You're better than that."

"I d-don't want to be shot."

"Tell me what the code is, and this all goes away." Sal smiles. "It's just a code, Vi. It's just a painting from one woman who won't miss it. You're willing to get shot because of her? Do you think she'd want you to get shot defending some silly painting?"

The exertion of digging the grave closes the distance and lunges for my vital points. My arms droop. My head feels so heavy. I can't fight. I can't move.

"Tell me what the code is, Violet." Sal's voice raises a notch. It's not much, but it's the loudest I've ever heard his voice go. "You want out of the con life? Fine. You can have that. But you need to tell me the code. This is your last chance."

Honesty.

"It's just money," Kerwin whispers in my ear. "Just give it to him. It's not worth getting hurt."

I've already gotten hurt.

Sal's finger pulls the trigger in slow motion, every millimeter taking years. It's going to hurt. It's going to hurt, but not as much as James hurt. Not as much as Taylor hurt. Not as much as Cass and Merril and Mrs. Silverman hurt. Leaving them hurt more.

Lying to them hurt more.

"Freeze!"

The word rings clear, then there are clamors of "Police!" and "Put your hands up!"

Sal jerks the gun away and points it a man in a trench coat: Mr. White.

Sal's gun squeezes three bullets off. Mr. White ducks, and from somewhere else several guns scream at once.

Sal gives a grunt and collapses onto the sand. It melds around his tracksuit. I scream—scream for him. Kerwin shouts his name, a keening scream. Children crying for a father dying.

The silence after he hits the ground echoes in my chest.

From behind Mr. White step two men in uniform—police. Kerwin bolts across the sand, the police sprinting after him. Mr. White rushes to me and cradles me in his arms.

"Did he get you?"

I glance at the motionless lump on the ground, my heart twisting around. "Is he . . . ?"

"I don't know." Mr. White shakes his head. "But you're okay now."

I give a wretched laugh, short and biting, and exhaustion starts to darken the edges of my vision.

"Erica's over there," I say breathlessly.

He nods. "Good work."

I'm going to faint. My head lolls back. "Violet."

Mr. White looks down at me. "What?"

"That's my real name."

The shouts of the officers fade. Mr. White's face and the sky framing it fade. The motionless body of the man who raised me fades. Blissful silence.

21: FIND IT

My new roommate watches as I unpack. The drawers are rusted, hard to get open. I shove my clothes in and throw the suitcase on the creaking bed.

"So." She snaps her gum. "What're you in for?"

"Technically? Grand theft auto. They gave me a year."

Her eyebrows quirk, a little impressed. She adjusts her sweatpants. "Guess what I'm in for."

I turn and study her face. Amber skin, thin lips. Pear-shaped but muscular. Her hair is a dead giveaway—kept in a low ponytail. Not vain.

"Definitely not shoplifting," I finally say.

"Aggravated assault."

"Your stepdad?"

"Yeah." She looks perturbed. "How'd you know?"

I smile and fold back the covers. They're thin and used and smell like strong bleach.

"I'm just good at reading people."

Los Amos Juvenile Detention Center is in the middle of nowhere. A small town is to the south, with a grand total of two blocks of main street. I drove though it in a police car on my way here. The officer pointed out the bank and laughed, telling me not to rob it. Like I would con a tiny place like that.

Like I would ever con again after what I'd been through.

The girls in this place are in for shoplifting, substance abuse or possession, and breaking and entering. Those are the top three. The food is little more than slop, the exercise yard is a seventy-by-seventy fenced-in mud pit, and the guards like to blow whistles in your ears, but it could be worse.

I've been in worse.

We all wear the same gray sweat suit. There's the same hierarchy you'd find anywhere—the bullies and those who allow themselves to be bullied. The really intimidating and abusive girls are kept in a separate wing.

I pick at my stew. Angela, my roommate, squirms.

"This is the fourth day in a row we've had stew."

I shrug and sip broth. Angela drops her spoon.

"Oh *shit*, Bren's coming this way."

I glance up. Bren—tall, wiry, a tattoo curving down her arm—approaches our table flanked by two other girls of almost equal height. Bren was—is—in a gang, has more connections to the outside than she can count, and runs the import of cigs, pills, makeup, decent tampons, and everything a girl might need. In exchange for equal favors.

She looks me over. "New girl."

"Bren." I smile. "I'm Violet. It's nice to meet you."

"Heard you were a con artist. The one pretending to be that missing girl."

"You heard right."

I feel Angela shrink away from me, like she doesn't want to be noticed. Bren takes my fork off my plate, stabs a piece of meat, and eats it. She chews slowly, thinking, and swallows.

"Lock picking?"

I nod. "Anything made before 2012."

"Hacking?"

"Not so good with computers, but I can turn them on."

"Fighting?"

"None of that, really."

"People?"

"Oh." I smile wider. "I'm the best at people. Would you like a demonstration?"

Bren narrows her eyes, but jerks her head at one of her lackeys. The girl steps up, a willing victim. She's wide, wider than most girls. Ridiculously huge thighs. Her rib cage is abnormally large; she breathes slow and even. Once a competitive swimmer, definitely. Her eyes flicker when I meet her gaze. A twitch of her jaw. Something to hide, but not from me. From Bren. Her hair is short and unkempt, and her fingernails are clean but bitten ragged.

"Pills," I say finally. "You used to swim. Liked it, too. But you weren't quite good enough, were you? So you took something to up your game one day. And the day after that. And the day after that."

The girl's face darkens.

Bren's eyebrow goes up. "That all?"

"She's still doing pills." I nod at her hands. "Uppers. Don't know where she's getting them, but she's taken some recently. Haven't you?"

"Shut up, bitch!" the girl snarls.

Bren slams a hand over the girl's chest. "I told you to quit taking that shit."

"I am! I swear, Bren, I quit! This little bitch is making shit up!"

"Where do you hide them?" I keep my voice calm. "Your pillow?" No response. "Your drawers? The toilet?" No response. "Hole in the wall, maybe?"

A twitch.

"Hole in the wall it is." I smile.

The girl's face lights red. "Fucking cunt! I'll kill you!"

"You won't touch her," Bren snaps.

"Do we have a deal, Bren?" I ask politely.

She glares at me for a few moments. "You come when I call you, work your shit when I need you to, and you won't get touched in this place. You got me?"

"I got you." I smile and pick up my tray. "Have a fabulous day, ladies."

It might not be much, but for now it's home.

They make us do art, home ec. We talk to shrinks, but none of them is as good as Millicent. None of them has that same little smile, that same encouraging presence that lets you say anything and nothing at all. No tea in this place. Just watered-down coffee.

There are no more voices.

No more cons.

No more Erica.

Here, behind bars in juvie, I'm freer than I've ever been.

We have two hours of computer time on the weekends. No instant messaging, no video chats or Internet access. Just e-mail and a word-processing program. Taylor's dad e-mails me—he's my lawyer. Said he felt sorry for me, said his "friends" (the mob) had always liked Sal. His representing me was a show of respect to one of Vegas's most influential con men.

The police let me have one of Sal's many rings.

I stared at it for four days then chucked it over the fence of the exercise yard. A crow flew away with it.

———

Cass and Taylor e-mail me the most. I don't think Merril's forgiven me, or will ever forgive me. She might when Cass talks her through it.

Time, and all that bullshit.

Cass is more understanding. She's warming up the more I e-mail her about my life with Sal—how I was raised. The more she finds out about the real me, the kinder her words sound. Taylor keeps me in the loop about everything at school, the classes I'm missing, who's going out with whom. She knows I miss the daily stuff. She hates gossiping but does it anyway. For me.

James hasn't e-mailed at all.

I expected that though.

Mrs. Silverman called a few times, but our conversations were always short, and she would always start to sob. After the third call, she stopped. Seeing her testifying in court was surreal. She didn't look at me. Later I learned she'd decided not to press charges. Instead of fraud, all the police could get me on was stealing the car from Home Depot's lot. Taylor's dad made me play the victim—wove the story of Sal and how he raised me. I put on a weepy face that wasn't all faked. The jury ate it up.

A care package arrived for me in juvie on day six, filled

with biscotti and fancy shampoo. The note was simple and in elegant handwriting:

Thank you.

— — —

Erica's funeral was held two weeks after my sentencing. Mr. Silverman attended. The newspapers said he was laughing instead of crying.

— — —

Taylor is my usual visitor during visitor day. Not today, though. She's off to New York to visit her mom. Today I'm alone.

"Violet?" A guard taps on my door. "You've got a visitor. I'll take you there."

Cass, maybe? Or maybe it's Mrs. Silverman. No, it wouldn't be her. She still has a lot of healing to do before she ever looks at me again. But she will someday. Or so I hope.

I step into the tiny white room, the door closing behind me. On the other side of the glass is a boy with a windbreaker and long blond hair. It's shorter, though. His face is thinner. His calloused hands fold on the table in front of him. I don't move, staring at him from the place where I stand. I should sit. Sitting would be good, but I feel like any movement will make him bolt. Make him break.

Slowly. I move slowly, pull the chair out, and curse it when it makes a screeching noise. Settle, smooth my sweat pants. We sit like that, neither of us looking at each other and neither of us willing to pick up the phone and start the conversation. Time passes, long and stretched. His hand moves for the receiver, and I take ahold of my end at the same time.

His lips open, eyes flickering up to meet mine.

"I lied," I cut him off, spit it like I'm spitting something foul from my body.

"I know," he murmurs.

Another silence. It's a good silence though. I can hear him sigh, clear his throat. It's all I need. It's all I can have right now.

"One year in here," I say. He nods. The soundproofed room is clean and white. A bandage. A point that holds together my two worlds—James and prison.

"I don't regret it." I swallow hard. "You, Taylor, meeting everyone and doing things with you guys was the best time of my life."

"Mine too," he agrees. A smile tugs at his mouth. I don't want to cry in front of him, but I can't hold the sadness back anymore. It's not just tears of regret for what I did, or for my situation now; it's tears for Kerwin, now on the run. For Sal, now dead. For Mr. and Mrs. Silverman learning to breathe now.

For Erica, who's with her family now.

Who's at *peace* now.

James can't touch me through the glass, but he wants to. I can see it in his eyes, his tensing muscles. He wants to say something. He bends down and brings out a guitar instead. He props it on his lap, puts his end of the phone on the table near it, and starts strumming. The song fills my tiny room.

And I start to cry.

ACKNOWLEDGMENTS

Long paragraphs of gratitude are the sort of thing that's hard to get into if you weren't there.

Thankfully, I was. Doubly thankfully, a lot of other people were, too.

Thank you to the crew at Viking Children's for tinkering lovingly with my book. Thank you to Sharyn November, my indomitable warrioress editor, for pointing at my small bean of a book and saying "This. This one." Thank you to Jessica Faust for her unending support, patience, kindness, and willingness to look Violet's way.

Thank you to Melanie Santiago, Jamie Blair, Dana Alison Levy, Kate Boorman, Jennifer Wood, Jennifer Walkup, and all the wonderful lady writers ensconced in the LitBitches Internet cave. You inspired and uplifted. A special thank-you to Laura Tims, Sarah Harian Raynor, and Leah Clement for trying your hand at friendship with a terrible weeb like me.

Thank you to Kate Fujimoto, Hannah Shimabukuro, Katie Aymar, Amanda Aymar, and Kristin Remington for being the best posse a girl could ever have while still learning how to bleed properly. Thank you to Niccole Medea

Long for raising her eyebrow and asking "Now what?" when I showed her the beginnings of a story.

Thank you to my family. Thank you to Michael Painchaud for your unwavering pride in me. Thank you to Deborah Painchaud, for your love and support in all things trying and difficult. Thank you to Cheri Painchaud for being a shining example of strength and tenacity.

Thank you to Griffin Weston for being the patient, captive audience my writing—and I—needed, precisely when we needed it most.

And finally, thank you to Violet. I heard your call. I hope I did it justice.

You're all right now.

Michelle Painchaud was born in Seattle but grew up gate-crashing parties in sugarcane fields in Hawaii. Cats and anime take up what little part of her brain isn't harassed by stories of teenagers kicking ass. She lives in San Diego, California, and you can find her on Twitter: @michelleiswordy and on Tumblr: michellepainchaud. tumblr.com.